K L CREAR

The Reinvention of Lottie Potts

Crear Publishing Ltd

First published by Crear Publishing Lts 2023

First edition

ISBN: 978-1-7392765-2-2

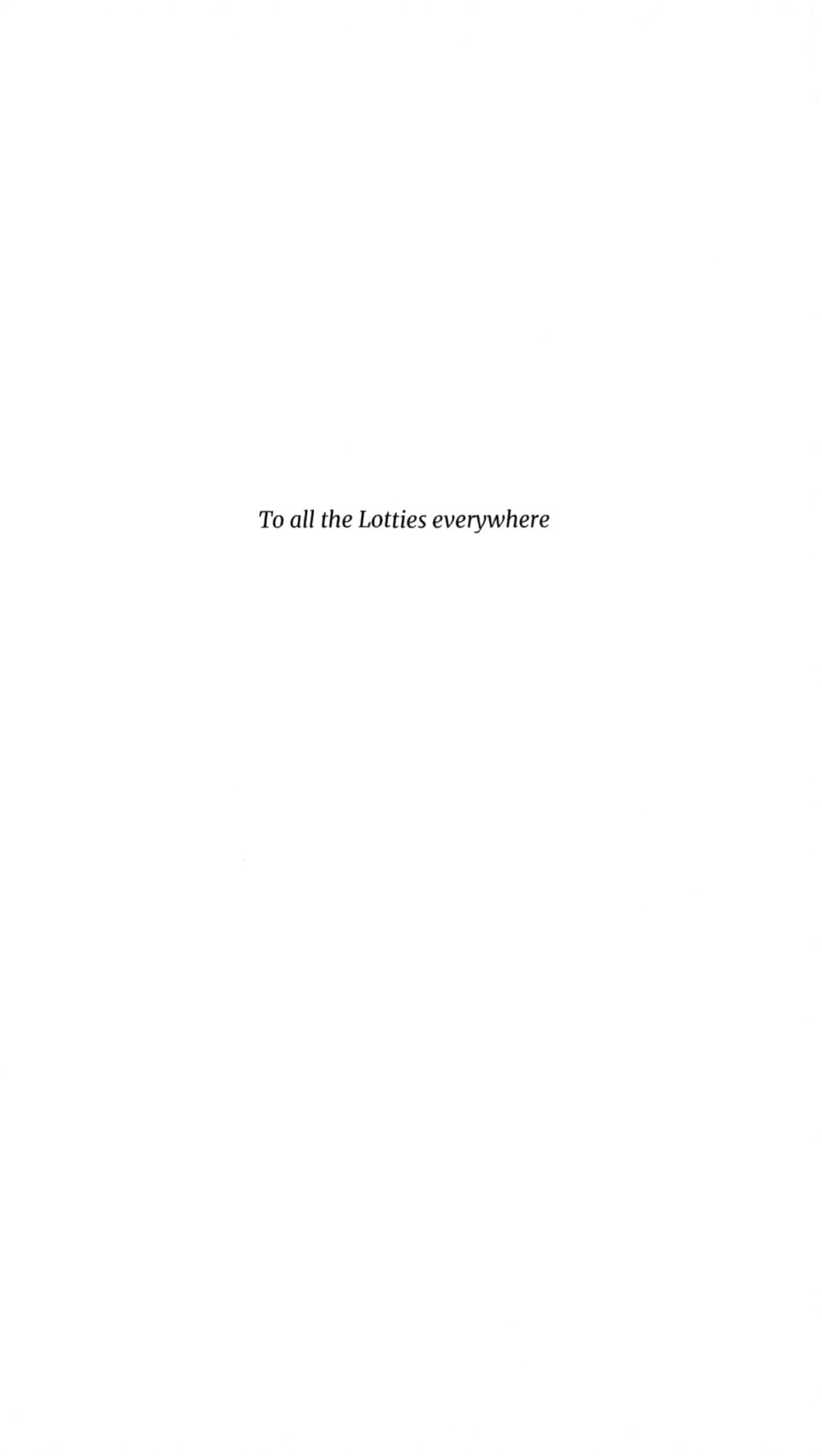

To all the Lotties everywhere

Contents

Chapter 1

"Why on earth did I say yes?" I asked myself desperately for the umpteenth time in half an hour. I was staring despairingly into the depths of my wardrobe and, boy, was it a depressing sight. A sea of shapeless black garments seemed to stare back at me menacingly from their hangers, cruelly mocking me.

I had reluctantly agreed to go out with my three girlfriends for cocktails on Friday night at a fancy new tapas bar in town, and I was beginning to really regret it. Don't get me wrong: I loved my friends, and the time we spent together was precious, but it had been such a very long time since I had been out on the town that the idea of getting all dressed up was seriously getting me down.

With a deep sigh I surveyed the wardrobe again. When exactly had I become so dowdy? All the clothes were long and wide and very, very black. There was the occasional hint of grey or navy going on, but no flashes of bright colour or anything that resembled any flair for fashion or fun. It was ridiculous: after all, I worked part-time in a fancy women's boutique in the centre of Leeds, yet my wardrobe would have made Queen Victoria feel frumpy. There was absolutely nothing amusing to me as I stared balefully at my meagre selection of garments.

I sank down onto the cream-covered double bed, the mattress sinking under my not inconsiderable weight and messing up the neatly placed satin throw cushions. I made a mental note to myself to make sure I arranged them perfectly again before I went downstairs. No point in giving Daniel something else to whinge about when he got home from work. He was always so damn grumpy these days, the littlest thing would set him off. Plus, it was Wednesday and my day off work, so the house was expected to be especially clean and tidy when he returned from his oh so important job in banking.

Once upon a time I had really loved fashion; it had been my passion from a very young age. I delighted in the way you could alter your mood so radically just by changing the fabric you put on your body. As a little girl I would spend hours browsing my mum's Littlewoods catalogue, circling all the outfits that I could only ever dream of owning. As I grew older, I would save my pocket money to buy copies of *Vogue* magazine. The models were exquisitely beautiful and the editorial photo shoots like stunning works of art. I had always harboured a dream of working in fashion, maybe as a journalist on one of the glossy magazines. I had imagined I would have such a glamorous life and sashay my way through it, effortlessly chic and wearing just the right shade of lipstick for whatever situation came my way.

I suppose I couldn't really complain. After all, I had realised my dream of working in fashion - although working part-time in Leodis Chic, a small boutique in a slightly run-down 1960s shopping centre in the busy hubbub of Leeds, wasn't really what I had envisioned. Then again getting married at 24 and having our son Jacob three years later hadn't been on my desired life trajectory either. I'd always thought I would be a career girl, maybe marrying in my thirties and having a child shortly after; but you have to adjust, go with the curve balls that life throws, or rather unceremoniously chucks, your way.

I sat upright on the bed again and stared into the spotlessly clean mirror above my dressing table. I squinted at my tired reflection - a sort of DIY Snapchat filter to soften the visage of the frump staring back at me with her sad green eyes. I hated to admit it to myself, but to use my mother's words I had "really let myself go". The woman staring back defeatedly looked every exhausted second of her 44 years of age. I was simply Charlotte Potts, a flabby, unglamorous middle-aged mum from a little village in West Yorkshire, and not the sharply dressed fashion editor I had always dreamt of being. From my shoulder-length brunette hair, desperately needing a cut and slightly greying at the temples, to the size 20 body encased in elasticated fraying jogging bottoms and unflattering crew-necked jumper, I looked like the sartorial equivalent of an ageing rich tea biscuit that had been left out of its packet too long. To sum it up, I looked thoroughly boring. I used to look good. I used to look at least like a chocolate Hobnob! Why and when had I become so drab? And why did my mind always go to food? At any given moment, I could be thinking of absolutely anything – world politics to *Love Island* – and suddenly, snap, I'm right back to dreaming about grub again.

I hauled myself up from the bed and repositioned the cushions in perfect order. A nice cup of tea and a chocolate biscuit was a pretty good idea, though; just a little break from finding an outfit to wear for Friday, and then I would be back on the quest with a vengeance. Who knows, I might find a little number hiding in the darkest corner of my closet that would be ideal: a sparkly size 18-20 something that would turn me into a statuesque supermodel, sucking in and accentuating exactly where it needed to. It was always good to dream.

Ten minutes later I was happily sitting in the lounge with a mug of tea in one hand and a plate of Viennese whirls settled on the arm of the faded blue sofa. I'd already scoffed down one, enjoying the crumbly texture and the little smidgen of jam in the middle. I didn't feel guilty, though; I had purposely not checked the calorie count on the side of the box but felt sure they couldn't be too sinful since they felt, and therefore must be, angelically light. Anyway, I was making a healthy chicken casserole in the slow cooker for dinner tonight, and I was determined I would only have a miniscule portion. So, all was good with the world.

I flicked through the TV channels, deciding on a *Real Housewives* show, and sank smugly back in the sofa. A bit of pure escapism – silly neurotic women with their designer bags and smooth expressionless faces arguing about complete nonsense as they tried not to fall off their stilettos and spill their Pinot Grigio. It was just the ticket.

I had an hour or so to kill before Jacob was due back from school. He would no doubt shamble into the house, drop his tatty old rucksack on the floor and then be snout down in a packet of Doritos before muttering he was going upstairs to his room until dinner and not to disturb him on pain of death. I smiled indulgently to myself; I really loved that boy. Seventeen years of age and currently at the local sixth form college studying for his A-levels. A complete teenage nightmare pain in the butt at times, but also incredibly sweet. Jacob was my little boy and I loved him with all my heart.

As I watched the TV drama unfold, I relaxed with a contented sigh. It was some fifty-something harridan with a face as unlined as a toddler screeching away. She was wearing a ratty blonde wig so long it could sweep the floor, and a skirt so short that the whole audience was her gynaecologist whether they liked it or not. She was shouting at her younger boyfriend, poking a bony bejewelled finger at him and informing the vacant-eyed toyboy with his dazzling white teeth to "own his shit".

My mind began to wander again for a second. Against my better judgement I felt a little stirring of excitement at the prospect of going out socially again with my friends. Well, it was either excitement or trapped wind from the Mexican food I had cooked last night – beans were never my friend. No, it was most certainly a little flutter of excitement. I was sure of it. And I should be excited too: my friends were an amazing group of women – well, most of the time. But the worry of what to wear and possibly being mistaken for their maiden aunt rather than their fashionable friend of a similar age was casting a dark cloud over my mood.

I used to take such a pride in my appearance. Even going out to Tesco to do some grocery shopping was an opportunity to be stylish. I would have my make-up applied impeccably and be dressed in a smart casual manner, conscious of who I might possibly bump into. But that was five years and four stone ago. Now it took all my effort to slap on a layer of Nivea cream as thick as a coat of emulsion paint and a hasty sweep of Chapstick along my lips, not caring if I bumped into Brad Pitt or Dame Judi Dench over the deli counter. I knew something had to give.

My mobile vibrated fitfully in the pocket of my sagging joggers, announcing an incoming message. I excavated it and squinted at the screen. It was a message from my best friend

Lila. I couldn't help but smile, just seeing her name.

"Looking forward to Friday! Can't wait to catch up with you and the ladies for a few small sherries – it's been waaaaaayyyyyy too long."

My mood jumped from elation to panic; I sighed dejectedly and typed out my reply, finishing it off with a sad-faced emoji. "I've missed everyone too, but I'm thinking of crying off as I haven't got anything decent to wear."

My phone immediately began to ring. It was Lila, and clearly messaging wasn't going to be enough for her; she needed to hear my excuses for herself.

"Hi, Lila, how's it going?" I greeted her warmly. "I'm just thinking I might stay in on Fri..."

"Absolutely no way in the world are you bailing out of our first night out in ages!" Lila's normally refined voice had a shrieky shrill edge to it. "I'm stuck in this office working with these absolute dickheads and the only thing keeping me going is dreaming of a nice chilled vodka martini on Friday night. You are not, repeat not, cancelling on me."

I had a mental image of what Lila would be doing at that moment: probably sitting at her heavy oak desk in her couture navy suit with her red-rimmed designer glasses on top of her head, a pile of vitally important legal documents spread out haphazardly in front of her. Her glossy blonde hair would be scraped up into a stylish chignon. She would be looking so chic, so professional and so bloody thin.

Lila was five years older than me at 49. She worked as a senior solicitor in Leeds city centre in one of the fancy firms where they charge like an angry bull with a migraine. She was a formidable woman to deal with – a veritable force of nature. Her male colleagues were in awe of her and somewhat terrified by her sharp business acumen. She had gained the nickname along the corridors of her smart office building of "Lila the Rottweiler", a moniker she was not supposed to be aware of, but of course she was and secretly rather revelled in it. Lila was nothing like a Rottweiler really, more of an amiable spaniel, but her work persona had taken an age to cultivate, and she was going to benefit from it professionally as much as she could.

We had met at our local park some twelve years before when our sons had made an instant friendship over the jungle gym, like only children can. They had been best of buddies from the first time they met, both grovelling up their nostrils and competitively comparing their bogies. Little boys were always such a delight. Lila and I had been forced to make halting polite small talk as our children played, but after we had chatted for an hour together we too were shaping up to be best of friends. Our lives were very different – me working in retail and Lila as a solicitor - but our personalities had gelled and that was that. At 19 Lila's son Thomas was two years older than my Jacob. Lila hadn't let having a child get in the way of pursuing the career she had always dreamt of. She was of the opinion that as a woman you could have it all if you wanted, or not – the choice was yours. Her son was away at university in Bristol now, studying Economics, and Lila was suffering from empty nest syndrome, something I was already dreading knowing that the time for Jacob to move out would happen all too soon.

Lila was happily single after the marriage with her accountant husband Duncan had ended some three years before. She had discovered her husband's predilection for meeting other women via dating apps on his mobile phone. One evening he had left his phone unattended while taking a quick shower and Lila had casually noticed the first line of a message on his welcome screen. He had been arranging to meet Kacey - a 29-year-old personal trainer from Huddersfield - for a romantic rendezvous at a nearby Nando's, of all places. No doubt Duncan was hoping to have Peri-Peri with a side order of passion.

He had suddenly realised the error of leaving his iPhone unlocked and unattended and had raced back to the kitchen to retrieve it. Naked and still wet from the shower, with suds of shampoo dripping from his receding hairline, he stopped in his tracks as he watched his wife scroll through his messages, her jaw set in steely determination. Duncan's terror at seeing his wife grip his phone was akin to her directing a loaded gun to his dangly bits. He knew that his life as he had known it was now well and truly over. Although Duncan thought he was hooking up with an energetic young personal trainer, it was Lila who really demonstrated her fitness that night as she agilely kicked her soapy, naked spouse out of the marital home and out of her life for good. Lila was not one for forgiveness; you crossed her at your peril.

I tried to think of the best way I could make Lila understand why I was so nervous about going out with her and the girls in two nights' time. I knew she wouldn't get it. How could she? She was always so confident and stylish; the thought of being self-conscious and embarrassed about one's appearance would be an alien concept to her.

"I've nothing to wear," I wailed miserably. "I'm fat, I'm old and everything I try on makes me look like Pavarotti with slightly less facial hair."

Lila exhaled impatiently. "Not this nonsense again. I've told you a million times you're not old, not fat and you look nothing like a dead Italian tenor!" She paused before continuing.

"You're a beautiful woman in your prime, even if that oaf of a husband of yours can't be bothered to put his newspaper down long enough to appreciate you. You're coming out on Friday night, sporting that jersey dress I bought you for Christmas, and I'm not hearing any more excuses or you and I will really fall out."

I knew that when Lila was determined there was no point in arguing. I could never win an argument with her, and I didn't have the energy to even try. Anyway, Lila was right: she had bought me an incredibly flattering black stretch wrap dress from one of her favourite upscale boutiques last Christmas. It had been stuffed to the back of my wardrobe as too nice to wear until I had lost some weight. It did fit though, as it was well made and had a bit of 'give' to the material. And it was black, which was a huge plus in its favour as this was the only colour I could manage to wear. And when I say the dress was black, I mean black. You know what it's like when you first wash a black top and it turns a dark shade of grey. To get a proper jet black that won't fade the first time you wear it, you need to spend your pennies and invest in quality.

I felt a modicum of enthusiasm rise up in me, as if I'd just taken a swig of an energy drink and the adrenalin was starting to pump through my veins. I was beginning to feel ready for this.

"OK, I'll come. I won't let my silly nerves get the better of me." I nodded enthusiastically although there was no one there to see. "For pity's sake, it's only a few drinks with my best friends on a Friday night; what could possibly go wrong?"

"Exactly," Lila enthused, "it's going to be a fabulous night and I can't wait."

I said goodbye and stuffed my phone back in my jogging

bottoms. She was right, of course: I was being ridiculous. Yes, I had put on weight, a lot of weight, as all my family and friends had obviously noticed even if they chose to deny it. But this didn't change my worth as a woman. I wasn't simply defined by my looks or my size. I had been an attractive woman in my day, and in a certain flattering light, preferably candle, I still was. Anyway, there was always Spanx knickers and minimiser bras, and I was booked into my hairdresser's tomorrow for my eight-weekly cut and colour, so soon the badger stripe would be no more.

I tidied away the plate bearing the last remaining Viennese whirl. I considered stuffing it in my mouth, which would save having to put it back in the biscuit tin, but decided against it. Small steps to a slimmer me. I stood up, brushed the crumbs from my clothes, turned the television off and strode purposefully into the kitchen to stir the chicken casserole. I smiled to myself: Friday was going to be good, I was sure of it.

Chapter 2

"What's this, Mum? It looks like prison slop." Jacob was peering unenthusiastically at my gruel like casserole, hoping that if he stared long enough it might turn into something he could consider eating.

"Don't be so rude," I scolded gently, replacing the lid on the pot. "It's chicken casserole – it's healthy... you know... like good for you."

Jacob grimaced at the imposition of healthy eating. "Can we at least have chips with it?" he asked, ever hopeful. We both loved our chips.

"No chips tonight: we're having new potatoes and mange-tout alongside the casserole." I smiled conspiratorially at Jacob as I let him into a little secret: "but your dad's out tomorrow night playing squash so I thought we could get a Domino's in for the two of us."

"Dope!" A broad grin lit up his face, revealing those dimples that turned him back into my little boy instead of the awkward 6-foot-2 man-child that had filled the kitchen till then. "I'll have a Pepperoni Passion with extra cheese."

I smiled happily and ruffled his shaggy hair till it stood out in cute random tufts. "Yep, it's like I always say, it goes down easy if it's nice and cheesy."

Jacob grimaced to indicate just how tragic I was. "Yeah, Mum, you may say that but in future can you please try not to? It's just next level cringe."

I couldn't help but laugh. What was the point of being parents if we couldn't embarrass our offspring all the time? "OK, OK, but just remember the pizza is a little treat, a one off. I'll be back to cooking healthy stuff again after that."

Recently my husband Daniel had become pretty health-conscious. He was often out at the gym in town or playing squash at the local sports centre with his work colleague Jon. He had also adopted a much healthier diet: long gone was his penchant for steak pie, chips and onion rings, or my home-made lasagne that he always used to say was "nearly as bellissimo as me". Lean chicken and grilled fish were now on the menu, alongside my standard casseroles hiding their five-a-day-veg to fool Jacob. My humble slow cooker was rapidly becoming my gadget of choice in the kitchen, and it was great that Daniel was embracing a healthier lifestyle. I was proud of him. He was looking good – really fit and healthy for his 48 years. He'd lost quite a bit of weight too, he proudly informed me while admiring himself in my dressing table mirror: he was now size 34 waist. I told him how amazing that was, while sucking in my own stomach to struggle into my size 20 jeans.

"Do you really need those, Charlotte?" Daniel had asked me a few evenings earlier as I'd emerged with a packet of pickled onion Monster Munch in one hand and a glass of Pinot Noir in the other. The look of disapproval on his face had made me flush as red as the wine. I had felt the sting of tears behind my eyes and hurriedly blinked them away.

"No, I don't need them, but I want them" had been my curt reply as I sank back on the sofa beside him. I had continued to munch my crisps and sip my wine as we watched TV, but I barely tasted them. Daniel's disapproval had made my favourite treats taste like claggy sawdust, and the wine wasn't much better. Damn him! Why did I let his words hurt me so much?

Since then, I had begun to hide my indulgences at the back of the kitchen cupboard where he wouldn't go looking, and try, at least in Daniel's presence, to exhibit a somewhat healthier diet. It wasn't easy though. I think the sad reality was that I was honestly greedy, and food was beginning to act like a crutch to me. Apart from my part-time job in the boutique, and looking after the house and my family, I didn't really have a lot going on. I was, I had to admit to myself, lonely. I did see my mum once a week, as she lived just a few streets away. I was an only child and dad had passed away five years ago. I liked to meet my mum for coffee and a catch-up every week we could manage. It was all dependent on mum's schedule, as she was quite the social butterfly these days: between playing golf, her many classes and lunches with her girlfriends, she often didn't have time to fit me in. Daniel's parents we only saw occasionally as they had retired to Spain, only returning to the UK sporadically. Anyway, Daniel wasn't particularly close to his parents, though they did keep in touch with Jacob, often on Facetime, which was good.

I checked the clock again on the kitchen wall: it was 7:10 pm. Daniel was a bit late this evening. I tasted the casserole and added a little salt to the rather bland concoction. He often was late these days. There was a time when you could have set your watch by him: he would walk through the door promptly at 6 pm, take off his highly polished shoes and leave them neatly by the stairs, give me a kiss on the cheek and enquire how my day had been. However, these days he was coming home later and later. I knew that he was extremely busy at work though, so I couldn't be a pain about it. He would tell me about all the extra work his supervisor was piling on him, and how under pressure he was feeling. He said his job was giving him executive stress, so the regular gym sessions and squash matches helped him to unwind and relax, which could surely only be a good thing? The last thing I wanted was him to be wound up and on edge. Daniel tended to be a little grumpy at the best of times.

I could hear Jacob stomping around upstairs in his bedroom, and the heavy bass booming from his sound system. "Maybe he's tidying up?" I imagined, but quickly dismissed the thought knowing this would most certainly not be the case. Jacob's bedroom was an epic disaster zone which I was not permitted to enter – not that I would have wanted to anyway. I did go in every few days to retrieve any dirty plates from under his bed and maybe dump his worn underwear in the laundry basket on the landing, but that was about it.

My mind drifted back to our night out on Friday. Lila was right: the black dress would be the best option. It was flattering, and with the right underwear hoisting everything in place and some tasteful jewellery I was sure I wouldn't look half bad.

As well as myself and Lila, our two friends Jasmine and Jayne would also be going. Jasmine I had known for many years, as our sons had gone through school together; we had met when the boys were first in reception class. She was a couple of years older than me and a stay-at-home mum. Jayne on the other hand was my oldest friend: we had first connected over the coincidence of being the same age, with birthdays only three days apart. We had lived next door to each other for a few years when we were teenagers and our parents had been best of friends. We'd spent all our time between the two terraced homes. It was now nearly thirty years since we'd been neighbours, but we'd always stayed in touch and tried to catch up with each other a few times a year. Jayne had her own business making bespoke jewellery and selling it online. She was incredibly artistic, and her creations simply stunning. Neither of them knew Lila particularly well, only having met her on a couple of occasions before, but they both liked her. Lila's natural confidence and charisma ultimately won people over and they both found her to be great company, if somewhat intimidating at times.

I heard the key in the front door and checked the kitchen clock again: it was 7:43 pm and Daniel was finally home. I listened for him pulling off his shoes and dropping his briefcase in the hall. He was sighing deeply as he entered the kitchen to greet me, tugging at his blue-striped tie as he made his way over to me.

"How's your day been?" he enquired in a bored tone and briefly pecked me on the cheek. "I've had another shitty day. I'm bloody knackered." He yawned in an exaggerated fashion to demonstrate just how bone tired he really was.

I smiled pleasantly at him. "I'm fine, love. Quiet day, really. I saw Mum for a bit this morning, but apart from that I've just been in the house pottering around. Dinner's ready whenever you are: it's chicken casserole."

Daniel waved his hand dismissively towards the door of the lounge. "Yeah fine, whatever, I'm so ravenous I could eat a scabby horse between two stale breadcakes. I'll be watching the TV; just bring it into me on a tray when you're ready."

His back was already to me as he made his way through to

the living room. I watched him walk away for a few seconds – tall and broad-shouldered with his wavy light brown hair shining under the hallway light before he disappeared into the other room and firmly shut the door behind him.

I looked despondently at the kitchen table where I had set three places for dinner. Sighing, I removed the plates and cutlery. I'd really hoped for a proper family dinner that evening, all sitting around the kitchen table exchanging our respective days. But now we'd be silently eating our food off our laps again, with the television as the only focus of attention.

Thirty minutes later the chicken casserole had been devoured. It didn't take long to eat as the length of time it had been bubbling away in the pot had rendered it a muddy-looking mush that could have been gummed down by a toothless octogenarian. It hadn't been the most palatable of dishes. In fact, it was dull: probably the culinary equivalent of being stuck in a lift with a tax inspector. No wonder Jacob had wolfed it down so fast, barely tasting it and then asked to be excused, desperate to bury himself upstairs with a packet of Jammy Dodgers. I'm sure he was grateful that Domino's pizza, not more of his mother's home cooking, was on the menu for the following night.

Daniel and I then sat side by side on the sofa staring at the TV in what I hoped was a comfortable silence. It was a documentary, though I couldn't really concentrate on it: something about the alarmingly high divorce rates in the country. Bloody hell, that really wasn't the ambiance that I was hoping for.

"Do you mind if I change channel?" I asked, fumbling down the sofa for the remote control. "I really should get a hoover down here sometimes," I mused to myself as my hand grazed what I hoped was a few grains of rice from the Chinese takeaway Jacob and I had enjoyed the week before.

"Suit yourself," Daniel yawned, not bothering to cover his mouth. "To be honest, I might call it a night and get myself up to bed; I'm completely whacked."

I was disappointed, but tried my best not to show it. I had been hoping we'd have an opportunity to talk, especially with Jacob now upstairs. We had hardly had a chance to be together as a couple at all recently: Daniel was always working late or out at the gym.

I used to love the good old days when we would settle contentedly down at night and watch movies. His arm would be draped over my shoulders, and I would snuggle into him. It had been an age since we had been like that. These days we sat right next to each other, our shoulders almost brushing, yet it felt like there was a gulf of a thousand miles between us. I hated it and I couldn't understand why we were like this now. I knew that Daniel was overworked and tired, but was it more than that? Did he not find me attractive any more? Was I just too big? Had I stopped making an effort with my appearance? I really hoped that wasn't the case. I knew we hadn't exactly been swinging from the chandeliers lately, and our sex life could not be called red hot; more lukewarm than lusty. I laughed bitterly to myself: it actually wasn't even tepid now. I brushed the unwelcome thoughts aside; I really couldn't think like that. I just didn't want to have to unpack that particular box in my head.

Daniel picked up his mobile phone from the arm of the sofa next to him and got ready to go up to bed. He was reading something on the screen and a small smile flickered for a few moments at the corners of his mouth.

I muted the sound on the television screen for a second and cleared my throat to get his attention. "Before you go to bed, I just wanted to tell you that I'm going out with the girls on Friday night for a few hours." I looked up at him expectantly.

"Mmmmm," he answered, his eyes still fixed on the phone in his hand. "Sounds good; you could probably do with a night out."

I nodded in agreement, even though his attention clearly wasn't on me. "I agree, and we're planning to go to the new wine bar and tapas place in town... you know the one? Olive Affair?"

Daniel was still distractedly tapping on his phone. "Yeah... yeah, that sounds good." He started walking towards the door before thinking better of it and stopping to turn towards me. "Actually, I'm going out on Friday night too. A couple of the guys thought we should have a few beers straight after work, wind down for the weekend, you know, talk about office stuff... pretty boring really."

"Oh... OK," I replied. At least that meant I wouldn't have to leave him any dinner while I was out, I supposed.

Daniel was about to leave the room when he stopped abruptly as if he had suddenly remembered something. He turned on his heel and came back over to kiss me swiftly on the cheek. "Night, love, don't forget to turn off all the lights before you come to bed."

And with that he was gone. I checked my watch: it was only 9:45 pm – far too early to go to bed. I decided that although I was on my own, I fancied watching a film. I had a great love of old classic cinema, especially romances. I knew straight away which film I would watch: after all, I had seen it only a few hundred times before. As the film started with the scene in the refreshment room at Milford Junction, I let out a truly contented sigh. You couldn't beat *Brief Encounter* for a bit of pure romantic escapism; the chaste yet passionate love that could never be.

I poured myself a glass of Chenin Blanc from the bottle we'd had with dinner, of which only a trickle now remained. Nothing for it: I was going to have to open another bottle. It just couldn't be helped. And you couldn't possibly have a nice, chilled glass of wine without something nibbly to accompany it. That was where a tube of sour cream and chive Pringles came into play. Bliss. My favourite black and white movie and my buddies "vin blanc" and "salty carb" for company. What could be better?

Nearly two hours later, the movie finished and its credits scrolled slowly down the black and white screen to the melodic strains of Rachmaninov. The wine and snacks had long been devoured, so with a yawn and a stretch I too headed upstairs for the night. I tried to make as little noise as possible as I undressed for bed. I really didn't want to disturb Daniel. I listened in the dark room for a few seconds, realising I couldn't hear the familiar low rumble of his snoring. Clearly he wasn't sleeping, as I suddenly heard a faint sigh of displeasure when I turned on my bedside lamp.

"Maybe I'm a little bit tipsy?" I thought to myself. I certainly seemed to be having more trouble than normal getting out of my unsightly underwear. I finally managed to get the knickers off and kicked them unceremoniously into the corner of the bedroom, in a messy heap for the laundry basket the following morning. I then tried unclipping my bra.

"Do you really have to make so much bloody noise?" Daniel

pulled himself upright in bed, disgruntled and blinking like a newborn dazzled by the light.

"Ooops... sorry," I apologised in a hushed voice, "I didn't mean to wake you." As I spoke, I pulled my bra off by one strap in what I hoped was a vaguely coquettish manner, ready to throw it in the vicinity of the abandoned knickers. A small item that had been nestling in the cup of the bra now managed to jettison its way from its bosomy home towards Daniel, as if my bra was a cotton/spandex mix catapult. It hit Daniel squarely on the left cheek.

"What the hell was that?" he demanded, picking the tiny potatoey missile off the duvet, where it had landed. "Is...is it a crisp?"

I nodded shamefaced. "I think it's half a Pringle," I admitted quietly. "After you went to bed, I felt a bit 'snackish' so I had a couple of them with a little glass of wine." I wasn't being completely honest. I had polished off two-thirds of the new bottle and hadn't stopped chomping the Pringles until I hit the dust at the bottom of the tube.

Daniel appraised me for a second with a withering look of pity before shaking his head and then settling back into bed with a firm "Goodnight, Charlotte!"

Despondently I pulled my pyjamas on as quickly as I could, my favourite ones with the hearts and unicorns. I slumped into bed myself, before turning off the light.

"Goodnight, Daniel." I turned towards him and leant in to kiss him on the cheek, but there was no reply; just the faint, steady sound of his breathing.

Sleep evaded me for the longest time that night as I lay on my side staring at the ceiling. The unevenly drawn curtains allowed a chink of light from the street lights below to cast shadows across the artexed ceiling. These shadows took on ominous forms in the dim murky light. As I lay completely still, listening to the low rumble of my husband snoring, I had a worrying feeling of unease. Why did I have this strange feeling of foreboding? I just couldn't shake it off. Dawn was already breaking over our little house when I finally drifted off into troubled sleep.

Chapter 3

"I'd love to be able to wear these." I could hear the longing in my voice as I felt the fabric of the satiny cream trousers that I was pricing up. They were as soft as butter between my fingers and simply stunning.

My colleague Morgan shook her head forcefully and let out a loud snort of derision. "Not me; you wouldn't catch me dead in 'em. You'd wear them out once for a night and they'd be ruined – all covered in cider and chicken kebab by the end of the night." She picked absently at her chipped black-painted fingernail as she continued to speak. "You'd forever be paying to get 'em dry-cleaned; nah, give me a pair of wipe-clean pleather jeans any day of the week."

Let me describe Morgan. She was twenty-four years old, and like me favoured black as her clothing colour of choice. Unlike me, though, Morgan was as thin as a rake and her favouring black was more out of her own sartorial choice than necessity. She was the niece of my boss Diane, who was the owner of Leodis Chic and two other struggling shops in the West Yorkshire area. Morgan was helping and sometimes hindering in the shop after being "let go" from her most recent clerical position, due to a difference of opinion with her boss.

Her boss was of the opinion that she should be behind her desk promptly at 9 am Monday to Friday; whereas Morgan believed she needed her beauty sleep in preference, hence why she was now assisting me in her aunt's shop. Diane was employing her niece part-time as a benevolent favour to her sister, until Morgan secured another job. However, what had started out as being a favour in the short term had now seen Morgan working in the boutique for over a year.

Morgan loved fashion, designing and making many of her own clothes. She had an eclectic personal style that managed to be both chic and edgy. She wasn't really suited to working in a boutique that catered for the thirty-plus yummy mummy/business lady model. The rails of clothing in the store were all pale muted shades, with tasteful jewellery adorning the mannequins: in stark contrast to Morgan's black suede miniskirt and chunky Doc Marten boots and her many piercings. Morgan looked like a fish out of water amongst the cashmere cardigans and patent high heels. Her style was as far from Leodis Chic as one could imagine, but that didn't stop her from looking simply fabulous. I sighed to myself, realising that I too now looked out of place in the store but not for the same reasons as Morgan. When I had first started working for Leodis Chic some eight years earlier, I had relished my generous staff discount and loved wearing the glamorous outfits the shop had to offer, always keen to follow what fresh stock came in. Now I homed in on the few items of black the shop bought in, whether they suited me or not, just so long as they fitted. Or more often than not I simply wore items from my own wardrobe that I had purchased online. It was part of my job description to wear garments from the store's collection, but embarrassingly most would not suit my current frame, if in fact they fitted at all. I knew Diane realised this was the case, and I was thankful she had not made a big issue of it, sparing my feelings.

I scooped up a pile of the cream trousers and started hanging them in size order on a rail next to the entrance, hoping they would seduce would-be shoppers with a passion for fashion and a generous credit limit not to walk by but to come in and browse.

Diane had been worrying herself sick about the current state of the business. It was clear from the lack of footfall in the shopping centre generally and especially this boutique that things were not looking good. Diane was a stylish fashionista in her late fifties who took pride in offering the customer an old-fashioned shopping experience. She felt, like me, that fashion could elevate the soul, so she endeavoured to make her boutique a little piece of heaven: an oasis of peace and tranquillity fringed by appealing single-breasted pant suits and chiffon scarves. However, not everyone shared her ethos, and custom in the boutique had been slow for many months now.

Diane could often be seen pacing around the shop floor wearing out the carpet with her nude stilettos, bemoaning the state of her finances and how her shops were on the "bones of their arse". There were mutterings of the evils of online shopping: how it bypassed the simple joy of retail therapy, and woe betide anyone who dared speak of Amazon's next-day delivery service – the evil that could never be mentioned.

I did worry about the real possibility of the boutique going under and my job with it. I knew the job wasn't much, especially compared with the likes of Lila's, but it was all I had: my precious bit of independence amidst the monotony of life, and the thought of losing it was very scary.

"Why don't you try them on?" Morgan was holding out a pair of the trousers in a size 20 – the biggest that the store stocked. "I'll hold the fort," she gestured over to the changing room. "Just because they might be something you'd wear to your granny's funeral doesn't mean you couldn't rock the hell out of them."

I smiled appreciatively at my younger colleague, but replaced the hanger firmly back in its place. "Thanks, Morgan, that's nice of you to say so, but just because they make them in my size doesn't mean I would wear them. Just because I can doesn't mean I should. I reckon I'd look like a walking three-piece suite in those."

Morgan sighed at me and shook her head, clearly perplexed. "I don't understand you, Lottie; you clearly love the strides, but you won't wear them because you worry about what other people will think of you. It makes no sense to me. Why do you even care? I couldn't give a shit what anyone thinks of me. I wear what I want for me, end of story, and if someone doesn't like it then they shouldn't bloody well look."

I cast my eyes over Morgan's appearance: her black hair shining like graphite, streaked randomly with lime green highlights, and the earnest look lighting up her pretty face. I remembered vividly what it was like to be her age: full of confidence and passion for life, before it had the chance to be eroded away. She was young and brave and looking forward to the many adventures that would come her way, happy to forge forward, blazing a new path. I sighed inwardly: I used to be like that too; I used to be young; I used to be brave; I used to be thin.

Morgan glanced down at the anime character watch that adorned her left wrist, noting the time. "It's 2.30 pm; aren't you finishing soon?"

I nodded vigorously and quickly ran my hand through my hair. "Yep, I'm off at 3 pm, heading along to Scissor Sisters to get my hair done. It'll be nice to get rid of my grey roots."

"I like the grey in your hair." Morgan was studying me approvingly. "It gives you a bit of an edge, like nature's highlights; you should definitely embrace it, be the authentic you."

"You must be kidding!" I shook my head emphatically. "Just because I feel about a hundred years old doesn't mean I have to look it too. I want to look less 'Miss Marple' and more 'Miss, are you old enough to be drinking in this establishment and can we see your ID please?'"

Morgan laughed. "OK, I hear you. Hey, do you reckon they're lesbians that own your salon?"

I stared at her, confused. What an odd thing to say. Morgan really did come out with some funny things sometimes. "I really have no idea, Morgan. You do say the strangest things at times."

We continued to work alongside each other for a few minutes in comfortable silence, lost in our own thoughts, when a voice rang out shrilly in the empty store, jolting me back to reality.

"Charlotte Potts, is that you?"

I turned towards the source of the nasal voice that had so rudely interrupted my daydreams. With a feeling of sinking dread, I realised who it was.

"Imogen, how lovely to see you," I gushed. The way I could lie with such ease sometimes worried me. I'm sure a psychologist would have something to say about it, and I doubted it would be good.

Standing before me, resplendent in a figure-hugging dress

and toting a high-end designer bag, was none other than one Imogen Dyer: yummy mummy extraordinaire, school governor and raging bitch to boot; all shiny blonde hair straight out of a Loreal advert, and a youthful face that probably came more from healthy living and an organic diet than Botox and fillers. And here she was in the flesh in my workplace, giving me a thorough once-over with her beady eyes, and clearly finding me wanting.

"Charlotte, it *is* you. I thought it was, but I couldn't be sure until I spoke to you." Imogen ran her hand through her glossy mane of hair; the light caught it and it shone like spun gold before falling perfectly back into place, as if it had its own muscle memory. If I ran my hand through my hair like that, I would look like Boris Johnson caught in a wind tunnel. Damn it, I remembered I'd done exactly that barely five minutes earlier.

I had known Imogen for a long time, longer than I cared to remember. Jacob and her son Damian had been friends for many years during school until a couple of years ago, when they suddenly became sworn enemies overnight. I remember there was a girl involved in it somewhere, there usually was. Anyway, due to our sons' friendship, Imogen and I had been thrust together over the years. I would naturally class her more as a frenemy, or someone I was extremely pleased not to encounter for the last couple of years - or that was until now.

Imogen hadn't changed a bit. In fact, in the past two years I think she had managed to become even younger and somehow more beautiful. How was that even possible? She must have made a pact with the devil; that had to be the answer, it just wasn't natural.

Imogen had a perfect life: perfect husband, perfect home, perfect pert little bottom, just perfect everything. And as such

I perfectly hated her. Oh, I know that's not nice to say, but boy was I jealous of her. I know jealousy isn't an attractive feature, and I'm pretty sure I was green all over with it; which was fitting as I'm sure Imogen believed I looked like Shrek or the Jolly Green Giant.

She smiled in that pouty girlish way of hers, which probably had grown men swooning the world over. Her eyes narrowed slightly. "Charlotte, darling, I didn't realise you worked here." She cast her eyes up and down me again, and I could feel the distaste radiating from her in waves.

"Yep," I replied hastily, tripping over my words. "I've... I've been here part-time for over eight years actually; it gives me something to do." I laughed as if I was somehow saying something that was desperately funny. "And it keeps me out of trouble."

She laughed politely herself. "How utterly fabulous! I've never actually been in here before." Her gaze drifted around the shop, her expression suggesting she'd got a whiff of something none too pleasant; a bit like the face Jacob put on when I waved a spoonful of parmesan cheese too close to his bolognese. "I don't tend to buy off the peg normally, you know, but I'm looking for a top to go under my new McQueen blazer." She thrust a silky hot pink camisole top towards me. "Do you happen to have this in size 8? I can only find these enormous sizes that look like something you'd see a family of four camping in at Glastonbury." She indicated the size 14 top she had laid on the counter and visibly shuddered.

I smiled politely. "Unfortunately, all we have is what you see on the rack; that top has nearly sold out, it's proved so popular with our customers."

"Really?" Imogen's eyebrow rose quizzically, well as much

as her Botox would allow. "Never mind, I'm going to go into Leeds city centre tomorrow; I'm sure I'll find something suitable at Harvey Nicks."

I nodded, my face a polite rictus grin of agreement.

Imogen glanced at her Cartier watch hanging off her elegant but rather bony wrist. It was clear that conversing with me was a huge waste of her valuable time. "It really is so lovely to run into you, Charlotte, after all this time. It's such a pity our boys aren't joined at the hip any more, but what can you do?"

I smiled again but said nothing. I did find it a pity that the boys had fallen out of favour with each other, but what I didn't find a pity was that this toxic witch wasn't part of my friends' circle any more.

"Do you still have my number, Charlotte? We really must go for lunch some time at Brasserie Bleu, have a lovely girly catch-up and put the world to rights. Why don't you give me a bell next week sometime?"

"That would be fabulous," I agreed, nodding my head vigorously, knowing damn well there was no way I would be doing anything of the sort. I couldn't imagine anything worse than spending a couple of hours nibbling undressed salad with Imogen Dyer. Anyway, I wasn't even sure if my ample derriere would fit into the miniscule booths at the chicest French restaurant in town.

"Well, bye, sweetie, it was amazing to see you; and you're looking so... so... well."

I physically shuddered at this. It felt as if someone had just tap-danced across my grave. I knew without a doubt that "well" was by no means a compliment from Imogen. By saying I looked well, she might just as well have said I looked like a suet dumpling on legs.

I kept my polite smile fixed firmly on my face as Imogen flamboyantly air-kissed me on both cheeks before sashaying out of the shop, trailing a lingering aroma of Chanel no. 5 in her wake.

Morgan had been quietly taking in the exchange, with a smirk playing out on the corners of her scarlet-painted lips.

"Who is that almighty cun…?"

I cut her off abruptly before she could finish her question. "Don't say it, Morgan. You know I hate that word more than any other. That was just a very old friend of mine."

"Friend?" Morgan laughed bitterly. "Who needs enemies when you have friends like that?"

I nodded in agreement and couldn't help laughing. "Yep, you're completely right. When I said friend, I should actually have said hatchet-faced old bint."

I glanced at my watch again, realising with a jolt that it was now after 3 pm. I had better get my skates on and get to my hairdressing appointment pronto if I was to get rid of my battleship grey streaks. The salon was within the same shopping centre as Leodis Chic, but I didn't want to be late. I hated to be late for anything. I liked to think it was out of respect for people and their time, but I realised that it was also because I wanted to avoid drawing any unnecessary attention to myself.

Five minutes later I was bursting through the door of Scissor Sisters, red in the face and gasping for air from my energetic gallop to my appointment. I must have looked a fright: like a huge scarlet tomato in a turtleneck sweater, or something equally unglamorous. Martina, the proprietor of the salon, looked up briefly from the reception desk as I made my grand entrance.

A warm smile cracked her heavily made-up face. "Charlotte, lovely to see you. Take a seat over there and Tabby will be with you in a minute; she's just finishing up with her client now." Tabby, the young auburn-haired stylist, gave me a cheery wave as she continued to blow-dry the hair of an elderly lady engrossed in reading a woman's magazine. I imagined her seduced by the story of meeting the man of her dreams at the ripe old age of 92 on the bucking bronco whilst holidaying in Benidorm.

"Thanks, Martina." I lowered my bulk into the slightly tatty leather seat, my breathing subsiding to a more normal level after my exertions. The swivel chair was positioned directly opposite the dreaded mirror, which stretched across the full wall of the salon. I tried to avoid looking at my reflection, but there I was in all my glory. What was it with bloody mirrors in hairdressing salons? Was it just me, or do they make everyone else look completely hideous too? Do they ship them in specially from the hall of mirrors at a funfair? Sitting looking at myself in the slippery black gown that encased me from neck to knee, I looked like a slug in a duvet. Not really a desirable look for anyone. I waited patiently for Tabby to join me, absent-mindedly thumbing through a copy of a glossy magazine which was several months out of date. I was humming away to Katy Perry's *I kissed a girl* as I soaked up all the fashions and dreamt of a much slimmer, younger, confident me wearing them all.

"OK then, Charlotte, what's it to be today?" Tabby's sing-song voice pulled me sharply out of my daydream and back to reality. She began running a brush through my hair. "Is it just the normal brunette tint and trim, or are you going to let me do something truly outrageous and exciting this time?" She gave me a devilish wink.

I laughed a little nervously. "Just the same as normal, thanks, Tabby. Keep it shoulder-length and just get rid of the greys; then I'll be good for a few more miles."

Tabby shook her head and sighed. "I'm disappointed in you, Charlotte, but I know that one of these days you're going to let me transform you." She moved my hair back from my face. "You've got such a pretty face; all you need is a few blonde highlights and some nice face-framing layers and I could make you into a super model."

"A super model? You've got to be joking. You're a hair-dresser, not a bloody magician," I snorted. I didn't have the guts to try a radical new look just now, even though there was a tiny nagging voice whispering in my ear, telling me to go for it. Live a little for once. What had I got to lose? Maybe it would make Daniel sit up and take notice of me for once. And what about the way that Imogen had looked at me barely an hour ago? That had really hurt, like I was a yellow-stickered item in the reduced aisle at Sainsbury's that no bugger wanted; an old egg and cress sandwich that was well past its prime with its corners curling up. But no, I kept quiet and let Tabby continue with banishing my greys and giving me my safe shoulder length boring brown do. Who was I kidding anyway? I was always going to stick to the nice safe option. It was what I did.

Chapter 4

Later that evening, Jacob and I were vegged out on the settee together, slowly demolishing our pizza takeaway. I felt lucky to be able to enjoy a few hours with my son in quiet, contented peace with plenty of cheesy carbs.

"Do you want that last chicken wing, Mum?" Jacob asked hopefully.

I grimaced and shook my head forcefully, looking down at the greasy remnants of our meal. "You have it, love. If I eat any more, I'm going to morph into a dough ball."

The zip of my size 20 jeans was already rolled down at the waistband, as the stiff material had been branding my skin like a purple marker pen.

We were watching a film on Netflix together. I had already checked it out on IMDB, hoping upon hope that it would have some good reviews. Damn it! It had a rating of 4.1. I was always adamant that I would only watch films that scored at least a rating of 6, but it was Jacob's choice and, *quelle surprise*, it was yet again some zombie thriller. I couldn't help thinking distastefully that the current victim being eaten alive looked uncannily like the topping from my Texas BBQ stuffed crust that I'd just wolfed down not five minutes previously.

It had been a lovely, chilled evening – spending quality time with my son was always a treat, even if it was in the company of the half-chomped undead. It was such a shame that Daniel couldn't be here too, I thought loyally, but at least he would be having a good time playing squash and expending some of his pent up energy in such a wholesome way. I knew I really should think about getting some form of exercise too, but that just felt a bit overwhelming at present. The idea of me joining a gym would be about as welcome as if I suggested to Jacob that we watched a nice rom com after the zombie carnage had concluded.

Jacob unfolded his tall frame from the sofa with a yawn and headed off towards the kitchen, his low-slung jeans hanging off his slim hips. I could hear him yank open the door of the freezer and furtively rummage around inside. "Getting myself some ice cream, Mum. Do you want some?"

I considered this for a few seconds: a nice scoop of praline and cream would go down very well indeed, but I I shook my head. "No thanks, Jacob, I'm stuffed, fit to burst."

I felt rather proud of myself: after all, let's be honest, there was always room for pudding if you really wanted it. It didn't matter how full you were; you could be absolutely pogged, but there was always a little pocket of stomach left to accommodate a scoop of ice cream or the tiniest sliver of chocolate cake. I ran my hand through my recently coiffed hair, as if expecting to find a glowing halo. I had to admit that Tabby had done a good job: all my grey was gone, and my shoulder-length waves were shining like a newly ripe conker. She was an extremely good stylist; maybe I should have been brave and let her have free rein on my barnet after all.

Jacob returned to his place next to me with a full carton of

Häagen-Dazs and a soup spoon sticking out of the top. He happily slurped some of the creamy dessert off the back of the spoon before a troubled expression clouded his youthful face.

"Doesn't it bother you how much Dad is out now?" He turned his attention fully towards me and his voice was verging on anger. "He never seems to be home any more; it's like we don't exist for him!" His eyes narrowed slightly. "He's out tonight playing squash again, and he's out for drinks tomorrow night too."

"Yes, but I'm out too tomorrow night as well... remember?"

"Yes, I know that, Mum," Jacob was shaking his head, "but you usually never go out. Whereas Dad... well, Dad is never here."

"I'm going to leave you some food on a plate for when we're out, love, so you won't need to fix yourself anything: maybe some shepherd's pie or a chilli."

Jacob rolled his eyes. "That's not the point I'm trying to make. It's not my stomach I'm worried about, Mum. It's just... never mind... it's nothing." He turned his attention back to the ice cream that was running down the outside of the container, perilously close to dripping onto his ripped jeans. He stopped it in its tracks with his finger before returning his gaze to the zombies on screen.

I sighed inwardly to myself. It upset me that Jacob was so concerned about how often his father was away from home. I had convinced myself that Daniel working such long hours was good for his career and therefore for the family; and the regular gym sessions and squash games were good for his health and mental well-being. OK, sometimes I did feel a bit hurt that he would rather have a few drinks after work with his colleagues than come home to his family, but he always reassured me that this was a positive thing: he was networking and making important work connections. I prided myself that I was a great wife for being so supportive of my spouse.

"Your dad works so hard so that we can have the best standard of life." I picked up the pizza box with the few dry crusts rustling in the bottom and took it into the kitchen. Standing by the chipped Formica worktop I gave myself a few seconds to compose myself before returning to the lounge. I smiled overly brightly at my son.

"It's good that Dad is getting so fit that he can kick a ball around with you better, not get so out of breath."

"Oh yeah?" Jacob rolled his eyes sarcastically. "When did Dad last do anything just with me?"

I thought for a few seconds and realised Jacob was right. Father and son used to go out just the two of them, having their "boys' time". I relished the opportunity to get rid of them both for a few hours so I could indulge in a box set uninterrupted, or dive head first into a juicy novel; but Jacob was right, they hadn't done anything together in months: no kick-arounds at the park, no ten-pin bowling, no trips to the cinema - nothing.

I guess I had just thought that Jacob felt it was a bit tragic to hang out with his dad at his age. The option of being with his mates was probably far preferable to spending time with the oldies; but maybe I had been wrong. Maybe Jacob had been missing his dad as much as I was, and I had simply failed to notice; too caught up in my own concerns. I felt deeply troubled by this.

I turned my attention to my son again. He seemed fine now after his outburst: his eyes were transfixed on the television screen, where a bouncy young blonde was running screaming through the woods, bizarrely zigzagging in her white nightdress, pursued by a horde of ravenous zombies who were eyeing her up like an all-you-can-eat brain buffet.

Chapter 5

"Would you just have a look at the state of that!" My own eyes and those of my two girlfriends Jasmine and Jayne swivelled to who or what Lila had noticed. A little further down the bar from us, at a high round glass table, two gentlemen in their early sixties were sitting on bar stools drinking brightly coloured cocktails and clearly trying to catch Lila's attention.

The one that was obviously displeasing Lila was resplendent in tight cream trousers and a vibrant pink shirt, the buttons of which were so tight that they were straining against his burgeoning belly, evidently ready to burst forth at any second. To add a little flair to his ensemble he also sported a gold medallion nestling in his greying chest hair. He looked like an ageing 70s porn star, and clearly wasn't Lila's cup of Earl Grey. Unaware of this fact, he held up his cocktail glass, his diamond signet ring flashing gaudily on his stubby finger, glinting under the fluorescent disco lights, and mouthed slowly at Lila, "Can I buy you a drink?"

Lila shuddered visibly and shook her head vehemently to indicate that she was not in the least bit interested in anything he might care to offer her, drink or otherwise.

She was clearly none too impressed. "Is this what it has come to?" Sighing, she picked the olive out of her martini glass and chewed on it slowly. "First night out in ages, I'm looking drop dead gorgeous, if I do say so myself, and the only man who gives me the faintest bit of attention is Mr Comb-over." She grimaced again for effect. "I can actually smell the Old Spice and Viagra from here."

It was 10:30 pm on Friday night and we were finally on our girls' night out. Jayne, Jasmine and I were sitting shoulder to shoulder in a cramped hot pink leatherette booth, enjoying our fifth, sorry make that sixth, overpriced cocktail of the evening. We had already consumed a lovely meal at the Tapas restaurant; then we'd decided to throw caution to the wind and head to Eduardo's nightclub to enjoy a dance and recapture a little of our lost youth. The venue was usually referred to as Desperados. I'd not been to this nightclub or any other in many years, and I was pretty sure the carpet hadn't been cleaned in just as long.

Despite all my fears over the past few days, I was having a simply splendid time. I was feeling on top of the world as I slurped down my porn-star martini and noted to myself that I was looking damn good too. I was wearing the black wrap-over dress, and I liked feeling pretty and feminine for a change.

Earlier that evening, as I had inspected myself from every angle in the hall mirror before departing to meet the girls, I had had my reservations. Did I look like mutton dressed as lamb? Could I really get away with such a bright shade of red lipstick? And were my magnetic false eyelashes that Morgan had given me and insisted I wear just a step too far? Did I look more Drag Queen than Beauty Queen? More cock and balls than belle of the ball?

Jacob had given me the confidence I needed to strut out of

the house feeling like a million dollars. Watching me turn this way and that in front of the mirror, he had given me a huge smile and a reassuring thumbs up: "Go and have fun, Mum, you look awesome."

I'd hugged my son with affection and given myself one final appraising look before pulling on a burgundy-coloured shrug over my dress, just to cover the possibility that my less than toned arms would have a swing of bingo wing to them. I then left the house feeling calm as I got into the taxi to make the short journey to the restaurant to meet the girls.

My outfit and I had met with general approval from my friends. They were all in agreement that I scrubbed up pretty well. There was only one fly in the appointment that Lila was quick to point out: "You've got to get rid of the bloody shrug." She gestured to my burgundy woollen cover-up. "It's spoiling the aesthetic. You've got a lovely dress on, and you've gone and shoved a bit of bad knitwear over the top. It's giving off crusty cardigan vibes."

I shook my head at Lila. "I need to keep the upper arms covered: they're a tad dinner lady." I poked at the top of my arms to demonstrate the wobble factor. "I want to look sexy and sophisticated, not like I should be doling out portions of pie and mash to a load of year 9s."

As always, Lila was adamant that her opinion was the only one that mattered and the shrug had to go; so reluctantly I peeled it off, feeling the static flying off with it. I stuffed it on top of my black patent handbag by my feet.

"Much better," everyone chorused in unison.

Lila drained her glass, caught the attention of a young barman with a wave of her hand and ordered another round for us all. "I never understood an item of clothing that could be called a 'shrug'. Could you imagine anything in fashion quite as boring and indifferent as a shrug?" She shrugged her shoulders as if to demonstrate. "The name says it all."

"Lila's right," Jayne commented enthusiastically. "That's a lovely dress, Lottie; it suits you so well that it's a shame to cover it up."

Jayne was looking pretty good herself. She too was heading out of her comfort zone for the night. As Jayne predominantly worked from home on her jewellery business, she usually dressed in a uniform of oversized T-shirts, jumpers and leggings, rather like how I chose to dress. Jayne had a great figure though, probably about a size 12-14 and all the curves in just the right places, with a little nipped in waist and a flat stomach – more from good genes than working out. I sighed to myself: if I had Jayne's figure, I would be dressed permanently to the nines. However, Jayne did not see herself as the world did. She hated her body: she felt she was too fat with short legs, so chose to cover up in layers of baggy fabric too. She was daft, but I suppose that's how the world is: women tend to be their own harshest critics.

That evening Jayne was wearing a long, coral-coloured silk blouse over some dark fitted indigo jeans; the combination of the orange top and her auburn hair and sparkling bright blue eyes was simply stunning.

Jasmine was looking amazing too. She was decked out in a silky halter-neck red jumpsuit with high black stilettos; the shade of red against her black skin was simply stunning. Her curly jet hair was pulled back into a bun, with little tendrils hanging prettily onto her face. She wore minimal make-up, but then with skin as flawless as hers, it really would have been gilding the lily to cover it up.

The sexagenarian lothario who had been trying to woo Lila with offers of a drink strolled purposefully past our table on the way to the bar, casting Lila a look of withering distaste before turning his attention to a group of cackling ladies dressed as schoolgirls for a 50th birthday celebration.

"Oh dear, looks like you've missed out there, Lila," Jasmine winked playfully at Lila as she stirred her Daiquiri with a wooden cocktail stick.

"Oh well, my loss." Lila grimaced. "I think I can live with it, though. And what I was inhaling wasn't so much Old Spice as a whiff of mothballs and desperation."

Jayne was nodding at Lila with a sage expression on her face. "You know, all joking aside, you shouldn't be so dismissive; he could have been a really nice guy. You never know, you might have just dissed your soulmate – the yin to your yang."

Lila crossed a slim tanned leg over the other as she shuffled her position on her high bar stool. Her expensive tan leather skirt was proving to be a bit of a slip hazard on the cheap vinyl seats.

"I can say with all confidence that that gentleman was not my soulmate." She sat forward slightly, as if to impart something of great importance. "And talking about yang, or should I say *wang*, check out a load of this."

Lila was holding her Prada-encased phone across the table for us all to scrutinise. There were a few moments of silence as the three of us tried to fathom what we were looking at. There were some tufts of ginger hair and what appeared to be a long pink column.

I nodded at Lila, pleased with myself for figuring it out so quickly. "It's Beaker from *The Muppets.* Jacob used to love watching him when he was younger, and Kermit and Miss

Piggy, before he moved on to *The Simpsons* of course."

My friends began laughing hysterically, trying desperately to stop the tears from running down their faces and ruining their carefully applied make-up.

Jasmine rubbed my arm affectionately, rather like the way you would humour someone none too intellectually blessed. "No, Lottie, it's not a Muppet, it's what is commonly known in the world of online dating as a dick pic."

I took the phone from Lila and studied the image more carefully. Yes, I could see now that it was indeed a male appendage in all its glory. But why would the owner have decided it was a good idea to send it by phone message? Especially to Lila? It wasn't exactly a thing of beauty; not worthy of being framed and gracing the wall above your fireplace anyway.

It was Jayne's turn to give her full attention to the small iPhone screen. "Surprised there's pubes," she commented thoughtfully; "he must be a bit old school."

Lila went on to inform us all that although she wasn't appalled to find the odd dick pic landing in her inbox, and it certainly brightened up a dull afternoon in the office, she certainly wouldn't date someone whose first point of contact was introducing you to his family jewels. She would rather enjoy a candle-lit meal of meat and two veg with a man before actually coming face to face with the... ahem, meat and two veg.

I soon learned that apparently in the world of dating, pubic hair had long become a thing of the past. Males as well as females were expected to be plucked down yonder, like a Bernard Matthews' butter ball turkey. Of course I could understand it from a hygiene point of view: no one liked to be unexpectedly flossing their teeth with an errant strand of pubic hair, but it all seemed a bit alien to me, and to be honest a tad chilly – especially in Yorkshire.

I imparted my view to my friends. "I don't like it; there's nothing wrong with a bit of hair down there, especially for men. It's like adding a nice faux fur trim to a pair of suede gloves; it just adds a bit of interest, takes your attention away from all the pink."

Lila was still laughing. "Might have known you'd like a hirsute fella, Lottie. I bet Daniel's never had a Bic razor down there in his entire life."

Lila's comment stopped me dead for a few seconds. Once upon a time she was right about Daniel. He had never been one for male grooming of any description, and he would have thought the notion of manscaping to be utterly hilarious. However, just lately he had been taking more care with his appearance. He had started tweezing his eyebrows of an evening in the dimly lit bathroom mirror and slapping on a liberal amount of night cream, even dabbing on eye cream in a circular motion to his crow's feet. His shelf in the bathroom cabinet was beginning to look like the beauty department in Boots, whilst my shelf bore solely a lowly pot of Nivea, that flat blue pot, the one my Grandma Agnes always used to use.

To be fair, as for his lack of pubes in that department, I couldn't really comment. His nether regions could very well now be sporting a short back and sides, but regrettably it had been a few months since I had seen them. Daniel was never one for parading around the house butt naked, but even he had been a little more conservative of late; it always seemed that his pyjama bottoms were firmly on and the drawstring waist neatly tied twice – once to be secure, and then once again for good measure.

The sound of Lila's laugh brought me back to the conversation around me, out of my daydream. Lila was proudly showing another picture on her mobile phone. This time thankfully it was a male face, and rather a nice face at that: a handsome man with a thatch of thick brown hair was smiling warmly from the screen. Next to his face was the name Adam and the age 36.

Lila looked like the cat that had got the cream and decided it wasn't lactose intolerant. "That lucky fella, ladies, is my date for tomorrow night."

I was a little shocked, I had to admit. "You're kidding, Lila? He's only 36, that's 13 years younger than you are. Are you going to have anything in common?"

Lila rolled her blue eyes, and they glinted like chips of sapphire. "Who cares if we have anything in common? Have you not checked out his face? He's absolutely gorgeous, and so what if he's younger? Haven't you heard that age is only a number, and anyway mine's unlisted!"

With that she attempted to shimmy her way off her high bar stool. Had she pulled it off gracefully, it would have looked effortless; but it was spoilt by the large farting noise caused by her leather skirt peeling off the vinyl seat, a sound rather reminiscent of a whoopee cushion.

"I'll name that tune in one," Jasmine commented, smirking. Lila coughed in a futile attempt to cover the noise and hastily grabbed Jayne's arm. "Come on, we're dancing," she announced, pulling her friend along with her, whether she was willing or not.

Within a couple of minutes Lila and Jayne were strutting their stuff on the dance floor, garnering appreciative glances from random men as they spun around to Pink's *Trustfall* blaring out from the DJ booth. They looked so happy and confident out there, really enjoying their best lives. "That should be me too," I thought, making the decision that I was going to head for the dance floor too. Everyone looked so happy and at ease. Even the woman dancing on her own just off to the right of Lila and Jayne was simply having the time of her life, dancing and singing to the pop music with wild abandon. My eyes were drawn to the outfit she was wearing: the tightest leopard skin leggings I had ever seen. Honestly, there must have been a camel limping around the desert somewhere that was missing its big toe.

I left my burgundy shrug on my seat and slung my evening bag over my shoulder before turning to my remaining friend. "Come on, Jasmine, let's have a dance too."

Jasmine shook her head. "You go, Lottie, and I'll see you on the dance floor. I'm just heading to the Ladies first. Anyway, knowing my luck there'll be no toilet paper in there, so I'll be shaking my ass before I even get near the dance floor."

I couldn't help but laugh at this as I watched her head off to join the queue. I picked up my glass of martini: might as well drain this first and give myself a bit of extra Dutch courage before I showed the world what a first-class mover and shaker I was.

The straw was just up to my lips when I first spotted her.

I didn't know her, but she was absolute perfection: from the long mane of icy blonde hair grazing her narrow shoulders to the slender heart-shaped face where everything looked in perfect proportion. No thin lips or wide nose here; everything was just as exquisite as Botticelli's *Venus*. And this vision of loveliness was in Eduardo's nightclub on a dreary wet Friday in March. She looked as if she belonged on a catwalk in

Milan, or delicately sipping champagne at a chic pavement brasserie in downtown Paris. She was elegantly attired in a knee-length Bardot-style black shift dress which showed off her long coltish legs as she walked confidently and purposefully on her vertiginous high heels. If I had worn the same footwear, I would have been stumbling around like a newly born Bambi or my Uncle Eric on Christmas Eve when he had been enthusiastically inhaling the Bailey's and sherry trifle.

I stared wistfully at her. She was everything I wanted to be all wrapped up in a perfect package of a person. She barely glanced in my direction as she made her way past me and towards the tables at the back of the club. She didn't even seem to walk, but merely glide. She briefly raised her hand to wave a greeting to someone she knew as she passed them by, and then she was gone.

I turned to catch another glimpse of her and could just about make her out in the distance smiling at her companion as she sat down and elegantly took a sip from her drink. I strained my eyes to get a better look at who her companion was; keen to see who such a beautiful woman would choose to spend her evening with, but I couldn't quite make him out as he was sitting behind one of the gaudy marblesque pillars that were dotted around the club to add a bit of class. Ha! Chance would be a fine thing.

I looked again and could just make out a black loafer poking out from behind the pillar. Suddenly I had a rather strange, unsettled feeling in my gut. Maybe I shouldn't have had the prawn pil-pil and the calamari at the restaurant after all. Too much seafood and cocktails could often have a rather unfortunate effect on me. But no, I wasn't feeling ill; it was something else, something I couldn't quite put my finger on.

And then I saw him. The man that the perfect blonde woman was sitting with had leaned in to speak to her, clearly needing to get closer for his voice to be heard over the warbling of Pink. Like her, he was also very attractive. A handsome man. A married man. My man. My husband.

My vision started to dance and white spots were swirling erratically in front of my eyes as I realised the man that Miss Perfect was sitting next to was none other than my Daniel.

Chapter 6

I have no idea how long I sat there, barely daring to even breathe. It could have been seconds, it could have been minutes, I simply had no idea. I do know that when Lila and Jayne returned from the dance floor I was still staring at the couple, my eyes unwavering and never leaving them for a second.

"Charlotte...are you OK?" Jayne touched me gently on my arm. "You look as if you've seen a ghost."

I turned my face towards her but just stared blankly. No words would come.

I was sitting in the loud, brightly lit nightclub, but I felt as if I was in a vacuum. Or that I existed and didn't exist at the same time. I know that doesn't make sense, but it was how I felt. I suppose it was the shock rendering my body incapable of anything. Suddenly I felt my emotions whoosh over me like a great tidal wave and I started to cry, great big snotty tears of despair.

"It's Daniel," I wailed.

By this stage Jasmine had also returned and was settling herself back in the booth. "What's Daniel?"

I shook my head miserably from side to side. I just couldn't answer. I didn't want to have to admit to them what I had seen.

Lila's eyes darted around the club, and her gaze fixed on Daniel and the blonde sitting at the back of the club.

Her eyes narrowed dangerously. "Is that Daniel?... It is. Who's that he's with?"

I shook my head again. "He told me he was going out for a few drinks with colleagues after work... I thought he was out with the guys for a few beers."

Jasmine and Jayne had also now fixed their glares on Daniel and his companion. Clearly Daniel and his *friend* were both oblivious to the interest that our table was showing in them as they chatted together, obviously exceedingly comfortable in each other's company. Daniel whispered something to the woman again and she threw back her head with abandon and laughed. She rested her hand on his affectionately.

"The little prick!" Lila's voice was high-pitched, and she was clearly angry. Little red spots had flushed both cheeks, which was always a giveaway that she was ready to go into full "Rottweiler" mode. "I'm going to kill him."

I took her hand in mine. "No, Lila, don't. Don't go over there... please... just leave it."

I knew Lila was angry on my behalf, but if anyone was going to make the short walk through the crowded bar and confront my husband, it was going to be me.

I looked over again at Daniel and the woman, willing for him to notice me, for shock to register on his face, but he didn't. He was clearly too interested in having a good time.

I needed to calm down. I could hear the blood pounding in my head.

"What do you want to do, Lottie?" Jasmine's large brown eyes were full of concern. "It's your call."

But what did I want to do? That was the million-dollar

question. I had such a burning desire to storm over to Daniel and confront him, but something deep inside me was stopping me from doing just that.

Daniel had said he was coming out after work for a few pints; "pretty dull" he'd described it. The blonde vision who he was sitting with certainly didn't fit that description. She was about as "dull" as a 10-carat diamond twinkling under a fluorescent spotlight.

I started to do what I always do in any situation, I started to rationalise. Of course, he had come out for a few drinks after work; they would have all gone to The Wiry Whippet pub just near his office, had a few pints, all work chums together, chatting about their colleagues and slagging off the boss. No doubt one by one the group would have trailed off, trains to catch, dinners getting cold at home on the kitchen table etc. etc. until only two remained: Daniel and the blonde. She must be a new member of staff, and Daniel had stayed out with her after everyone had departed for home so that she wouldn't feel left out. The Wiry Whippet would probably have had a band starting at 9 pm and it wasn't a genre of music that either of them appreciated, so they had moved on to Eduardo's. That was all it was. Just work colleagues. All perfectly innocent, nothing to see here.

I looked over at them again. Who was I kidding? I knew that I was usually the queen of denial, but this time I couldn't kid myself. What do they say, "There's no fool like an old fool"? Well, I was fooling myself no longer.

I had known things had not been right at home for ages: Daniel's distant behaviour with me; his lack of interest in the bedroom, or anywhere else for that matter. I had always blamed myself; put it all down to me not being good enough.

But how could I ever be good enough against her? There was no competition. She was gorgeous; everything I could only ever dream of being, and she was there with my husband: the man I thought I would spend the rest of my life with; the man who I would take Saga cruises with; who would sit next to me in our 70s at National Trust houses, where we would share a flask of stewed tea and eat tuna and cucumber sandwiches together and talk about our grandchildren. All the banal and comfortable dreams I had for our future together evaporated like a puff of smoke from one of those ridiculous cocktails that the barman was currently preparing. I felt like my life had now ceased and the future I had envisaged for us was being clumsily erased from our life story.

I knew deep in my heart that this woman was not merely a work colleague; they were much more than that. I felt that the woman had stolen my husband's heart and therefore had stolen my future. I felt angry at her, but not nearly as angry as I felt towards him. The anger I felt towards my husband was monumental.

I started to get out of my seat. I was going to bloody kill him. OK, not literally, I didn't really think the cocktail stirrer I had jammed in my fist would do all that much damage anyway. Give him a good old poke, I suppose. I laughed bitterly to myself; after all, it had been a bloody long time since he had given one to me.

As I clambered down from the booth, I caught a glimpse of my reflection in the mirrored wall on the back of the bar. Let's just say I was not looking my best. I had been so pleased with my appearance several hours ago, but now I looked like a red, bloated-faced disaster of epic proportions. It was always the same: as soon as I started to cry, my face would puff up like a crimson marshmallow and my carefully applied make-up ran rivers down my face, pooling in the cups of my bra.

I was definitely not going to confront Daniel looking like this. I was going to wait, bide my time, do it my way and in my time. I needed the opportunity to lick my wounds first and get my head around all that I had seen. I turned to my friends who were looking at me with a mixture of concern and morbid curiosity. "I want to go home."

Chapter 7

I didn't go home though, I went back to Lila's house instead. She insisted that I shouldn't go home in the state that I was currently in, as I would just alarm Jacob. She felt I really needed to talk things through with a friend first. I had to agree, so reluctantly accompanied her back to her beautiful detached bungalow in a fancy part of town.

Jayne and Jasmine had both returned home. After seeing Daniel with his *friend,* it had put rather a dampener on the evening. They both hugged me and kissed me copious times on the cheeks, then got their respective taxis home, while urging me to phone them if I needed anything at all, or just to talk at any time. I really did have good friends. For that I had to be thankful.

Lila and I continued to drink well into the night. We ransacked her drinks cabinet and were now drinking out-of-date crème de menthe with shots of tequila on the side for good measure. I fooled myself into thinking that the mint in the liqueur would somehow have a soothing effect on my stomach. There I was again, always looking for the positive in things. That would really need to stop.

We also pillaged Lila's fridge, and she was now drunkenly dunking cocktail sausages into a pot of red pepper hummus and devouring them as if it was *haute cuisine.*

"What are you going to do then, Lots?" Lila went to take a bite of the mini sausage, but missed her mouth completely as it fell down into the recesses of her silk top, never to be seen again. She picked up another sausage and continued dunking.

I threw back my tequila shot in one. Wow it burned, but in a good way. I pulled my shoulders back purposefully. "I'm going to find out exactly what's going on, that's what I'm going to do."

I had decided that I really needed to pick my timing when confronting Daniel. He always had a way of wriggling out of things and somehow making it seem like the fault was with me. I wanted to catch him again with Miss Blonde and see what he would say then. But until then I was going to have to keep my counsel and not let him know that I knew anything. That was going to be difficult. I was going to have to act my ass off. And as someone whose acting credentials only ever went as far as playing "random villager" in my Primary School Nativity, that was going to prove quite the task.

I had let Jacob know that I wouldn't be returning home that evening. I'd sent him a text message two hours earlier, at just after midnight, saying that Lila was a little "worse for wear" and that I was going to stay the night at her house just to keep an eye on her.

Jacob had responded in his usual way: "Ok Mum dad's not back yet c u in the a.m. x"

So, Daniel wasn't home yet. *Quelle surprise!*

When Lila and I had polished off the remainder of the green liqueur and the tequila and had demolished half a partially defrosted strawberry gateau, it was finally time for bed.

Lila escorted me to her pristine guest bedroom with its

luxurious cream cotton bedding. It looked like something from a top-end chic boutique hotel, certainly not the Travelodge I was used to. I rapidly pulled off my black dress and climbed into the bed in my mismatched underwear. Blimey, this bed was comfortable, and the bedding felt like I was being wrapped in a fluffy cloud.

"If there's anything you need, I'm just next door," Lila instructed.

"Thank you, Lila," I mumbled tipsily. "I do normally wear ear plugs when I sleep, but I guess I won't need them sleeping on my own tonight - no Daniel snoring."

Lila indicated the chrome and wood bedside table next to me and started to laugh. "Well, you'll find some plugs in there if you want, but I wouldn't advise putting them in your ears." I could still hear her laughing to herself as she shut the door and stumbled drunkenly into her own room.

With that I fell into a deep, dreamless sleep. The effects of shock and a brewery's worth of alcohol had rendered me virtually catatonic.

Chapter 8

It was after 11 am the following morning when I finally walked through my front door. Jacob, not an early riser at the best of times, was sitting at the kitchen table eating enough cornflakes to fill a washing up bowl and scrolling through TikTok.

"Morning, sweetheart." I greeted him with a brief kiss on the cheek and then flopped down on the seat next to him, my head pounding as if *Riverdance* was performing in my skull.

He gave me a thumbs up. "Good time then?"

A wave of pain shot though me that actually hurt my heart, and I felt the sting of upcoming tears as I remembered the events from the previous night. I hastily stopped them in their watery tracks. "Yes, it was good, so lovely to see the girls, but we all had a few too many cocktails."

"As long as you had a good time." Jacob's attention was back to his phone, and he was chuckling at a short video of a pug dog dressed in a tutu, seemingly signing in tune with Miley Cyrus.

"Where's Dad?"

"Lounge," Jacob replied without looking up from his phone.

I filled a glass with water from the tap and swallowed down a couple of paracetamols before heading off to find my darling husband.

Daniel was indeed in the lounge reading his paper. He looked up from it briefly when I entered the room. "Good night?" He made no comment about the fact that I had stayed at Lila's house for the night rather than coming home. Quite clearly it wasn't an issue for him.

"Yep," I nodded brightly at him, "and you?"

"Mmmm." He turned the page of his newspaper slowly. "What? Oh yeah, me...it was very quiet; work talk, that sort of stuff... putting the world to rights, you know? Boring really."

I nodded again at him. I didn't trust myself to speak for a few seconds. When I had recovered my composure, I smiled brightly at him. "What are your plans for today? We could do something nice together as a family... if you like?"

I felt like I was testing him. Giving him an opportunity to put us first, to think about his family before himself for once.

He sighed regretfully. "I wish you'd said earlier that you wanted to go out, but I've made plans now."

"Plans?" I enquired sweetly.

Daniel folded his paper neatly and placed it on the coffee table. "Just a game of squash again with Jon. I'm meeting him at the sports centre in about an hour or so."

I picked up the newspaper, took it into the kitchen and deposited it in the recycling. Was he really going to play squash with Jon? I sincerely doubted it. I needed time to think, to decide what it was best for me to do.

I began to prepare a beef chilli for dinner that evening. It just gave me something practical to do, to keep my hands busy and away from Daniel's neck. I could focus on preparing the meal and then it could bubble away for the remainder of the day in the slow cooker.

I was feeling as if I was on autopilot as I chopped onions and deseeded chillis, when a little devil seemed to whisper quietly in my ear.

I took some of the seeds from the green chillis that I had been chopping and began to grind them in my marble pestle and mortar until they became a powdery dust. I then placed them on a saucer and made my way upstairs to our en suite bathroom. I felt like I was in some sort of trance-like state.

I found Daniel's day cream on the shelf in the bathroom cabinet where it always was. I picked it up and read the details on the side of the fancy silver pot. "With vitamin C and peppermint to refresh your skin and leave you tingly and revitalised" it stated. I unscrewed the cap. Hah! I'd show him tingly and revitalised alright. With that I dumped the chilli seed powder into the cream. It sat on top of the viscous gloop, so I grabbed an ear bud and stirred it in well until it was undetectable. I then tossed the ear bud into the rubbish bin next to the bathroom scales. The scales that I avoided like the plague.

With that I made my way calmly back downstairs to finish preparing the dinner.

Chapter 9

Less than an hour later, I felt like an ersatz Sherlock Holmes as I followed my beloved husband, at a fair distance, as he briskly made his way to the sports centre for his game of squash. I pulled the collar of my coat up against the wind that was picking up and swirling around some random litter. Could I possibly be any more of a cliché? Dressed in a mac with my collar turned up, tailing my husband as he made his way to a romantic rendezvous?

I still had the faintest glimmer of hope that Daniel was indeed making his way to the sports centre; that in the next couple of minutes he would turn left into the road that housed the newly refurbished sports centre that still managed to smell like old plimsoles and wet dog.

My heart was in my throat as I followed him furtively along the road. I needn't have worried about him clocking me though, as he was very much in a world of his own, humming away to himself happily. I couldn't be sure, but the tune sounded very much like 'When a Man Loves a Woman'.

Albert Avenue was coming up on the left and Daniel would need to be turning into it in approximately 20 seconds. But he continued past the avenue and carried on along the road before turning right onto the High Street. Clearly, he was not going to the sports centre after all. Although I had known all along that this must be the case, it still felt like a physical blow to my gut.

Daniel checked left and right for oncoming traffic before he dashed across the main road. I stood perfectly still as I watched him, waiting to see where he would go next. He meandered past a few shops – the hardware shop, the newsagent's, the old-fashioned little bakery that always smelt like sugary heaven when you passed it and sold the most amazing apple turnovers. He strode purposefully along until he reached the entrance to Moonlight Lounge, the intimate cocktail bar that had sprung up on the High Street about six months before, having been a childrenswear shop in a previous life.

He paused for a second to adjust his collar and check that his hair wasn't too windswept, then disappeared inside.

At this point I made my way to the zebra crossing to cross the road. Unlike Daniel, I was not going to play fast and loose with my physical well-being and casually jaywalk.

I felt my nerves jangling as I made my way along the parade of shops. I passed by the hardware shop, the newsagent's and the cake shop – my favourite. Strangely the tantalising aroma wafting out of Sweet Buns Bakery did absolutely nothing for me this time, and I felt no desire to go in and buy myself something.

When I arrived at Moonlight Lounge my anxiety was through the roof. I felt timid and terrified simultaneously. I stood rooted to the spot for several seconds and tried my best to steady my breathing and reduce my heart rate. Nervously I peered through the frosted window into the glamorous world within. As it was a Saturday afternoon the place was rammed. There was the whole spectrum of humanity there in front of my gaze: twenty-something groups of fashionable girlfriends sipping away on neon-coloured cocktails, older women with their smart couture and gin and tonics, and a few groups of men drinking wine or having a pint. There were even a few football supporters who looked like fish out of water in their team stripes as they sipped their drinks, probably wishing they'd gone into the Wetherspoons down the road instead.

Then I finally spotted them. They were sitting about halfway down at an intimate table for two. Daniel was gesticulating to something on the cocktail menu as a young waitress nodded and took their order. And there she was - Miss Blonde. She was more casually attired than the previous night, with fitted indigo jeans encasing her long legs and a smart cream blazer. She looked just as beautiful though, I thought with a sigh.

I took another deep steadying breath and placed my hand on the doorknob ready to enter the premises. It was at this point that I spotted the little chemist's shop next door and a thought flashed through my brain. It was the little devil whispering to me again, and I chose that moment to listen to him once more. I walked away from Moonlight Lounge and entered the chemist's shop instead, the bell above the door jangling and alerting the staff to my arrival – there was one little purchase that I needed to make.

Five minutes later and I was back at the doorway of Moonlight Lounge. I took another deep breath, said a little prayer and this time walked into the bar as purposefully as I could manage on my shaky jelly legs. It was only a short distance to Daniel's table, but it felt miles as I made my journey over to them. It was as if I was walking towards something truly terrible – a root canal at the dentist's or an Adam Sandler film perhaps.

Miss Blonde glanced up at me as I stopped at their table, with a quizzical look etched on her beautiful face. Daniel failed to notice me for a few seconds, but when he did the expression on his face was utterly priceless. He looked as if he had been slapped in the face with a wet haddock. He appeared stupefied, as if he just couldn't compute what was happening. Then his face paled slightly, and his demeanour changed to shame; just how I imagine he would look if his mother had caught him in a quick after-school wank as a boy. Finally, his expression turned into annoyance, and bright spots of colour appeared high on his cheekbones.

"Char...Charlotte, what are you doing here?"

I took in his defiant pose and facial expression and had an overwhelming desire to slap his lying cheating face, but I didn't. That just wasn't my style.

"What am I doing here?" I somehow managed to keep my shaking legs in check and my voice was dripping with saccharine sweetness. "What are you doing here is more the question, surely? I didn't realise this place sold Sea Breezes with a side order of squash, or is it a Screaming Orgasm you're really after?"

Miss Blonde's eyes were darting between myself and Daniel, and she gave me a withering look of contempt. "Babe, *who* is this woman?"

Babe??

I turned my attention back to Daniel, as did she. He looked aghast.

"I... I... I'm sorry, Roxy, but this is my wife, Charlotte."

Now it was Roxy's turn to look aghast. "Your wife?" Her voice was so shrill that I was surprised we could actually hear it. It should have been only audible to dogs. Quite fitting for her, really. I'm not saying for a moment that she looked like a dog – the complete opposite, in fact. But what sort of a name is Roxy? Surely that would have been more fitting for a Staffordshire bull terrier than this thirty-something blonde totty in her designer jeans.

Roxy was shaking her head back and forth vigorously, and her dangly earrings caught in her thick mane of hair. "I don't understand, Daniel. You told me you were a widow."

Of all the things I had expected to hear, this was not it. I imagined that Daniel would have told this woman that we were separated or divorced, or maybe she would know he was married and would find it a bit of a thrill to be the other woman. Not this, though. I had never for a solitary second contemplated the fact that he might say I was dead! My darling husband had chosen to kill me off so that he could embark on a liaison with another woman. The filthy lying prick!

I stared Daniel straight in the eye, hoping that my glacial glare would possibly give him frostbite of the nether regions. "No, not dead at all. I had a bit of a cold a few weeks ago, but I think you can see that I'm very much alive and well."

Daniel's head was now in his hands. "I'm sorry... I'm just so sorry?"

Who was he apologising to? I had this awful sinking feeling that it wasn't me. How could I have been so wrong about someone? How could I have loved him so completely for so much of my life, yet he could do this to me? What was wrong with me? No, I thought angrily, what was wrong with him? That was the real question.

Foxy Roxy was not happy. "You lied to me... How could you? You said you loved me. We talked about marriage, and all the time you were still married to *her*." She thrust an accusing finger at me.

This was not going at all the way I had imagined: I had envisioned that I would storm over to the pair of them, confront the lying cheat of a scumbag spouse and his bit on the side, and have my moment of glory. Stoically, with a breaking heart I would have the small consolation of knowing that I was now taking control of a horrible situation. However, it now felt as if this woman was considering herself more of an injured party in this triangle than me – his wife and the mother of his child. The absolute barefaced cheek of her!

I glanced around the subtly chic furnishings and soft lighting, and it suddenly dawned on me that I must look a right state: standing in the middle of this chic up-scale bar in my tatty old mac, with my hair piled up on my head in a messy bun and the remnants of last night's make-up smeared over my face. But I simply didn't care. I felt great. I felt like a warrior. And I was not having this woman play the victim. Not on my watch.

I pulled out the paper bag I had got from the chemist's from my coat pocket and extracted the contents.

"Obviously you will not be welcome back home tonight, Daniel," I informed him with a sarcastic laugh as he continued to sit stock still with his head in his hands. There was just the faint sound of jagged breathing coming from his vicinity. I turned my attention back to his companion. "I suppose he'll be staying at yours from now on?"

Roxy nearly choked on her frozen daiquiri and looked absolutely appalled by this notion. I gave her a wide smile that I hoped would pass as friendly. I sincerely doubted it though. My rictus grin would probably resemble something straight out of her worst nightmare: the bogeyman in size 20 stretch Lycra, no doubt. I tossed the contents of the paper bag towards her, and the box landed just adjacent to her cocktail glass. She picked it up, examining it and clearly not understanding what it was.

"It's his special ointment," I explained pleasantly, "for his psoriasis. He gets it particularly badly on his bottom, the poor love. Just make sure he rubs it in often, or you can do it for him if that's more your bag. The main thing is just to apply it regularly, as if the psoriasis isn't treated his arse cheeks will flare up and resemble a flaky old Hobnob biscuit. Not a pretty sight, I think you'll agree."

A slow grown emanated from Daniel, and I realised with elation that he was mortified. Hah! Good. Bloody well served him right.

I suddenly realised that we were proving to be quite the entertainment for the other customers: a thoroughly entertaining floor show for them to enjoy alongside their overpriced beverages. I heard a few muffled giggles coming from the next table, where a group of twenty-something girls appeared to be surreptitiously filming the exchange on their mobile phones. Normally I hated to be the centre of attention, but for some reason today it wasn't a problem for me. I seemed unflappable. I was just too angry in that moment to feel embarrassed or humiliated. No doubt that would come later, as would the tears.

Roxy's face was a picture of shock. She looked absolutely appalled. Somehow, she was beginning to look less and less attractive to me as time went on. A bit of a reverse Dorian Grey phenomenon, and I didn't think her portrait was going back in the attic any time soon. Yes, she was still an incredibly beautiful woman, but I was getting the definite impression that this woman was extremely self-absorbed and selfish. It's true, the old adage that real beauty comes from within.

Ideally I should then swing my hair elegantly over my shoulder, turn on my heel and sashay out of the establishment like the wronged heroine from one of my favourite old black and white movies. And I still felt I'd done a decent enough job as I strode out of the place with my messy bun, my shabby mac and my scruffy trainers. I felt simply invincible and incredibly proud of myself.

Back out on the dirty pavement in front of the bar a few moments later, it was a different matter. The soaring elation I had felt was quickly abating, and grim reality was slowly beginning to register. The realisation of what I had just encountered and what it all meant for me and my life began to sink in.

What on earth was I going to do?

Chapter 10

Fifty minutes later, I was back sitting in the same tatty leather swivel chair at Scissor Sisters that I had vacated only a couple of days before. Somehow, though, it felt as if I had lived an eternity since then. On a whim I had decided to call the salon and see if there was any chance that I could be squeezed in for a last-minute appointment. I didn't know why, but I just felt compelled to do something spontaneous, something just for me.

"It's really fortunate that I could fit you in, Charlotte," Tabby commented, combing my windswept tangle back from my face. "I just had a lady cancel with a dicky tummy from a prawn madras she'd had last night, so you're in luck."

"Not so lucky for her," I mumbled with a tight-lipped smile, thinking to myself I would much rather have an attack of the raging biryani squirts than the rumbling inner turmoil I was currently experiencing.

Tabby threw her head back and let out a booming laugh. "Yeah, you're spot on there. That's why I always stick to a korma; much less chance of the 3 am toilet trots with something nice and mild."

Tabby continued to comb my hair as she hummed along to K D Lang warbling in the background on the antique-looking stereo system. "Why are you back so soon though, sweet? You've only just had it coloured and trimmed; I didn't think we'd have the pleasure of your company again for at least another six weeks."

That was a very good question. Why was I back in the salon so soon? When I had left Moonlight Lounge and found myself back on the rain-spattered High Street, I had felt completely alone, cast adrift in a sea of noisy shoppers and pedestrians. Standing almost trance-like, I had kept playing back our conversation in my mind. I had the most overwhelming feeling that I was at a critical juncture in my life. Things were spiralling out of my control, and I needed to get a grip of something - of anything. Evidently I had relinquished all control in my marriage. I had become a doormat, a bit player in the story of my own life; a sad, pathetic version of the woman I was really meant to be. I had to take up the reins of my life again and steer it on a course that suited me. I had to put myself first for once.

I had started plodding towards home. I dreaded getting into the house and having to tell Jacob all that had happened. I just didn't think I could face it. To see his face crumble when I explained what I had discovered about his father was really something I did not relish. I was going to ruin his Saturday too, but did I really have to? I could leave it for a few hours, let him enjoy his weekend before I dropped the bombshell. Really, what was the rush?

In the distance I could just make out the blurry, green, blob-like shape of a double-decker bus slowly approaching. I had reached the shabby old bus shelter, with its broken windows and fragrant whiff of stale piss and cider, where a sweet-looking old lady was waiting. She offered me a friendly smile that crinkled her face into a thousand little furrows. "Is that the bus coming in the distance, dear? I think it is, but my poor old eyes aren't what they used to be."

"Yes, yes, it is," I replied, smiling warmly at her too. Right then I made up my mind that I wasn't going home after all. I turned to address the kindly-faced woman. "I'm getting that bus too."

"Champion." Her pale eyes twinkled at me. "I'll sit next to you, and we can have a nice old chinwag on the way to town."

Oh dear. That really wasn't what I had in mind. In truth, I just wanted some quiet time, a chance to stew on things and wrap my mind around everything. But as I looked at the diminutive anoraked form of the old dear, I just couldn't be mean. It didn't come naturally to me.

"Lovely." I held out my arm to stop the bus; and then pulled out my phone to make the call to the salon.

As I sat down on the crowded number 12 bus to Leeds city centre, I decided that I would only engage in a bit of small talk with my companion, about the weather and what not. I would not discuss anything to do with the state of my marriage. There was no way I would be discussing what I had seen last night and what had occurred when confronting Daniel and his girlfriend today. It was just too awful. As I dabbed my red-rimmed eyes with a crusty old tissue that I had fished out of the bottom of my handbag, I was still sure that the topic of my marriage was strictly off limits, and most definitely so to strangers. I was keeping it all to myself. I was going to be tight-lipped on the subject and definitely not crack. It was all just too embarrassing and humiliating to mention out loud.

My plan was working fine while I discovered that my companion was called Daisy and lived on her own in sheltered accommodation with her two Persian cats, Laurel and Hardy.

Then she had offered me a Werthers Original sweet, and this small act of kindness made the dam burst in my heart. The whole sorry story spewed out of me like a torrent. Daisy was so sweet in a warm, motherly sort of way, with her compassionate eyes and offers of old-person candy. She was the type who would surely bake her own bread and feed the ducks on the pond in the park. She was such a sweet, nurturing figure in her tartan-lined boots and eccentric bobble hat. She listened intently as I told her my tale of woe from start to finish, occasionally nodding her head and waiting patiently for me to end, which I did with a soggy, snotty snuffle.

"The ruddy buggering little shite!" she exclaimed angrily, little shards of Werther's caramel hitting the threadbare head-rest of the seat in front of us. "I hope you hoofed him hard in his wedding tackle." Oh dear. Not quite the sweet, mild-mannered old lady after all, it would appear. Her vocabulary was more like drunken sailors on a stag night.

Anyway, as I had already spewed everything out to Daisy in my tearful attack of verbal diarrhoea, now that I was sitting with Tabby in the salon it seemed only fitting that I should also let her into the pantomime that my life had become. When I had once again finished the tale, she let out a low whistle.

"Wow, that's certainly a lot you've had to deal with in a short period of time." She turned to Shannon, the junior stylist who was sweeping up hair and trying to give the appearance she hadn't been earwigging on our entire conversation. "Shan, go and get Charlotte a cup of coffee; and add a big slug of the Bailey's left over from Christmas; I think she needs it."

Shannon nodded in agreement and shambled off to get my drink.

Tabby continued to comb my hair. "So, what are we doing

to your hair today then? Something radical? Something that'll royally piss off the hubby? Number one buzz all over perhaps? Or can I get really creative with colour? I've always thought you would look awesome with lavender locks."

I turned to Tabby, and as I tried desperately to stop the tears that were collecting in the corners of my eyes from sliding down my cheeks, I said, "I just want you to make me beautiful."

She smiled kindly at me. "Well, my darling, that's the easiest job in the world."

Three hours later and I was finally done. I hardly recognised myself as I took in my appearance in the long, smeared mirror. I looked good: not just "good for me", but good.

Tabby was standing a little way back from me admiring her handiwork. "Well, tell me you aren't beautiful now?"

I couldn't. She had worked wonders. It was amazing how a different colour and a shorter cut could transform someone so much. My mousy, flat as a pancake, brown hair was no longer; it was replaced by a shorter flippy do, with long face-framing layers and highlights of toffee and caramel running through it like threads of gold. As I moved my head back and forth, letting the tresses swish, the light bounced off it like it was on fire. Yes, I still had the puffy eyes from crying, my face was a tad blotchy and bloated, and we won't even get started on my double chin. But I felt good; and more importantly than that, I looked good.

Martina, who had been busy sorting out boxes of conditioner by the till, now came over to give her opinion too on my transformation.

"Girl, you look fine." She gave a proud nod of her head, the green reading glasses perched on top of her spikily cropped red hair looking perilously close to sliding off. "All those years you've been coming here, and damn it if there wasn't a babe lurking in there just needing to escape. I tell you, us stylists are better than therapy any day, and a damn sight cheaper."

Tabby laughed. "I wouldn't go that far, Marti, but I've got to say that for a confidence boost we might just have helped our girl here."

I smiled at them both. The new hair had certainly lifted my mood. After my contretemps with Daniel, I had felt the need to do something radical. Well, radical for me and certainly out of my comfort zone; and a haircut with new colour were about as rebellious as I got.

"You need a new outfit to go with the new look," Tabby commented. "Something a bit va va voom, to give you a little pep in your step."

I shook my head vehemently. Not a chance. There would be no shopping for clothes. I couldn't bear the thought of rummaging desperately through rails of too small clothes looking for a size 18-20 that didn't resemble an awning from the village fair. No thank you. What was it with clothes designers anyway? Why would they imagine for a second that anyone over a size 16 would want to wear jumpers emblazoned with "babe" or "hot stuff" across the front? The only time I ever felt "hot stuff" was due to my size and the blasted peri menopause. And what was it with thinking that every curvaceous woman wanted to wear leopard print? Or waterfall cardigans? Or cowl necklines? I shuddered at the thought.

Clothes shopping was out, but what about make-up? I used to love experimenting with make-up in my youth, and thinking back I'd had quite a flair for it, but that was so long ago. However, you didn't have to be a size 12 to fit into a mascara tube, did you? I fished out my little shiny make-up case from the bottom of my cavernous shoulder bag. It was a beady little number that Jacob had made me for Mother's Day at school, donkey's years ago. I opened it up and peered critically inside, half expecting a couple of moths to fly out. There were, however, three tampons, a dried-up mascara wand and a Boots 17 lipstick in the shade Twilight Teaser that must pre-date Tabby's existence on the earth. Of course, there was also the requisite mini tub of Nivea cream and some Vaseline and bizarrely a random piece of red Lego. I almost half expected to see some 80s leg warmers and a couple of shoulder pads in there for good measure. Some of my make-up was so old and out of date that I was lucky it hadn't killed me already. Hah! That would have played right into Daniel's hands. Eradication by eyeliner perhaps? Death by dusty old blusher? He wouldn't have had to fib about my demise then to get his leg over, would he?

I could go to Boots right now and treat myself to a few new items of make-up. It wouldn't break the bank, as they always had their 3 for 2 offers, so in fact I would be saving myself money. It was the fiscally responsible thing to do - an absolute no-brainer. Plus, putting my old, tired make-up on with my new hairstyle would be an act of criminal proportions; and, as I'm sure you're aware by now, I am nothing if not a good law-abiding girl.

I hugged Tabby and Martina warmly, and thrust a generous tip into Tabby's hand, which she amply deserved. She then whispered quietly in my ear, "If you really want to get back at your husband, why don't you let me take you out for the night sometime?"

I can only imagine the shock that registered on my face. I felt an embarrassed flush spread up from my neck to my cheeks.

Was she flirting with me? I know I can be a bit slow off the mark, but I really think she was. As I pushed the heavy glass door open and entered Boots, I could feel the beginning of a smile twitching the corners of my mouth and spreading all over my face. Maybe I wasn't such a lost cause after all?

Chapter 11

I was heading past Leodis Chic when Morgan spotted me and waved enthusiastically through the window. I'd really wanted to enjoy my purchases and slink off home. I had put off speaking to Jacob for long enough now. I needed to sit him down and have a serious heart to heart with him about our family and the future. However, it would be rude to ignore my young work colleague. Anyway, I was really fond of Morgan, and the big smile plastered over her pretty face suggested she was happy to see me. I couldn't just walk past, leaving the lights of the shopping centre for the darkening street beyond, to wait for my bus.

"Holy shit, Lottie, you look on fire." Morgan ran over to greet me as I entered the shop. She was dressed in a black shiny latex bustier top with sprayed on jeans and heavy red boots covered in studs. As always, she looked amazing but rather out of place in the elegant yet rather restrained boutique.

She spun me around until I was dizzy so that she could examine my new hair from all angles. "It's the dog's bollocks!" she proclaimed. "You are popping, lady."

"Errr...thank you." I hoped that the words were compliments. They were said with an encouraging smile, so it certainly appeared that way. However, it sounded like gobbledegook to me; but then again, what did I know?

I gave a quick glance around the store. It was worryingly quiet for a Saturday afternoon. There was only one customer, a furtive-looking man in his late fifties who was examining the lingerie selection with a rather anxious eagerness, running his fingers over the satin gussets with his cigarette-stained digits. Maybe he was buying a birthday present for his wife, but then again did it matter? Just as long as he was buying. The shop really did need an influx of purchases and some money ringing in the till.

Diane was striding over to me on her high heels. "Charlotte, your hair looks amazing. Have you just had it done, dear?"

I nodded at my boss. "I needed to do something; I needed a change. Maybe if I look different, my life could be different too." I knew I was babbling, but I couldn't stop. "But I'm fooling myself if I think a new hairstyle can change anything at all."

The tears that I had been suppressing for so long began to creep in salty rivers down my cheeks, and I dabbed at them with the same old tissue that had been wrapped around my fingers all day.

"Morgan, get the kettle on, we need tea," Diane instructed in a businesslike tone. "And bring the biscuits - the nice ones with chocolate on, not those diet ones that are like chewing on old bath mat."

Diane smiled sweetly at me. "Come into the back, Charlotte. It's nearly 5.30 and I'm shutting the shop early. Why don't you tell me all about it."

The three of us sat huddled in the small staffroom at the back of the shop with its chipped Formica cupboards and stained carpet. An hour or so later and we had drunk several cups of tea and demolished the entire packet of fancy biscuits. By that time, they'd also both absorbed chapter and verse of "The life and times of Charlotte Potts". It really was a depressing tale.

Diane shook her head sadly. "I'm so sorry, Charlotte. I know how much you love him. It's such a betrayal, and you've been together for such a long time. It's been over twenty years, hasn't it?"

I nodded glumly at her.

Morgan's eyes were flashing angrily. "The pompous twat! Fancy saying you were dead. Shit on a stick, Lottie, how did you manage not to punch him in the face? I would've knocked the bugger right out."

I shook my head sadly. "Yes, I was riled up; but now I just feel sort of numb. It's the betrayal and the hurt. I gave him everything and always loved him and he does this to me. He's humiliated me, stamped all over my feelings. And she is just so young and beautiful. I feel like a worn out bit of dry toast in contrast to her; she's like a... a... fancy *pain au chocolat* in comparison."

"More like a cheap tart from the seconds stall at the back of the market," Morgan rejoined loyally.

I wondered why I had referenced food again in my analogy of Roxy. One thing for sure was that I was no longer hungry. I had managed just half a biscuit with my several cups of tea, so my appetite had disappeared as fast as my belief in a loyal husband. Maybe this was what people talked about when they mentioned the heartbreak diet. Only time would tell. My appetite had never failed me in the past. Even in times of despair I had always eaten. It had always been comforting, or so I had thought.

Morgan's face then morphed into a smirk as she let out a

tinny, high-pitched laugh. "The thing with the cream for his arse was hilarious though, Lottie – really inspired; I didn't know you had it in you."

I smiled despite myself. "I know, right? It just came to me when I saw the chemist's shop. It felt good to embarrass him though, give him a bit of his own medicine, quite literally; and the girlfriend looked mortified, which was also a bonus."

"Now you've got a lovely new hairdo, why don't you get yourself something new to wear too?" Diane suggested. "Retail therapy is always good for the soul when you need a bit of a lift, and we've got some lovely new items in that might suit you."

I shook my head. "No, I've just bought some make-up and that will have to do me. I couldn't face trying clothes on too, that would just depress me even more. And no offence, Diane, but I couldn't fit one leg into most of the stuff we stock."

Diane had a thoughtful expression on her carefully made-up face. "Maybe that's where I've been going wrong," she admitted with a sigh, "not catering for a more diverse clientele."

"Hello!" Morgan rolled her eyes theatrically. "I've been telling you that for ever, Auntie Di. You need to get something a bit more edgy for girls like me who like a rad look; and something for the chubbier, fluffy lady like Lottie."

I laughed despite myself. "Is that what I am, fluffy?"

Morgan nodded seriously. "Well yeah, I guess you are."

I liked that - I really wasn't fat at all, I was merely fluffy. It made me sound cute, like a little bunny rabbit. However, whether fluffy or chubby or any of the other well-meaning euphemistic terms that could be trotted out, I knew the truth was that I was fat. But so what? Fat didn't mean unattractive, and as I checked out my appearance again in the little cracked mirror above the microwave, I knew without a doubt that I wasn't ugly.

The new hairdo helped, of course, but it wasn't just that. I had allowed myself for far too long to believe I was unattractive. My husband had certainly made me feel that way. What the heck! I had made myself feel that way, but no longer. My husband should have cherished me, loved me for who I was through literal thick and thin. Seeing Daniel today with his beautiful new paramour by his side should have made me feel much worse about myself, but surprisingly it didn't. It was as if my eyes had finally been opened. Charlotte Potts had been sleepwalking for way too long; dreaming her days away with sweet treats and wistful regrets, feeling lonely and alone. But no more; no longer would I allow myself to feel like that. Charlotte Potts was coming back. Amen, sister.

Meanwhile Diane had been speaking, and as I watched her scarlet-coated lips forming words, I forced myself to concentrate on what she was saying.

"I know you're right, Morgan. I really must do something radical to get the customers back in. I can't keep haemorrhaging money like this. I mean, I can probably limp on for another month or two, but if things don't improve soon, I'm going to have to close. The stuff we're selling just isn't cutting it any more. They can buy it all cheaper online, so we're simply not unique." She sighed and sipped at her cold cup of tea. "Or should I say, I'm not unique."

Morgan took her aunt's hand in hers and gave it a reassuring squeeze.

Chapter 12

Twenty minutes later I was standing at the bus stop shivering in my thin coat when my phone began to ring. I retrieved it as quickly as I could, fumbling with my thick fur-lined gloves and squinting at the little screen. It was Jacob. My heart sank. I would need to tell him now, explain about his dad, explain why I hadn't come straight home. I hoped he would understand that I'd needed some time on my own; a little retail therapy as well as having my hair done; a chance to talk to friends and have them make me coffee with Bailey's and tea with luxury biscuits whilst I licked my wounds.

I shouldn't have worried for a second though, as Jacob completely understood. I might not have much, but I had a great son. We talked intently on the phone as Jacob told me that his dad had come back to the house several minutes before. He'd hurriedly collected some belongings for a couple of nights and stuffed them into his gym bag. He of course hadn't had the decency to explain to his son what had happened; he just instructed him to "ask your mum". Typical of Daniel to leave the hard work to me. Didn't like to get his hands dirty. His willy? Well, that was a different matter.

I felt terrible as I confided in Jacob what had happened, what I had witnessed at Eduardo's the night before and what had transpired at Moonlight Lounge today. I didn't go into too much detail. I wanted to spare him as much hurt as I could. However, he was seventeen years old and as smart as a whip. He had the right to know what was going on. It impacted on his life too, after all.

"I knew there was something." I could only just make out Jacob's voice as the reception on my phone was appalling. "It all makes sense now."

"Are you OK though, Jacob?" I implored. "I'm just so sorry this has happened."

I heard Jacob sigh. "You know what, Mum? I'm all right. I knew something was wrong, I've known it for a while. But you deserve better than this; we both do."

I couldn't have agreed more.

"Anyway," Jacob continued, "Ivy from next door popped round. She asked if you could drop in and see her when you get a chance."

"Oh... OK I will, probably tomorrow or the day after."

"You might as well do it when you get home. I'm going round to Ben's house in a bit to play *Call of Duty* with him. He's asked if I want to stay over. Is that OK, Mum, or would you rather I stayed at home with you and kept you company now that we know Dad won't be here?"

I insisted that Jacob should go to his friend's house and spend the night. I would selfishly have liked him to stay in with me, of course I would. Maybe another horror-themed evening with junk food to numb the feelings? Carbs, sugar and bloody zombie carnage? But no, I knew that I no longer wanted to feed my feelings in such a destructive way. It would be good for Jacob to spend some time with his friend. And he would only be a few streets away if I needed him. It was important that he wasn't burdened with all of my woes. He was a young man, and the last thing he needed was to fret about his poor old mum and what a selfish arsehole his father was.

I told Jacob I loved him and he reciprocated, even though I knew it must have embarrassed the hell out of him. Bless him. With that, the conversation ended. I popped my phone back in my bag and shivered again through my coat. The evening air was feeling decidedly chilly.

In the distance I could see the number 12 bus approaching. I picked up my bag of new cosmetic goodies and waved down the bus.

For the whole thirty-minute bus journey I pondered on my life. So much had changed in such a relatively short period of time, it was quite a lot to wrap my head around.

Was my marriage really over? Did Daniel love this new woman? He certainly seemed enamoured by her, but was that just the glitz and sparkle of new love? Especially new love with a younger, sportier model? I didn't know. What if it was just a fling? What if it ran its natural course and he wanted us to try again? After all, we'd been through so much together for so many years, would I really want to throw it all away? So many questions, for which I had no answers. I just had this overwhelming feeling of floating above myself. I felt numb. My entire life was falling apart in front of my eyes, yet I felt so detached, as if I was merely an observer. It was a surreal feeling.

The bus slowly crept its way along the busy High Street with its merriment and bright lights. Was my husband in one of the many bars and restaurants that we passed? Was he back out on the town again for another night with Roxy, barely giving a thought to how his long-suffering wife was feeling? I felt a shiver of regret run through my body and pulled my mac more tightly around me, as if it would give me a hug. Boy, did I need a hug.

My stop was quickly approaching, so I rose disheartened from my seat and pressed the bell. A few minutes later, I was at the end of our street. I could see our little house in the distance. I loved that house; it was my home and my haven from all the bad things in life. I'd been safe in there, in my sanctuary - or so I thought. I hadn't realised that the person who could hurt me the most was living with me in our little home all along.

I had something to do before I went home, though. I was first going to visit my neighbour Ivy, a lovely woman in her eighties who had been our neighbour for the whole time we'd owned our house. She had lived in the semi attached to our property for going on fifty years. She often said the only way she would leave it would be kicking and screaming or in a box. She had so many happy memories in her home from when she had lived there with her late husband Tom. He had passed away over ten years ago, but Ivy often said how she still felt his presence there in every room and that gave her comfort. They had never had children, not for the want of trying; it was just wasn't meant to be. Her house was also her safe place, her sanctuary, and meant much more to her than simply bricks and mortar. I could never imagine Ivy feeling that her home had been sullied the way I felt mine had; that her home was no longer her safe place. But then again Tom would never have betrayed her like Daniel had done to me. Tom had worshipped Ivy. They had genuinely found true love together.

I walked up to Ivy's smart, red-glossed front door and rapped on it sharply to alert her. Ivy was a little deaf, so it sometimes took a few knocks before she appeared at the door in her housecoat and slippers. Her lined face would always break into a warm smile upon seeing me, and I really was looking forward to a smiling, cheerful face to greet me.

I had barely finished my first knock when the front door swung open. I'm sure my face must have looked a picture as I jumped back with shock as if I had been electrocuted. The figure standing in the doorway in pyjamas was not the tiny five-foot frame of Ivy but a rather large, bearded man of at least six foot two. A little shriek of surprise left my mouth before I could muffle it with my furry gloves.

"You... you're not Ivy," I stuttered. What a ridiculous observation to make.

The large hairy gentleman standing at the doorway laughed warmly. "Indeed, I am not."

Chapter 13

I took a few awkward steps backwards and my eyes darted up and down the darkening street. Had I somehow stupidly come to the wrong house? Been caught up in my daydreams again and dawdled up the wrong path? Let's face it, taking the wrong path in life seemed to be my wont at present. But no, I was standing outside Ivy's neat brick semi with this big bear of a man filling up the doorway in his fraying Foo Fighters T-shirt and checked pyjama bottoms.

"You'll be wanting Auntie Ivy," he smiled at me pleasantly, his warm blue eyes twinkling and creasing slightly at the corners. He beckoned me into the porch. "Come in, she's just in the lounge doing her crossword."

I smiled warily and stepped into the house, carefully wiping my boots on the coarse doormat before making my way down Ivy's pristine hallway smelling of furniture polish and bleach. I entered her cosy lounge to find her relaxing in her favourite floral recliner with her glasses perched on the end of her nose. The newspaper with the half-completed crossword was open on her lap and the television was on in the corner of the room, its volume turned right down, but I could clearly make out it was *Emmerdale* - one of Ivy's favourite soaps.

As soon as she spotted me, a large smile spread across her

kindly face. She hastily folded her newspaper and put it on the arm of her chair.

"Charlotte dear, how lovely to see you." She gestured towards the dented sofa next to her. "Sit down, sit down and I'll get Leo to make us a nice cup of tea."

The man who I now knew was named Leo and must be her nephew nodded his head agreeably. "Glad to, how do you take your tea... err... Charlotte?"

"Milk, no sugar," I replied evenly, still unsure why Leo was staying in Ivy's home. Apart from myself and a couple of ladies that Ivy played bridge with on a Friday afternoon, she never normally had visitors. I studied his large frame as he loped off towards the kitchen to make the tea. I could hear him whistling pleasantly to himself as he filled the kettle from the combination tap.

Ivy then proceeded to fill me in about Leo. Ivy's youngest sister Rachel was Leo's mum and they had been living in Canada for many years. Sadly, Rachel had passed away a couple of years before. And for the last few years Leo had been working in hospitality in Vancouver, as well as doing some charity work here and there. He had returned to the UK a few days before to attend a close friend's wedding and was stopping with Ivy for a few weeks: a chance to catch up with family and friends and have a bit of a holiday too. This was all news to me. I vaguely remembered Ivy mentioning about family living in Canada, but not any nephew. Hang on a minute, though; now that I thought about it, when Daniel and I were first married, I remembered Ivy's sister coming to visit with her son, so that must have been this Leo. That would have been at least twenty years ago, when I was in my mid-twenties. Surely that skinny little teenager that used to hang around Ivy's house listening to grunge music and picking his acne couldn't be this domesticated man who was now making tea? He had really grown up and up, and then up some more. He must be about thirty-five years old now. The thought made me feel like an ancient fossil.

Leo reappeared momentarily, his towering frame completely filling the doorway. He was holding a flowery tray with three steaming mismatched mugs of tea and a plate of chocolate digestives, which he gently lowered onto the coffee table and passed round the mugs.

I accepted my mug with a small smile. "I don't suppose you remember me, Leo?" I suggested self-consciously. "I live next door; I met you before many, many years ago, but you were only a kid then."

Leo beamed at me as he took a large bite out of his chocolate biscuit, crumbs lodging in his thick auburn beard. "Of course I remember you, you were the lovely lady next door who was always singing when you hung out the washing."

I blushed at this memory. He was right though, I did always sing back then. There was so much to be happy about then, but now I couldn't recall the last time I had hummed a note.

Leo was smiling as he reminisced. "I remember how you were always so kind to me when you saw me hanging around the garden. I was a bloody nightmare back then, so full of teenage angst and hormones, a right miserable little bugger. But you always took the time to stop and talk to me."

I returned his smile. "You've certainly changed a lot from how I remember you."

"Just as well really." Leo threw his head back and laughed. It was a nice laugh, all deep and mellow. "I'm just back in the country for a few weeks, and I couldn't miss out on the chance of visiting my old Auntie Ivy."

Ivy smiled fondly at her nephew and leaned forward to pat his arm. "Not so much of the 'old', thank you very much." As she admonished him, it was clear how much she cared for her nephew. "It's wonderful to see you, lad." Her voice was thick with emotion. "I might not have had any bairns of my own, but this fella here is as loved as if he were my own born."

Ivy's eyes had gone a little misty and she gave her head a shake before turning her attention fully towards me.

"Well, Charlotte dear, what's been going on with you since we last had a blether?" She took a large swig of her tea and looked at me expectantly. "You're certainly looking as smart as a carrot: new hairdo, I see." She nodded appreciatively. "It fair suits you, it does; takes years off you."

I caught Leo looking at me intently. Was he checking me out? No, of course he wasn't. The very thought of it. To Leo I must have seemed as old as the hills, the nice old dear who lived next door to his Auntie; the rotund neighbour with the dress sense of a dowdy librarian. Him finding me attractive? Hah! The very thought of it. However, it didn't hurt for me to give him the quick once over, did it? After discovering what my darling husband had been getting up to of late, no one would blame me if I took to tripping up random blokes in the street and launching myself at them like a mid-life menopausal missile.

The trouble with Leo was that you couldn't make out too much of him under all that facial hair. Don't get me wrong, I like a bit of beard on a man. For example, Johnny Depp without a beard just doesn't bear thinking about, and George Clooney with a beard, "Well hello, Mr Swooney." But with Leo there was maybe too much facial hair; his shaggy unkempt look was going on in abundance. But his eyes were a lovely shade of oceanic blue, twinkling amongst the whiskers. It was just that his beard seemed to go right up into his monobrow without pausing. Oh, how I would love to get a flat razor and some tweezers at that face. The little devil was back on my shoulder again as I wondered just how much hair there was in the places that I couldn't see: those manly zones covered up with his band T-shirt and pyjama pants. I was incredibly glad at that moment that neither aunt nor nephew could read my salacious thoughts. Uh-oh! Lila was really beginning to rub off on me.

Leo had abruptly pulled his gaze away from me, clearly realising that the women folk needed to talk. He took this as his cue to leave, swiftly unfolded his large frame from the rather small armchair and politely excused himself; he was going to his room to catch up on some emails, but not before leaning over to shake my hand warmly. As his large warm hand gripped my smaller one, our eyes met and locked for several seconds. I felt a small shiver run through me briefly, like a stab of electricity. What on earth was that? Static from Ivy's 1970s brown and yellow acrylic carpet, maybe?

As I watched Leo bound up the stairs two at a time, I felt a pang of what I can only describe as regret at seeing him go. What was going on with me? A pleasant man making a bit of small talk, and I was going gooey around the edges. I really needed to get a grip. With a deep breath I forced my attention back to Ivy and started telling her everything that had happened in my world of late. She nodded encouragingly every time I needed to stop and dab my eyes with a tissue. She had such a kind and patient look and radiated such genuine concern that I felt the need to give her a hug.

"You know I think of you like a daughter," Ivy said, patting my arm affectionately, "but I could give you such a bloody good shake at times."

Her scolding words made me nearly drop my cold mug of tea. "What do you mean?" I was aghast at her words, even though they were not spoken harshly.

Ivy sighed. "For too long you've put up with Daniel's nonsense, let him get away with far too much."

She picked up another chocolate biscuit and began to munch on it thoughtfully. "You're such a lovely girl, but you've let yourself become a doormat. And you know as well as I do what happens to doormats?"

I sighed inwardly before replying quietly, "They get walked all over."

"Absolutely they do." Ivy nodded her head emphatically. "They get trampled all over, worn out, and the odd bit of shit ground into them too for good measure. You need to stop being a doormat and start being what you are."

I laughed bitterly. "Yeah, and what's that?"

The kindness on Ivy's face made my eyes begin to water again. Her voice was low and measured, but full of meaning. "I'll tell you exactly what that is... a fabulous, beautiful woman that that miserable old fecker doesn't deserve."

I hugged her small frame again, not wanting to let go. There's nothing like a hug when you feel your world imploding in on you and you don't know which way is up any more.

I checked the time on my watch - a Christmas present from Daniel many years ago, and now it was looking a bit worse for wear. Not unlike its owner. The brown leather strap had frayed at the edges. I remembered how happy I'd been when I unwrapped it that Christmas Day morning and how I had planted a delighted kiss on my husband's cheek. We had been so in love then, and Daniel would always surprise me with wonderfully thoughtful gifts. Now I was lucky if I got bath salts or gift vouchers. In fact, my last birthday had been an all-time low for me: he gave me a pair of fluffy socks and a diet cookbook. On the bright side, I could always keep my feet warm while I chopped the celery. The scratched watch face told me it was already 8.30 pm. There was nothing for it: I really needed to make tracks home. It was only next door, but even that felt like a monumental effort. With as much strength as my tired old bones could muster, I dragged myself up from my chair.

"Thank you for being such a good friend, Ivy." I glanced surreptitiously up the stairs. "Please say goodbye to Leo for me."

She nodded and the little twinkle was back in her lovely blue eyes. "You can be sure I will."

Chapter 14

I slept surprisingly well that night. I had imagined that once I finally got myself to bed I would be tossing and turning all night, fretting about everything and replaying all the humiliation repeatedly in my head. However, that was not to be the case: as soon as my head hit the softness of the pillow, I succumbed to sleep almost immediately, and slept like a baby for a good eleven hours straight. When you think about it, it's a funny saying, "sleep like a baby": after all, babies are the worst sleepers ever, always squawking and waking up to be fed or burped.

The bright morning light was determinedly forcing its way into the pervading gloom of my bedroom through the chink in the curtains where I had failed to pull them closed properly. It was going to be a glorious day, well, at least weather wise.

I stretched like a cat and yawned, blinking the gritty sleep from my eyes. It was Sunday, and normally Sundays were my favourite day of the week: lovely, relaxed days for losing myself in the Sunday papers and preparing a nice big roast with all the trimmings for lunch. A family favourite had always been lamb, fragrant with rosemary, and my roast potatoes, always just the right side of crispy. However, with the family having adopted a healthier eating regime, we'd recently turned to organic roast chicken instead; as soon as it was out of the oven, crispy and smelling divine, Daniel would rip off its skin and deposit it straight in the bin with mutterings of "fat content" and "unnecessary calories", and replace my crunchy roasties with baked potatoes sans butter.

Anyway, I had no plans to cook Sunday lunch today. No, today I had something much more pressing to do: getting to grips with the car crash that was my life.

I hauled myself out of the cosiness of bed and walked across the room to open Daniel's wardrobe. As I peered inside, I felt my stomach lurch: all my husband's good shirts were gone, including a few of his work ones, plus the trousers he kept for best. His aftershave was missing too, as was the pot of moisturising cream. Realising its absence, I felt a slight fizz of anxiety that I quickly suppressed.

Closing the wardrobe, I reached for my fluffy grey dressing gown off the back of the door and pulled it firmly around myself, knotting it tightly. I loved my dressing gown; it was as cuddly and warm as a lovely big hug. Daniel used to shake his head when he saw me wearing it, telling me I looked like a woolly mammoth; I admit that hurt a bit, but I wore it anyway for its cosiness. Sliding on my slippers, I made my way downstairs, opening curtains and drawing blinds as I went. Jacob probably wouldn't be back from his friend's house for a good few hours. Sunday mornings failed to exist for my teenage son; he didn't usually rise from his pit until well after midday.

In the kitchen I made myself a strong pot of coffee and decided that I fancied some toast with marmalade. Daniel would always scold me that it was full of sugar and empty calories, so rebelliously I ladled it onto my sour dough with wild abandon.

I took my breakfast into the lounge and sat down on the settee. I didn't put on the television as I would normally do; instead I embraced the silence of the room, trying to calm the turmoil of my inner thoughts.

What was I to do now? Was our marriage really over? How was I going to manage financially? And what about family and friends, how on earth was I going to explain all this to them? I felt that I wanted to cry, but there were simply no tears left. I'd become a dried-up old husk, and if anyone touched me, I would disintegrate into dust and cease to exist.

Why had Daniel done it? I couldn't understand how he could hurt me so much. Hadn't I always been a good wife? I'd always supported him in his career, even sacrificing my own dreams so that he could pursue his. I had always been loyal and faithful to him. I knew that in the last few years we hadn't exactly been love's young dream, but then again who was? It was hard to be spontaneous and keep the romance alive when you had bins to empty and skid marks to wash off teenage boys' pants. But I always thought the love was still there. Yes, Daniel could be rather abrasive and cutting in his attitude towards me, but I thought that deep down that was only because he cared. Probably he was worried that I'd put on weight, lost my spark or whatever. Surely, though, if that was the case, we could have talked, worked things out? But to betray me like he had was truly devastating.

I knew my marriage hadn't been perfect. Ivy was right that I had been a bit of a doormat. But I had truly felt that the sacrifices I'd made were for the greater good of our marriage and our family. So for him to cheat on me, and with someone like that woman, that was just too much.

"I think we really need to talk."

Daniel's sudden voice made me jump. How long had he been standing there watching me as I mindlessly chewed on my toast and marmalade, ruminating on my problems? Of course, he could just let himself back in the house; he wouldn't consider what had happened the day before, that it might have been more reasonable to knock on the front door for once.

I felt a myriad of emotions course through my body when I heard his voice. I longed to hug him, for him to convince me that everything would be OK, that he had made a huge mistake. I wanted to shake him too, to slap him across his smug, cheating face. I wouldn't slap him though; that just wasn't something I would ever do, and anyway it looked as if someone had got there first. Daniel's face was a rather disconcerting shade of red. He was literally as red as a beetroot, quite fitting really, considering the amount of them he ate in his never-ending bloody salads. Then I remembered his face cream and my little cheeky addition of the chilli. I didn't know whether to laugh or cry. His face most certainly had the radiant glow he was always desperately trying to achieve; yes, you would be able to see his face radiating from outer space.

Besides being such an alarming hue, though, his face was wearing a rather puzzled expression. He was looking at me intently as if something wasn't right, but he couldn't quite figure it out. Clearly my new hairdo had thrown him, but not enough to compliment me on it. I decided to break the awkward silence. "Daniel, are you OK? You look a little flushed." A rather unnecessary question from me, but I really didn't know what else to say.

Daniel looked agitated and a scowl sullied his regular features. "I don't know, I think it's stress or an allergy to something, and I didn't sleep too well last night."

Poor wee lamb, losing out on his beauty sleep, what a nightmare for him. Was Roxy keeping him up all night with her frisky demands? This thought brought me down to earth with a bump, making me feel empty and very, very sad.

Daniel ran his hand through his dark hair and sat down heavily on the edge of the coffee table. "I stayed the night at Jon's, and he only has a blow-up mattress in his box room. Every time I turned over it sounded like I was breaking wind, and to add to that it was extremely uncomfortable."

So Daniel hadn't stayed at Roxy's house after all. I doubted it was due to his sense of loyalty to me, or any sense of guilt. More likely she was annoyed to discover he still had a wife on the scene and a teenage son, and had refused to let him share their love nest for the night.

Daniel reached over and tried to take my hand. I hastily pulled it away from him, as if it had burnt me.

"Look, Charlotte, I know it must have been an awful shock for you to find out about me and Roxy. For that I'm sorry, but you know our marriage hasn't been great for a long while, with not much happening in the bedroom." He sighed deeply. "But I'm a man who has needs..."

I cut him off mid-sentence. "So what if our marriage had gone a bit stale? We've been together most of our lives. We made vows to each other, remember? Vows that I for one took very seriously. How could you do this to us? To our family? You've destroyed everything I held dear, tarnished all our happy memories. And for what? For a tumble with a young floozy?"

The tears that I thought had dried up burst forth again. "I know I don't look like her, don't dress like her, but I'm your wife. I thought you loved me. I thought we meant more to each other than a cheap fling."

Daniel had the good grace to look shame-faced as well as red-faced. Talk about a scarlet woman, there was a scarlet man sitting right in front of me.

"It's just that Roxy is so young, fit and vibrant," he responded. "She makes me feel young again and full of hope." Daniel's eyes shone as he waxed lyrical about his bit on the side. "I'm sorry that you feel hurt, but you've changed, Charlotte. You're not the person I married. You've become tired and dull somehow, and then there's all the weight you've put on too." With that Daniel glanced meaningfully at my half-eaten toast and marmalade.

I couldn't speak. Even now he was finding fault with me, my looks, my failings in his eyes, making me believe that everything was my fault. He was criticising me to make me believe that he was the victim here. Was this what I'd heard referred to as gaslighting? It sure as hell felt like it. In that moment I wanted to ram my half-eaten toast and too sugary conserve down his smug, patronising throat.

I'm sure Daniel didn't realise how angry I was getting. He seemed to be getting emboldened by my silence, imagining that I was accepting all he was saying without question. That was the thing about me: I could play a great hand of poker, could hide my feelings very well. It certainly helped to be married to such a selfish prick who failed to notice what was going on in the world around him; unless of course it concerned him and only him.

Daniel was speaking more confidently now, convinced that he was making perfect sense to me and that he was talking me around to his way of thinking.

"The thing with Roxy is," he began with a little fond smile as he spoke about his girlfriend, "she's young and she's a little infatuated with me because, well," he gave a modest laugh, "I'm an older, professional man. I have status and wisdom and she truly appreciates that."

"I hope she appreciates your cabbage farts and leaving your toenail cuttings on the side of the wash basin too," I silently raged.

Daniel continued holding fort. "No doubt things will fizzle out in due course. She's just temping at the firm at the moment, but she's talking about travelling with some of her flatmates once she's saved enough money, so she'll be gone soon and then you and me can get back to how we were."

I stared at him incredulously, shocked by what I was hearing. Was he seriously saying to me that once this woman left the country, we would just go back to how we had been? Carry on in our lives together? Even after how he'd stated in no uncertain terms how bad our relationship had become, or rather how bad I had become?

"But I can't stay at Roxy's place," Daniel explained with a grimace. "It's a bit of a dump. And obviously I can't keep sleeping on a blow-up mattress at Jon's place either. So I thought I should come back home. No doubt Roxy will be travelling in a couple of months' time, and then that will be that. I just want to keep seeing her for as long as I can." He looked at me expectantly. "After all, I don't play golf or go fishing or anything like that, and surely every man needs a hobby?"

I imagined that this final statement had rendered my face redder than my husband's. I probably resembled an old-fashioned tea kettle with steam coming out of my ears. Had I heard right? Did he just say what I thought? Was he justifying his affair with his young lover as not a big deal? Did he normalise it as just a "hobby"?

I didn't recognise my voice when I eventually brought out a response. My words were shrill and high-pitched, like Minnie Mouse having a meltdown. "A *hobby*?" I screeched, pacing around the lounge. I couldn't remain seated any longer, with the adrenalin pumping through my entire system. "If you wanted a hobby, you should have tried stamp collecting, not bloody tramp collecting!"

Daniel's eyes were darting around a tad nervously now. Evidently the penny was beginning to drop, and he was realising he no longer had control of the situation. "Does this mean I can't stay after all?"

It was at this moment that I spotted his blue sports holdall sitting out in the hallway. He must have expected to replace his clothes and toiletries, and there would be no harm done. Everything back to exactly how it had been. Oh, apart from the fact that his foolish old hausfrau of a spouse now knew all about his extracurricular activities of the leg-over variety. However, in his mind that wouldn't cause a problem as I would be fine with all that; hell, why not? I might even start making slow-cooker meals to freeze for her and her housemates, for when she was too busy shagging my hubby to be bothered to cook. And of course she would need some good nutritious food to keep her energy levels up.

Daniel had really misjudged me this time. Yes, certainly I was a doormat. Yes, indeed I was a mug. But now this worm had well and truly turned. This worman, sorry woman, had finally decided to become a warrior. Oh, you are in for one hell of a shock, Daniel Potts! It was as if the scales had finally fallen from my eyes. Too long had I made excuses for this man, made everything my fault, tried to see the very best in him. Sticking up for him in front of family and friends, believing that I knew the real him and he had a good heart and soul deep down. Now I saw him for what he really was: a cheating, lying, edamame-eating scumbag. And to use our son's vernacular, he could go and eat a great big bag of dicks.

I slowly turned to face Daniel. Outwardly, I was the very picture of calm, not revealing the inner rage that was threatening to spew out of me. "I'm going to take my turn to speak now," I told him with quiet, steely authority that quite impressed me. "You will not be staying here tonight, Daniel, or any other night for that matter. I don't care if you go to your fancy piece or stay at your mate's, just as long as I don't have to see your odious purple face around here for a single moment longer."

I picked up his sports holdall and threw it at him with such force that he stumbled backwards. It wasn't as heavy as I expected, so clearly he'd never intended staying away for more than a couple of days. He really thought I was such a pushover.

My husband was staring at me as if he didn't quite recognise the woman in front of him. But he said nothing, so I continued.

"We clearly need to sort out how things go from here financially, and what we do regarding Jacob. But you made a huge mistake underestimating me, Daniel. I loved you so much, and I would have loved you to the day I died. But the way you've treated me, I just can't excuse any more. I deserve better than this. I deserve better than you. I deserve..."

It was at this moment that the doorbell interrupted us.

Chapter 15

"Who the hell is that?" Daniel demanded. I shook my head. How should I know? I didn't expect Jacob to be back for hours, and we never normally had guests on a Sunday morning.

"Must be a delivery or something." I straightened my dressing gown and neatened my hair with my hands. "I'll get it and you can leave at the same time."

Daniel scowled at me. Clearly he was surprised by how our verbal exchange had played out, but nevertheless he slung his holdall over his shoulder. He looked as if he was going to do as I wished and leave now. He probably thought that if he gave me some time and space to calm down, I would see sense. I was just being an irrational woman. No doubt it was my "time of the month": that was always his fall-back position when my opinions were not completely in line with his own.

I got to the front door just in front of him and swung it open fully. On the doorstep stood the large, handsome form of Leo, all big and hairy with a wonderful warm twinkling smile like a big old teddy bear. As soon as I saw him, I felt my mood lift. He was wearing another band T-shirt, this time Nirvana, and ripped, faded jeans with a pair of battered old converse.

Although my heart soared upon seeing him, I couldn't

understand what he was doing here on our front doormat at barely 11 am on a Sunday morning. I hoped Ivy was OK: she could be unsteady on her feet, prone to take the odd tumble.

"Leo... what can I do for you? Is everything OK with Ivy?" I heard my voice rise in concern.

"No, Ivy is fine," Leo reassured me; and then I noticed the large enamel cooking pot he was holding, wrapped in a tea towel. "I just brought this for you." He held the pot out to me, and I accepted it gratefully.

"Thank you, Leo, that's really kind of you. But what is it?"

He lifted the lid so I could peer gingerly inside. It looked like a rich, tagine-type stew, and the tantalising aroma emanating from it made my stomach rumble slightly, despite my earlier toast and tête-à-tête with my husband.

"It's my signature curry," Leo informed me, beaming with obvious pride. "It's a lamb dish using Balti and Madras spices and seasoning. I call it..." he paused for a few seconds, as if there was a silent drum roll playing, "the Badass."

I took the proffered pot from Leo and laughed despite myself. "It smells lovely, and I'm sure it will taste amazing, but why are you bringing it round for me?"

Leo rubbed his thick beard thoughtfully. "Oh yeah, that was Auntie Ivy, she reckoned you might not be up to cooking at the moment, and I always make enough to feed a small ravenous village, so she thought you might appreciate it, you and Jacob."

Just then I became aware of someone impatiently clearing their throat behind me. I had completely forgotten about Daniel, still lurking behind me in the hall. I turned back to address my husband, noting the sour expression on his face.

"Daniel, this is Leo, Ivy's nephew. He's staying with her for a few weeks."

Leo stepped forward to greet Daniel with an outstretched hand, but as Daniel reached out from the confines of the shadowy hall to shake it, Leo recoiled slightly in shock.

"Pleased to meet you, dude... but I gotta ask, what the hell's happened to your face? You do know you're unbelievably red, right?"

My husband's pained expression seemed to ramp up a notch, and he looked as if he was sucking half a lemon through an old sock. He proceeded to shake Leo's hand almost aggressively.

"I'm fine, just fine... it's nothing." He dropped Leo's hand as if it repulsed him. "I'm Daniel, Charlotte's husband."

I saw Leo furtively cast a glance from Daniel to myself and then back to Daniel. I wondered what thoughts could be crossing his mind. I hoped he wasn't thinking that my husband was a fine-looking specimen and that I was punching well above my weight with him. God, I hoped not; that would have to be one hell of a knockout punch, for one thing.

However, I noted that Daniel was giving Leo the once over too; almost as if they were stags sizing each other up, picking their moment to lock antlers. I could almost feel Daniel's body bristle as he studied the competition. Competition? I was being ridiculous now. Maybe Daniel was right about the marmalade, and it had given me a bit of a sugar rush to the brain. One thing for sure was that I was letting my fanciful imagination run away with itself. But it couldn't be denied that each man certainly appeared to be trying to evaluate the other. Daniel, for one, was not looking too impressed with the younger stud as he clocked Leo standing there in all his splendour: with his ripped jeans and non-ironed band T-shirt. I could feel the waves of superiority burning off Daniel: evidently pretty underwhelmed with Leo's general appearance and deciding he was way beneath him.

When Daniel spoke, his voice had dropped a few octaves and taken on the plummy edge he reserved for people he deemed unworthy of his attention. Where on earth did his air of superiority come from? He'd grown up in a small Yorkshire village, as had I, in a smart but modest semi, and his school had most certainly been more sink estate than country estate. "You're Ivy's nephew then? I don't recall seeing you around much."

"No, I've been in Canada for a few years, working in the hotel business. It suits me fine and the weather isn't bad either," Leo replied amiably. "I'm just back for one of my pal's nuptials, and it's great to crash with Auntie Ivy for a bit. I'll probably only stay a couple of weeks, or maybe a month at most." He shrugged his wide shoulders non-committedly.

Daniel nodded his head slowly, and I could almost hear his thoughts turning over in his brain. Quite clearly he had written Leo off as a bit of a slacker: a loser working in a hotel, who didn't even have the gumption to commit to a date to return to his employment. Most likely a cleaner or a barman or some such position; in his eyes, menial jobs. Daniel always loved to feel better than everyone. I had guessed this stemmed from insecurity on his part, but I'd usually banished these thoughts as disloyal. However, now I was beginning to see my husband more clearly and giving my thoughts and feelings free rein. The truth was that my husband could be quite a snob.

But Leo didn't appear to have noticed Daniel scrutinising him; he was entirely distracted by the ruddiness of his complexion. Daniel was extremely red, and the colour clashed terribly with his emerald green polo shirt. I remembered how as a child I was told never to wear those colours together: as my old Northern Irish grandmother would say, "Red and green should never be seen, except upon an Irish Queen." And Daniel most certainly had no regal blood in him, he was just behaving like a bit of a Count.

The whole situation felt a little surreal. Daniel and I had been having a heated exchange not ten minutes before, and now we were standing on our doorstep conducting polite small talk over a cooling pot of stew. I decided I needed to bring the conversation to a close, and quickly.

I let out a small laugh. "I must say this pot is getting really heavy. I need to get it into the kitchen before we have a curry-tastrophe."

This seemed to work the trick, as Leo's gaze was distracted from Daniel's burgundy-hued face.

"Yeah, I need to be making tracks too. I'm catching up with some pals and I'm running late." He glanced at his watch for effect. "We're going to that new place on the high street - Moonlight Lounge." He laughed and shook his head. "I don't really fancy it, to be honest. I've heard it's full of pretentious wankers and gold diggers."

Daniel's face was a picture on hearing these words. I thought it impossible for his face to have turned any redder, but once again I was proved wrong. His face was the picture of embarrassment. Thank God it wasn't Halloween: he could have scared the neighbourhood children into therapy with that face.

Was it just a coincidence that Leo had mentioned the Moonlight Lounge? Obviously I hadn't said anything to him about the unfortunate incident there, but had Ivy told him last night after I left? I seriously doubted it, but then "pretentious wankers" and "gold diggers"; if Leo had spoken in total innocence, it didn't change the fact that his words were utterly priceless.

Leo gave a cheery wave to us both and was about to leave when Daniel got spurred into action: he shoved past me in his desire to get out of the house.

"Bye, Charlotte, we'll speak later," were Daniel's curt parting words as he barrelled by me in his haste to follow Daniel down the garden path.

I shut the front door and deposited the cooking pot on a shelf in the fridge, next to Daniel's wilting spinach and quinoa which would soon get dumped in the kitchen bin. I returned to the lounge and pulled at the edge of the linen curtains to peer curiously out of the window.

Leo and Daniel had only made it as far as the garden gate, and appeared to be in deep conversation. I felt butterflies flitting about in my stomach: what on earth could they be talking about?

For the first time ever, I cursed the effectiveness of our double-glazed bay windows. Yes, they kept all the heat in and the annoying street noise out, but they were too blooming effective when you actually wanted to earwig on a conversation.

I continued to watch the two men in what appeared to be animated conversation for a few minutes, until Leo casually strolled off down the street with his hands thrust in the pockets of his tatty jeans. Daniel in turn pulled his car keys out of his smart chinos and jumped into his swanky red BMW, revving the engine and driving off at speed, leaving a little cloud of smoke in his wake.

I dropped the curtain back into place. I was starting to have a weird woozy feeling in the pit of my stomach, the way I usually felt when a thunderstorm was brewing.

Chapter 16

The next few weeks passed in a bit of a blur. What would previously have seemed unthinkable was now becoming reality. My husband was gone, still living at Jon's house and by all accounts still seeing the fragrant Roxy. And I, well I was just having to get on with things the best I could.

Daniel came round a couple of times a week to see Jacob, and they would do "father-son" things: go ten-pin bowling or see a film at the cinema, stuff like that. In truth, Jacob seemed perfectly happy with the arrangement. He had confided in me that although he felt slightly guilty that he wasn't more upset about his dad leaving, he really wasn't. He was seeing more of him now than he had in ages, plus they were actually doing fun stuff. In Jacob's words it was "cool AF".

I was continuing to plod along with my little life, housework, working part-time at the boutique, just the general run-of-the-mill things that made my life my own: my own little kitchen sink drama, but I had an inkling, or rather more than an inkling, I knew with certainty that something fundamental had changed within me.

I thanked God every day for my family and friends and the lovely work colleagues that I was lucky enough to also call friends: the people in my life who made everything seem not so bad. Circumstances were still a bit shit, but not the sewage works of effluence that things had first seemed.

Daniel was persisting at trying to persuade me to let him move back in, to make efforts to repair our marriage and get things back on an even keel. But of course with him still having a mistress on the side. Him keeping things going with Roxy was non-negotiable, and me being unwilling to even discuss a reconciliation was quite clearly unreasonable in his eyes.

It hurt me to think that Ivy had been right: that I had allowed myself to become so much of a doormat that he thought I could agree to this. But I had no intention of giving in. I knew I deserved better than that, and it was as if my eyes were finally opened and I was seeing things as they were for the first time in years. I was realising the sad truth that my life was much more pity than pretty.

It was Wednesday, my usual day off work, and I was due to meet my mum at a local café in an hour for our weekly catch-up. In fact I hadn't seen her since Daniel left, and I was dreading having to confide in her the whole sorry story. Actually my mum had never been Daniel's most ardent fan, but she believed in the sanctity of marriage and reckoned that once you'd made your bed you had to lie in it, come what may; and if that meant no hanky panky to speak of, then so be it. I knew she needed to be brought up to speed though, as if she found out from someone else, she would be incredibly hurt that she hadn't already been told. But I was not looking forward to it in the slightest.

Daniel had now been living at Jon's for just over three weeks. At first I had found the loneliness and the sense of uncertainty about the future overwhelming. However, it's amazing how the human mind can adapt to any situation. And adapt I had. Of course I was still missing my husband at times, but not nearly as much as I thought I would.

I was sitting at my dressing table, looking at my reflection in the rather cloudy mirror. My mania for housework just hadn't seemed so important of late. Life was short and there would always be time to dust. It was just four short weeks ago since I had sat there studying my reflection and finding much to complain about. Only four weeks, but it seemed an eternity.

I ran my hand through my hair, and the light caught the beautiful highlights of caramel and gold. It was some weeks since I had been to the salon, but it still looked lovely. It cascaded down to rest just above my shoulders in all its shimmering glory. The shorter choppier style had really lifted my spirits and accentuated my looks too. My skin seemed less washed out now, less like an undercooked Yorkshire pudding. And was that the merest hint of a cheekbone? I studied my reflection again: my face was certainly looking more defined now, and there was only one negligible chin rather than the two I was used to seeing. In the past I had referred to them as the "jowly twins", but now there was only a glimpse of chins and with a flattering camera angle in a selfie I would be able to have the profile of an elfin supermodel. Well, not quite, but you get my drift. And after all, who didn't love a flattering selfie? They were as old as the hills when you thought about it. Didn't Henry VIII insist that Holbein paint him with a girthy codpiece? What was that if not a bit of selfie self-promotion in Tudor times? A dick pic of its day. We all succumbed to a bit of vanity, if we only admitted it.

I had to admit that it was amazing what four weeks without Daniel had achieved. I wasn't relying on comfort food as much as I had previously, but I hadn't been consciously dieting either. I had been eating amply and plentifully, but maybe not relying quite as much on the old beige junk food I once devoured. I had most definitely lost some weight: I didn't know exactly how much, and wild horses wouldn't drag me into the bathroom to stand on the rickety old scales to know the truth, but just from my face and the fact that my jeans no longer gave me vicious red welts around my midriff, I knew I had lost a fair bit.

Daniel, on the other hand, was quickly discovering that our separation was having a detrimental effect on his waistline. Without me on hand to prepare his healthy dinners and his three-bean packed lunch salads for work, he had chunked up a little. The bachelor lifestyle was proving rather at odds with his normal healthy fitness regime. Living with Jon and sleeping on the fold-out mattress each night was playing havoc with his old sciatic back problems, and he no longer felt the enthusiasm to race around a squash court after a hard day at work. Two men living together in a small flat with a miniscule grubby kitchen meant they relied on takeaways from near Jon's home. And as for work lunches, it was now more Pot Noodle for Daniel than my one-pot home-made vegetable soup that he used to zap in the office communal microwave.

When he made the twice-weekly visits to see Jacob, his whole demeanour was different. He'd lost his previous self-assured cockiness and taken on a shameful shuffle: his shoes needed a polish and his hair needed a good trim.

I studied my appearance in the mirror again. I had to admit that I was looking reasonable. Yes, I still applied the usual Nivea, but now embellished with my new make-up: the stuff I had bought in Boots the afternoon I discovered my husband's infidelity. I had learned the skill from watching videos on

YouTube and could now perfect the cat's eyeliner flick and the blended smoky eye. Generously, Lila had donated some unused cosmetic items of her own, luxury designer brands that would have made me wince at the price, but she'd bought them on a whim and had tired of them already.

I opened my wardrobe to audit the murky contents. There was still the same slough of black garments, but now there was the occasional flash of colour. Careful not to spend too much money on myself, I had taken to frequenting the charity shops on the High Street. There really were some amazing bargains to be had if you didn't mind a good old rummage. And as I could now squeeze comfortably into a size 18, it meant I had more options too. I always made a beeline for the sale rack where you could often pick up a little gem for less than the price of a small glass of wine.

I had discovered a lovely Monsoon maxi dress with the original price tags still attached, now at the ridiculous price of £2.50. I was over the moon with my find and held it up to the light in the shop window so I could admire it better. The shades of ruby and dusty pink in the silken material were so exotic. At this exact moment none other than Imogen Dyer had passed the window, all slim legs and sky-high stilettos, her long blonde hair and designer shoulder bag swinging in the breeze. Her face had been a picture of surprise at seeing me there inside the shop. But the stunned look soon changed to one of withering pity; she must have thanked her lucky stars for the platinum credit card nestled in her designer purse, and wondered how I could have fallen so low as to shop second-hand. She hated to buy off the rack even in designer stores, but the sale rack in Help the Aged would be a fate worse than death in her eyes. I uttered a little shrieking noise like a petrified mouse at seeing her, and scurried over to the bric-a-brac display to hide until she had gone.

I chastised myself later for letting her make me feel that way, and gave myself a good old talking to. I was on a budget, and charity shopping was a great way to build up a lovely new wardrobe. It was win-win all round. You got a bargain while recycling and looking after the environment and your carbon footprint all in one fell swoop. If Imogen thought this warranted her pity, then more fool her.

That being said, I didn't announce my preferred retail venues to all and sundry. I just graciously accepted their compliments when they admired a new outfit I was wearing. And I definitely wasn't going to confide in Lila that I had taken to trawling the local charity shops like she trawled the upmarket cocktail bars for men. I could just imagine her horror if she found out while sipping our Pinots that I was clothed head to toe in charity vintage chic for the princely sum of £30, whilst she was in the latest couture costing thousands. Of course when I say head to toe in charity vintage, that doesn't include the underwear; I do draw the line somewhere, and second-hand knickers are a definite no-go. Anyway, there was a "gentleman" I often spotted on my shopping trips who seemed to enjoy furtively checking out the ladies' winceyette nighties and other frilly bits. I had nicknamed him "Pervy Pete", and was convinced he would snap up all the lingerie the charity shops could offer, leaving none for the other customers.

I had of course bought that dress, despite seeing Imogen. It was just so pretty and too much of a bargain to let it slip through my fingers just because she had caught me indulging in discount retail therapy. I had forgotten all about her until a message from her good self pinged up on my mobile phone that very evening. The text was dripping with saccharine sincerity, concerned about me having to lower myself to shop second hand, didn't realise that money must be so tight. Obviously thinking Daniel was paid a pittance and we were as poor as church mice. She wanted to offer me her sympathy and a shoulder to cry on and how things were bound to get better. I was to keep my "chin up". At least she hadn't said chins, so I took scant comfort from that. She finished the long-winded missive by kindly offering to lend me any of her dresses so I wouldn't feel the need to shop second-hand. To Imogen it appeared that charity shops were one step up from being on the streets, tapping up strangers for the price of a cup of tea. I could almost hear her sighing with faux regret as she typed the last line: "But I fear they may all be too small for you, it's such a pity."

I had childishly stuck my tongue out at the screen, as if somehow Imogen would be able to see me. That message was so passive aggressive; or let's face it, Imogen being her customary self, a big old bitch. I could imagine her gazing around her palatial home at her perfectly groomed family and idyllic lifestyle, thanking God that she wasn't me. Being me was for her a fate not worth even contemplating. And that was without her knowing that Daniel and I had split up. She would probably spontaneously combust when she heard that nugget of juicy gossip.

I turned my attention back to my choice of dress for the coffee shop date with my mother. I really needed to get a move on and stop daydreaming or I was going to be late. I automatically reached for a V-necked black jumper and pair of darkest indigo boot-cut jeans to wear with my Chelsea boots. OK, I knew I was playing safe with black again, but Rome wasn't built in a day and at least I was starting to add some colour to my wardrobe. But I was only taking baby steps so far.

I dressed quickly and gave myself a final appraising glance in the mirror before leaving the bedroom. It was lovely to be able to breathe so well in my clothes again, and for them not to be so tight they were pinching me all over like a cantankerous land crab.

It was a brisk ten-minute walk to the café where I was meeting Mum. I felt in surprisingly high spirits as I made the journey. It was a warm, crisp April day, and fortunately the risk of April showers had failed to materialise so my umbrella could stay safely packed away. I hummed to myself as I paced the streets. I most certainly had a little "pep in my step", as Tabby would say. Yes, I had the sword of Damocles hanging over me: having to inform my mother that my marriage of over twenty years was down the toilet. But on a more positive note, I had discovered the day before from Ivy that Leo had decided to extend his stay in the UK for a couple more months.

I hadn't seen much of Leo in the past few weeks since he had brought round his home-made curry. Which by the way had been delicious; the man could really cook. Jacob had been in gastronomic heaven when he tasted his first mouthful. I watched him glance dubiously at the slow cooker lurking in the corner of the kitchen, scarcely believing that the ominous grey pot that in the past had offered up so many gruel-like casseroles could produce something so wondrous; until I told him that it wasn't his mother's masterpiece at all, but Ivy's nephew Leo who had created this culinary alchemy. Nevertheless, Jacob was so impressed that he returned the pot to Leo to say thank you in person. That thank you had turned into several hours, and I had eventually ventured next door to check if all was fine, and that my only child hadn't vanished into some sort of Bermuda triangle situation never to be seen again.

It was a good excuse for me to see Leo too. I just thought it would be neighbourly to have more of a chat with him and make sure he was enjoying being back in the country, that sort of thing. That was all, nothing more to it than that.

Ivy had ushered me into the house with a knowing little smile and gestured into the lounge where Leo and Jacob were both sitting cross-legged on the psychedelic carpet with a large pile of vinyl records between them, deep in conversation and oblivious to my arrival, discussing the virtues of Nirvana against the Foo Fighters. They were getting on like a house on fire: sharing similar tastes in music and a penchant for distressed ripped denim and band T-shirts.

I saw Leo a couple more times over the following weeks: pulling the bins out on a Thursday night or bumping into each other when I left the house to go to work. Apparently Leo was happy to stay at his Auntie's for a few more weeks until he decided what he wanted to do next career-wise. He was taking a bit of a sabbatical, as Ivy called it. I could only imagine what Daniel would call it. Something along the lines of "malingering, lazy wastrel", no doubt.

I was glad Leo was staying around though, for Ivy of course, nothing else. She had a contented glow about her with her nephew being back. She said it was so nice to have a man around the house again after all this time, and it had taken years off her. Instead of bemoaning the noise and lack of privacy that came from having a house guest long term, she seemed to be absolutely thriving on it.

I had been so lost in my thoughts of Leo that I came to

a skidding halt once I arrived at my destination: the cosily, or cringingly, named Old Fanny's Pantry. Taking a deep breath and stealing myself for the onslaught of questions I expected from my mother, I entered the warm interior of the café. I spotted Mum almost immediately, her instantly recognisable dark copper hair elegantly drawn back from her face in a chic updo. She was impeccably dressed in a smart navy two-piece trouser suit, with a choker of pearls around her neck. Her habitual leather bag was on the table where she was rummaging around for her glasses.

"Hi, Mum." I reached the table in a few short strides and dropped down on the padded chair opposite her just as she located her glasses. She popped them on before looking up to greet me. The shock that registered on her face was priceless.

Chapter 17

Evelyn Weaver was a smart, sophisticated woman and I loved her dearly. We didn't really have that much in common, looks wise or personality, but as a mum I wouldn't have changed her for the world. She was most certainly old school though. You didn't show your emotions: "dirty washing should never be aired in public" was one of her all-time favourite sayings, and life was usually to be endured rather than enjoyed.

I had always taken more after my father, Andrew: a mild-mannered man who loved his car magazines and his ploughman's lunches in the local, and would avoid an argument the way Jacob avoided the washing up. He had been a bit of a people pleaser too, just like me. He had been simply the loveliest man, and my mother and he had been the most perfect couple, enjoying a near idyllic life together. Well, that was the story my mum would tell, anyway. As a child I had known a rather different version. Yes, they were happy, but that was more down to my father biting his lip when my mother was nagging and taking refuge in the garden shed. He would flee there with a flask of tea with a little nip of whisky in it and one of his John Grisham thrillers when she was in full flow.

We had been a close-knit family though. My dad always

referred to us as the "Weaver Three", and Mum and I had been heartbroken when he died suddenly five years ago from a heart attack at the age of 68. I remember that Daniel had made an untimely remark at the funeral: that his love for cheese and pickle sandwiches and single malt had maybe been his downfall. How the tables had turned, now that Daniel's daily diet consisted mostly of cholesterol and cans of Carling lager.

"Charlotte, dear, you're looking well."

"Well": the compliment that curvaceous women around the world shuddered to hear. It never felt like a compliment, more like an observation that you had good wide hips and could arm-wrestle a rugby player. However, on this occasion it did rather sound like a compliment. Mum was not one for gushing accolades, and when she told me I looked well I was inclined to believe her. I felt really chuffed; it was nice to hear some positive words for once after the sting of Imogen's earlier text message.

"You've lost some weight... you look good." She nodded her head appreciatively. "You could stand to lose a little more though, so keep up the good work."

That was typical of Mum, bless her. I felt my bubble of joy begin to deflate slightly, but Mum still had more wisdom to impart.

"Don't lose too much, though, or it will look very ageing. You're over forty now, after all, dear, and a bit of padding on the face can work wonders."

I had to agree with her on this. I had, even at my slimmest, had a slightly round face and I was blessed to be pretty much free of the dreaded crow's feet around the eyes and forehead furrows. Sometimes there was something to be said for a chubby face. I called it my "Biscuit Botox".

"Thanks, Mum." I picked at the corner of the floral place mat in front of me, playing for time. I knew that I needed to grasp the nettle and tell Mum what had been happening, so with a deep breath and a vandalised placemat in front of me I did.

Mum listened intently for forty minutes as I poured my heart out and she poured the tea. She kept offering tissues from a little plastic packet that she kept on the table. Every time she thought my misty-eyed sniffing might turn into snotty-nosed wailing, out came the tissues; but overall I managed to keep my emotions in check.

Mum reached over and placed her delicate, pale hand over mine. It made my heart ache slightly to see the pronounced blue veins on her papery skin: she too was getting on in years and wouldn't be around forever. I didn't dare think about a world where I no longer had either of my parents.

"I'm so sorry, love." Mum squeezed my hand gently. "It's such terrible news." She dabbed at her own eyes, rimmed with unshed tears of their own. "I just can't believe that Daniel would do this to you and Jacob. I know he's always been a bit of a selfish swine, but I thought deep down he was a decent chap. It appears I was totally mistaken."

Mum closed her eyes for a few seconds and steadied her breathing. It was clear she was trying to calm her thoughts so she wouldn't become too emotional, as that simply wouldn't do.

"It is what it is," she announced firmly, sliding deftly back into her calm, unflappable Evelyn mode. "We just have to make sure that you and Jacob are OK. And you know that I will do whatever I can to make sure you two don't suffer."

I smiled gratefully at my lovely old mum. I was truly blessed in so many ways. So what if she didn't wear her heart on her sleeve and was more of the stiff-upper-lip school of thought? She was a good woman and a decent person, and I was very lucky to have her in my life.

Yes, it would be nice if she sometimes let loose a bit, threw caution to the wind and ate a whole Kit-Kat in one go rather than wrapping half up to take home to ensure she didn't exceed her 1,500-a-day calorie limit; or maybe occasionally had a glass of wine with lunch, rather than giving me her judgmental look as I ordered my second Sauvignon Blanc. That would hardly be shocking behaviour and unlikely to knock Prince Harry off the front of the tabloids, but she was who she was and way too long in the tooth to change now. And after all she could still fit into the wedding dress she wore at 21 years of age. Not that she would ever wish to wear a high-necked fishtail gown with slightly yellowing lace around Waitrose, but she damn well could if she so pleased.

Mum was looking at me thoughtfully. "I suppose this explains the weight loss and the smartening up of your appearance." She nodded her head again approvingly. "You certainly look good; you've lost your husband but found your spark again, I see. It's nice that you're putting yourself first for once. I always thought you saw yourself as a bit of an afterthought." She paused for a second, seemingly unsure whether to carry on, but she did. "You were starting to look like a sad carbon copy of my Charlotte, and I feared you'd lost yourself."

Mum was spot on. I had lost myself: lost myself in the endless slow-cooker meals and the monotony of the ironing basket that never seemed to empty; lost myself in the loneliness of the marital bed that seemed more like a war zone at times than a place of warmth and safety. I'd just lost me for a while. But it was as if I was emerging from an elaborate maze that I'd been trapped in for too long. I felt I was finding my way back to me.

I sighed deeply and was back to picking at the placemat again. "I'm not trying to lose much weight. A bit would be nice, but I like having my curves; they're just me, and I'm learning to like me again. I'm enjoying discovering make-up once more and thinking of myself as an attractive woman. For too long I've just thought of myself as Charlotte Potts – wife, mother and... well... object." I laughed bitterly. "You would think that after all these years of being neglected by Daniel, finding out that he was bedding a girl not long out of high school would have sent my self-esteem plummeting; but bizarrely it seems to have had the opposite effect and I now want to take time for me."

As I spoke the words to my mother, I knew that they were true. I had been sleepwalking through my life for far too long. Life was a privilege, and I'd been doing myself a disservice living this dull dishwater existence. I'd been really letting myself down. I thought of all the strong heroines I so admired in my classic black and white films. Hell, I felt like I was letting them down too if I'd continued to live this half-life. What would Bette Davies or Joan Crawford do in my position? Sure as shit they wouldn't just shrivel up with a family-size bag of Maltesers and fade away; fade away as my body conversely ballooned.

Mum was now trying to get the attention of the middle-aged waitress, propped up at the counter thumbing through a tatty paperback. "I'm going to order us some cake; blow the blessed calories, the gooier the better," she announced.

This was a turn-up for the books all right, and I smiled

warmly at my mother, feeling closer now than we'd been in ages.

The waitress eventually noticed my mother beckoning, dumped the paperback and grabbed her pad and pen. "What can I get for you ladies?"

Mum pointed to the over the counter sign announcing a "cake of the day" special offer. "What's your cake of the day, dear?"

The waitress thought for a moment then replied, "Home-made coffee and walnut."

"We'll have two of your biggest slices then, and another pot of tea, please." Wow, Mum was really throwing caution to the wind.

Ten minutes later we were scraping our plates clean, nearly removing the pattern from the chinaware in the process.

Mum spoke with a disappointed edge to her voice. "Well, I ate it all, but I can't say I really enjoyed it. I ask you – cake of the day? What day was that? A week last Thursday, I bet. The sponge was as dry as a bone. I need another cup of tea just to wash it down."

We laughed together at this and chit-chatted about our lives for another good hour or so. I even told Mum all about Leo staying with Ivy and how well he and Jacob were getting on. Mum gave me a little knowing smile, but then her face became serious again.

"The important thing, Charlotte, is to retain your independence. It's imperative that you keep working. You enjoy your job, so that's good, but you need to feel you have a place in the world, something that is just yours."

With a sigh I explained to my mother just how precarious my current employment situation was and how Diane might have to close the boutique leaving me and Morgan with no pay or position. Mum listened to me silently, but she had a thoughtful expression on her face.

Our catch-up had gone surprisingly well, telling Mum about Daniel. My fears about her reaction had proved unfounded. It had been a lovely few hours together, and when I returned home that evening, a feeling of peace settled over me.

Jacob had been home from school for an hour or so, and we chatted for several minutes, him telling me all about his day and the ridiculous amount of coursework he had to do for chemistry. I bit my tongue rather than say that if he spent less time on his computer games and more time on his schoolwork it wouldn't be such an issue, but I chose to stay quiet. That was a conversation for another day.

We enjoyed a hearty dinner of lasagne, not one made by my own fair hands but a ready meal, with garlic baguette, salad and oven chips on the side. I felt ravenous for the first time in weeks, and even after the gargantuan slice of coffee cake I'd had with Mum, I polished off my dinner with gusto. Daniel would have had a fit at the meal we'd just enjoyed: all those E numbers and additives and enough salt to kill an army of slugs. I wouldn't have heard the end of it. But I didn't feel guilty at all. Anyway, I was ensuring that Jacob and I ate healthily for the most part; but after all, a little of what you fancy does you good. Everything in moderation.

We talked and laughed together, mother and son comfortable in each other's company; it was a blessing that he felt at ease talking to me so openly, filling me in on his day – what his mates had said, even shyly telling me of the girls he liked. I savoured this time, as I knew it wouldn't last and he would soon be heading for his room. He was a teenage boy after all, and much as he loved his mum, I was still an oldie so could only be tolerated for so long.

I tried to talk to him about his father, encouraging him to open up to me, but he shut the conversation down immediately, saying he didn't think Daniel seemed that happy. However, he'd made his decision and would have to live with it.

Once Jacob had left the room, I was alone again, alone with only the leaning tower of dirty plates for company. I grabbed a pair of rubber gloves from the draining board, then thought better of it and tossed them back down. I decided the dirty plates could wait until the morning. I closed the kitchen door firmly – out of sight, out of mind – and made my way through to the lounge. I settled down on Daniel's side of the sofa. It was the unspoken rule in the house that this was "dad's seat". Well, not any more. I indulgently stretched my slippered feet out, taking up both seats, and cuddled up under a fleecy throw.

I turned on the television, knowing precisely what I was going to watch. It had been that sort of day, and it needed a certain film to round it off. Within a couple of minutes I was mesmerised by *All About Eve.* I had enjoyed it countless times before, and would no doubt enjoy it countless times in the future. You just couldn't beat a bit of Bette Davis, especially in her acclaimed role as Margo Channing. I needed to channel Margo Channing more: a woman in her forties, well just turning, who felt she was past her prime but refused to be overlooked and put out to pasture. I was sick of being a bit player in my own life. I had made a damn good start, but I was now going to take centre stage: the leading lady of my very own masterpiece.

Chapter 18

I took a sip of instant coffee and winced slightly; it was scalding hot. I ought to have let it cool down, but speed was of the essence as I was running late for work. I should have set out already, but here I was still in my dressing gown, scoffing down a piece of buttered wholemeal toast and inhaling Nescafe as hot as Krakatoa.

I'd found it so difficult to drag myself out of bed, my warm safe cocoon. I had been enjoying such an amazing dream when my alarm clock had rudely interrupted it. I'd been relaxing on a tropical island with Chris Hemsworth, enjoying fruity cocktails and even fruitier canoodling when the clipped tones of a refined male voice had rudely interrupted our passion. I was confused by this sudden *ménage à trois*. Foggy-brained and reluctant to be dragged from my lovely dream state, I woke to the reality of my alarm substituting Radio 4 and the 7 am news. In my desire to return to the tropical island, I had hit the snooze button several times.

Anyway, due to my excessive torpor, I was now in real danger of being late for work. Although I knew Diane wouldn't be too concerned with a bit of tardiness (we weren't exactly busy after all), I didn't want to be late; it just wasn't me.

Jacob was still snoozing away. I'd rapped on his bedroom

door twenty minutes before, but been greeted by a grumpy teen grunting at me to get lost. He didn't need to go to sixth form that morning; it was study periods and revision time apparently.

I finished my crust of toast and wiped my buttery fingers on some kitchen roll. I still hadn't done last night's washing up, but to hell with it; it could wait till I got back from work. What was the worst that could happen? Kim Woodburn appear in her rubber gloves and give my work surfaces a good going over with vinegar and fresh lemon? On second thoughts that would be pretty amazing. I loved Kim.

I closed the door to the kitchen to conceal the mess and hurried upstairs to get ready for work.

Thirty minutes later and I was finally leaving the house, fumbling with my huge bunch of keys. It was really only two keys: one for the front door and one for the patio doors that led into the back garden; everything else was just a massive random collection of novelty keyrings I had managed to acquire over the years – little trinkets that weighed my shoulder bag down and gave me a bit of a stoop. When exactly had I decided that a miniature plastic pork pie and a tiny metal Blackpool Tower would help me stop losing my keys? The mind boggled.

"Good morning, Charlotte, and how are you doing this fine day?"

The deep warm voice startled me slightly. I turned to see Leo leaving Ivy's house at the exact moment I was setting out too. He was dressed once again in his casual band T-shirt and jeans, this time with a military-style cord jacket over the top. His blue eyes twinkled and his teeth were straight and white when he smiled. He was clearly ready to face the day, yet his wild hair gave the impression that he'd been dragged through a hedge backwards and then pulled through again forwards for good measure. Did the man not own a comb? He most certainly wasn't the most sartorially polished of men, but I still found him adorable (platonically of course, I hasten to add).

"Hi Leo, I'm not doing too bad, just running a little late for work." I tucked my hair behind my ear in a manner which I hoped gave me a nonchalant air, only then realising I'd forgotten my earring on that side. So I quickly let my hair fall back into its previous position.

"Oh dear, if you're late I won't keep you. It's just..." Leo paused for a few seconds, seeming a little unsure of himself, which really wasn't like him at all. He ran his hand almost nervously through his thick thatch of hair. "It's just that I was wondering if you'd like to come out with me for a spot of lunch on Saturday at this new brasserie I've heard about in Harrogate. I know it's a little out of the way, but I can get a car. What do you think?" His eyes were looking hopefully into mine. "It might be fun."

Leo had caught me totally off guard. I hadn't expected this at all, and I was probably staring at him open-mouthed with all the grace of a stunned halibut. He seemed to take my stupefied expression as me declining his invitation.

His cheeks quickly reddened. "It's completely OK if you don't fancy it. It's just that, apart from catching up with old mates, I don't really know many people around here any more." He was looking at his scuffed trainers now; anything to avoid looking into my eyes again. "You're always so nice to talk to, I just thought it might be a bit of a laugh." His eyes were no longer fixed on his footwear, and he looked at me again, his brows raised hopefully, giving him an endearing boyish quality. "It's just some good food and a couple of drinks with a mate, what's the harm?"

I pondered on this for a few seconds. What was the harm indeed? Leo had come right out with it and confirmed we were just friends, so there could be nothing wrong with spending a few hours sharing a nice meal and a few drinks. After all, God alone knew what my errant ex would be up to, but I was pretty sure it wouldn't be anything as innocent as a cheese and pickle sandwich and half a lager.

I smiled at him warmly. "That would be lovely, Leo. I'm actually at a bit of a loose end on Saturday anyway as Jacob is seeing his dad. So apart from the dreaded housework, I'm free as a bird." A little giggle escaped me as a bizarre image of myself in a chicken outfit popped unsolicited into my mind.

Leo laughed too, but with a rather confused expression on his handsome face. "What did I say that was so funny? Go on, let me into the joke."

I couldn't admit to Leo the bizarre inner workings of my mind, he'd think me crazy. Hell, half the time I thought I was crazy, the crazy lady from next door. All I needed was a herd of stray cats.

So I thought on my feet: "Nothing really, Leo. But of all the things I thought might happen today on my way to work, you inviting me out was not on the list. Though I must say I'm glad you have. It's nice to have something in my diary for a change; it's not exactly bulging with social events at present."

It was true that Jacob was due to go bowling with Daniel on Saturday, and normally a day like that would be filled with me cleaning the skirting boards or bleaching the tea mugs. But lunch with a charming male friend sounded so much more appealing than Mr Muscle and a bucket of suds.

Leo was nodding his head and seemed perfectly happy with this answer. "I'm glad; it will be good to get to know you better, and I hear this place in Harrogate does wonderful seafood."

"Amazing, I love seafood," I gushed enthusiastically. "Well, any food really, apart from celery; that stuff is the work of the Devil... oh and avocado, can't understand why everyone raves on so much about it... it's just green mush; and don't even get me started on its texture. And avocado with poached egg... yuck; poached eggs on a fishcake I can just about get my head around, but avocado, no, it's utterly wrong and..."

I stopped myself abruptly, realising I was rambling on about absolute nonsense. Thankfully Leo had an amused look on his face and didn't seem to mind my verbal diarrhoea in the slightest.

"I've got to go or I'll miss my bus." I pulled myself together and set off towards my bus stop. "I'll see you on Saturday, Leo."

Leo waved at me, still wearing the same bemused expression. "Have a good day at work, Charlotte. I'll pick you up at 1 pm on Saturday. I'm looking forward to it already."

I must admit I had a spring in my step as I made my way to work. After barely five minutes, along came the double-decker – result. This was turning out to be a very good day indeed. As I stepped on the bus and scanned my card, I gave a cheery "Good morning" to the driver, who returned my happy greeting with a "Good morning to you too, young lady."

Young lady! Maybe I should have felt morally affronted at being addressed in such a manner. After all, I wasn't exactly young, and should he be gender-specific in this day and age? But in all honesty I was delighted. I felt I was a teenager again without a care in the world and so much to look forward to.

I edged myself into one of the few available seats, next to a truculent-looking youth in a baseball cap who threw me a surly glance at having to remove his backpack from the spare seat. I beamed back at him. Nothing was going to dull my spark. I felt on top of the world.

Chapter 19

Three hours later, and my spark was not just dull; it was well and truly extinguished. "So, it definitely looks like the store is going to close then?" Morgan's normally confident voice wavered slightly, and she sounded on the brink of tears.

Diane had just held a short staff meeting. The three of us had huddled together with mugs of strong tea as she imparted the news that we had all been expecting but dreading for months, that the store would soon be no more.

Diane simply didn't have a choice; she was haemorrhaging money hand over fist. There just weren't enough customers to sustain Leodis Chic in the long term, and even the customers who entered the boutique didn't seem keen to part with their hard-earned cash to buy the items we had to offer.

"I know this job was only supposed to be a short-term thing for me, Auntie Di, but I love working with you and Lottie," Morgan sniffed. "We make such a great little team." Her large green eyes were brimming with unshed tears, and she ran her index finger along the edge of them to try to stop them from escaping down her pale cheeks in a murky river of eyeliner.

I was gutted too. We knew it was coming, but I'd been trying to prolong the ignorant bliss for as long as I could, hoping that something or someone would come along to save the shop at the eleventh hour. But disappointingly that was not going to be the case.

Diane sighed heavily. "I have loads of stock left that I could probably try to sell off in my other stores." She didn't sound overly convinced as she spoke. "But those shops just don't have the same vibe as this one."

Diane owned another couple of outlets that were also struggling; but unlike Leodis Chic, they could limp on for a while, hoping for a miracle to turn up. One stocked mainly ladies' accessories: handbags, fascinators and the like; and the other offered baby apparel, from birth to five years of age. So the chance of offloading a ton of A-line skirts and tea dresses more suited to middle-aged mums seemed highly unlikely.

Diane sighed and continued, her voice low and full of regret. "My lease here is due to run out in a month or so, and I reckon we'll be shutting up shop for good then."

It all seemed such a shame. Diane had worked so hard over the years to make the business a success, but unfortunately it had come to this. The rise of online shopping had seriously hurt the business, and then Covid had proved the death knell.

I'd had such a blast working for Diane for the last few years, and with the addition of Morgan to the mix, it had felt like my workplace was another home from home. Well better than home, as dealing with Daniel's moods and bouts of silent treatment had become to feel like hard work, so my actual work was a bit of respite.

Diane returned glumly to the shop floor in case of a stampede of customers - highly unlikely – so Morgan and I stayed to finish our mugs of stewed tea over the bad news.

Morgan was twisting a tendril of her green-streaked hair

around her index finger and looking thoughtful. "It's just a shame that we won't be working together any more, Lottie. In another lifetime I could have seen us opening a little shop together: you know, one where we could stock the sort of clothes women like us would really want to wear." Her eyes went a little misty, and I could see she was imagining our retail emporium in her mind. "There would be cool edgy designs, you know, stuff that really slays; and then for your demographic, flattering stylish gear for plus size beauties, clothes that would really accentuate and make you feel fabulous, not like you were wearing a duvet cover."

I couldn't help laughing, I knew that Morgan's last comment was in relation to my black and tan maxi dress that I had worn pretty much to death last summer. I'd bought it from one of the rather frumpy plus-size shops on the High Street and I always referred to it as my "duvet dress". It was unflattering and cut in the worst possible way for a voluptuous figure like mine. Even though I now had more choices since I had lost weight, I was still most definitely big. And that was OK with me for the most part, but it still made clothes shopping tricky at times. Online there were a multitude of options that couldn't be found on the High Street, but I never felt that any of the models really represented me. Yes, they were over a size 16, but they still had washboard flat tummies and defined abs, not at all like me.

"Yes, Morgan, it's a lovely dream to have, but unfortunately that's all it is – a dream."

Truthfully, I did feel a little gutted. Morgan was right that it would be wonderful. The thought of us having our own little fashion empire was amazing, and I had always dreamt of working in fashion after all. But alas it was nothing but a pipe dream. Neither of us had any money for a start; well, Diane did, and I felt pretty sure she would be happy to invest in her niece's dreams, but I sincerely doubted that would include bank rolling the fashion fantasies of her middle-aged, plus-sized employee. "Plus size" - I had never cared for that expression. It sounded like such a utilitarian way to describe a woman's curves. I much preferred the word "zaftig". I had discovered it when trying and failing to complete a crossword in one of Daniel's highbrow magazines. Zaftig meant having a curvaceous, full rounded figure, and how much nicer did that sound than fat, plus size, hefty or any of the other terms that were trotted out for us larger ladies? I liked zaftig much more; it sounded rather exotic.

Knowing we couldn't put off the inevitable, I rinsed our mugs and we made our way back onto the shop floor. Morgan got busy organising the jewellery display, her face set in steely concentration as she untangled a stack of silver-plated bangles. She was uncommonly quiet, and I knew she was still digesting Diane's news. I studied her for a few more seconds. She really was exceptionally pretty: her face even paler than usual against her ivory foundation and her bee-stung scarlet-painted lips. She was wearing a mini black denim pinafore dress over a Victoriana style blouse that her great grandmother would have coveted, given half the chance. She even had a cameo style brooch at her neck. The demure outfit was offset by the addition of thick green tights that perfectly matched the streaks in her jet-black hair. The outfit was finished off with a pair of minute black dangly bird earrings.

I pointed at her earlobes. "I like your earrings, Morgan. Are they supposed to be budgies?"

This had the desired effect of pulling Morgan out of her

apathy. She laughed and rolled her eyes, but with affection as if she couldn't quite believe how much of a wally I was. "No, they're not budgies; they're my raven earrings. You know how I love Edgar Allen Poe, and they fit in with my gothic vibe."

She started to recite a few paragraphs from *The Raven* to elucidate her point.

"Aaah, I see," I replied. I had forgotten just how much of a smart cookie Morgan was, and well-read too.

The rest of the day passed at a snail's pace, a very lazy snail at that. But finally I finished my shift and was ready to head home. Diane had already left, needing to check on one of her other shops; and Morgan was heading out to meet a date at a local bar, some boy she'd found on Tinder. So we said our goodbyes and I made my way out of the store as Morgan locked up. I walked slowly through the shopping centre, noticing with alarm just how many of the outlets were now standing vacant. I was headed in the direction of my bus stop. The optimism I'd felt this morning after seeing Leo had dissipated over the course of the day. I had felt so light and on top of the world back then, but now I was weighed down with despond, almost as if my boots were filled with quick-drying cement.

As I passed Scissor Sisters, I could just about make out Tabby forcefully straightening the long glossy mane of a client. I raised a hand in greeting as I caught her eye, and gave her a little wave. She grinned and waved back and mouthed some words to me. I'm sure they were "looking fab", but couldn't be entirely sure. Maybe she had said "looking fat", I thought with a jolt of alarm. But no, Tabby didn't have a mean bone in her body, and anyway I wasn't looking fat; well I was, of course, but less fat than I had once been.

I felt my mobile begin to vibrate erratically against my leg, so I fished it out of my shoulder bag. It was a text from Jacob saying that he was going to get a burger with some mates so wouldn't be home for dinner. With a sigh I deposited the phone back into my bag – ready meal and a glass of wine for one then. I was just about to zip my bag closed when I thought better of it and pulled the phone back out again for another look. I had a sudden desire to check my socials. I wasn't really one for bothering with Facebook or Instagram, hating the type of people that felt the need to inform the world when they were having beans on toast or an adequate bowel movement. It all felt rather self-obsessed to me. Plus, I never came away from a good old stalk on Facebook feeling any better about my own life. Too many people seemed to have it all – perfect family, idyllic life, wonderful job. Even though deep down I knew they were only highlighting the best bits of their life, a sort of "must see" trailer, it still made me feel envious and inadequate about my own existence. Seeing perfect people with their perfect lives left me feeling perfectly crap.

I strolled along scrolling as I went, keeping one eye on where I was going so as not to collide with any of the harassed shoppers rushing by. Suddenly something caught my attention and I ground to a halt. Hang on a minute, I just couldn't believe what I was seeing. Daniel had changed his Facebook profile picture three days ago. It had previously been a snap of Daniel, Jacob and me on holiday in Gran Canaria a couple of years ago. We had been laughing at the camera as the wind had just blown off my sun hat, and we appeared tanned and happy. But now that picture had gone and been replaced by a photo of Daniel and Roxy. He had his arm draped casually around her shoulder and was grinning like a loon; she on the other hand was pouting, probably imagining it was seductive. The expression that was designed to be alluring actually made her look like a constipated duck.

And he had updated his relationship status too from "married" to "single". Single? I ask you. Not even "it's complicated" or "separated". The cheek of him! He'd left home barely a month ago. His side of the bed was still warm; OK, that was the electric blanket, but still. How could he? It was no time since he had been trying to persuade me to take him back, as Roxy was only his "hobby"; it would run its course once she'd gone travelling to Lake Titicaca, or wherever she was heading. I was absolutely gobsmacked. He had changed his profile status without a single thought for me or Jacob and how it would make us feel. We really didn't feature at all.

I scrolled further down his feed. There were countless posts of Daniel on nights out with Roxy - in restaurants, night clubs. Good grief, there was even one of them at an open mic night with Daniel wearing skinny sprayed-on jeans with no socks and deck shoes; he looked like a right bell-end. He definitely appeared to have put on a little heft with all the good living, and he must have had to shoehorn himself into the denim. It was not a good look on him.

"I'm not going to cry; I'm not going to cry." I repeated the mantra to myself over and over in my head. I tried to remind myself that I was glad that Daniel had gone. And I really was glad, but this still hurt. It felt like yet another betrayal. I had fooled myself for too long that we had been happy, when I knew that was very far from the truth. But to see this new life of his so blatantly exposed for the whole world to see felt like a massive slap in the face.

What should I do now? Go home to an empty house and brood on it? The thought of that seemed so depressing, and I didn't think one of my black and white weepies and a gallon of mint choc chip was really going to cut it tonight. I tossed my phone back into my bag and kept walking. A few steps further and I had once again stopped. There was the most delicious aroma wafting up my nostrils. I sniffed the air like a hungry bloodhound. Where was the smell coming from? The mystery was quickly solved as I spotted a little bakery a couple of shop units further down. I opened my bag again to reach for my purse and entered the shop, knowing it was guaranteed to make me feel a bit better; it always had in the past.

Five minutes later, I was leaving the shopping centre and approaching my bus stop with my little paper bag of goodies nicely warming my hand. My heart sank as I noticed there was only one other person waiting at the stop, clearly indicating that I had just missed a bus and there wouldn't be another for at least half an hour. On reaching the stop my heart sank even further: the other person was the morose-looking youth from this morning who had resisted moving his backpack from my seat. I nodded a greeting to him, but it was met by a blank stare. He wore a pair of those big old headphones that made him look like a wannabe DJ from Ibiza. I certainly wasn't going to get any witty repartee from him. Oh well, at least I had a little treat to keep me going until the bus eventually turned up. With a mounting feeling of anticipation, I unwrapped the contents of the paper bag. It was a delicious-smelling sausage roll, lovely and warm and with the most divine looking golden pastry. After forgetting lunch, due to the drama of the staff meeting, I was so ravenous that I could happily have eaten a scabby horse between two slices of wholemeal.

I was already salivating as I held my treat aloft, ready to sink my teeth into the flaky pastry goodness. But at that very moment a fierce gust of wind surged along the street, sending leaves and crisp packets dancing and twirling with its sudden force. Worse was still to come, as it blew the pastry clean off my sausage roll, straight into the face of my teenage companion. The look of shock on his face was priceless as he tried to register what had just occurred. He stood stock still, his expression quickly turning to displeasure at the same time as mine turned to regret. What remained of my savoury snack now appeared to be a phallus-shaped piece of flaccid sausage meat of an extremely unappetising shade of pink (the same shade as Peppa Pig but probably less porky). The wind had blown all the pastry off my sausage roll – the perfect metaphor for my entire, disastrous day.

Chapter 20

"What do you fancy then?" Lila was studying the cocktail menu, which was thick as an encyclopaedia. "There's one here called the Valiant Vegan I like the sound of," she pointed out with her French manicured finger.

I squinted at the miniscule lettering, thinking it was about time I invested in some reading glasses, but it was the price that soon drew my attention. "Thirteen quid for what's basically a liquidised salad. You'd have to be bloody valiant to pay that! Are they joking?"

Lila threw her head back and hooted with laughter. "I can tell you don't drink much in city centre wine bars any more, Lottie; £13 isn't that pricey, you know. Anyway, you're paying for the vodka in it, not just the mushed-up veggies."

"OK... so that's what you're having then? The Valiant Vegan?" I really didn't fancy that myself: imagining sloppy baby food in a martini glass adorned with a cocktail umbrella.

"Nope, on second thoughts it's a bit healthy for me." Lila raised her eyebrows suggestively. "I like my cocktails like my men: nice and stiff, plenty of spirit and not much else."

I rolled my eyes at her as I resumed scanning the cocktail menu. It was making my head spin. Unpronounceable names with spirits I'd never even heard of, with a muddle of this and a twist of that and garnished with micro-herbs and such like. Whatever had happened to the joys of a simple gin and tonic?

So here I was in this achingly hip cocktail bar at a whisker past 6 pm, rather than trundling home on the number 12 bus. After I had pebble-dashed the teenage boy with flaky pastry, I'd decided that a stiff drink was most definitely in order and had given Lila a call. She had been more than happy to power down her computer, grab her briefcase and meet me for a post-work snifter in a trendy bar in the business district. The venue had been her choice, of course: just around the corner from her office. It was quiet, save for a few smart executive types in their knock-off Armani suits sipping colourful concoctions and tapping furiously on their laptops for the latest deal. It really wasn't my sort of place, and I would have much preferred to have gone to the cosy old pub down the road: it was half the price and did a great line in salty bar snacks, even boasting a jar of yellowing pickled eggs for the brave or rather foolish punter. You really did have to be valiant to snaffle one of those bad boys. No, this place was a bit out of my comfort zone. Not my cup of tea, or rather glass beaker filled with neon liquid, foam and smoke bubbles.

"Should we just order a bottle of Chenin Blanc?" Lila eventually asked, her patience clearly wearing thin as I took forever to make my selection. I still couldn't make head nor tail of the menu.

I nodded gratefully. My head was starting to hurt from the effort of deciding what concoction to choose, and anyway I just wanted some mind-numbing alcohol and didn't fancy the inevitable wait as the waiter conjured up something that I would probably drain in one disappointed gulp.

The customer ahead of us was just paying for his drink. It really looked quite spectacular, akin to something from my GCSE chemistry class. There was a syringe of pink liquid stuck in one side and a large smoke globule billowing out of the top like a toddler's snot bubble. He looked a little in awe of it, as if he didn't quite know whether to drink it or put in on display in the Saatchi gallery.

Lila reached across the bar to him with a devilish grin. "You do realise it's not magic, don't you? And unfortunately, it won't make your cock any bigger."

"Lila!" I protested, my face flaming with embarrassment; I turned to the man as if Lila was my naughty child and it was my duty to apologise on her behalf. "I'm so sorry."

My words were understandably met with a huffy stare. I nodded at the man again and chased after Lila who was already striding away, her stilettos click-clacking on the wooden floor as she scoured the bar to find us a suitable table. She was carrying the wine bucket and glasses and I followed in her wake with a little bowl of olives and some scraps of flatbread that were clearly going to serve as our hearty dinner. As it was a Thursday, most of the tables were vacant so we had our pick.

"You really are the limit, Lila." I was hoisting myself up onto the high swivel stool, with all the elegance of an upturned woodlouse as I struggled to get my bulk seated comfortably. "That chap looked mortified."

"He'll get over it." At last she was pouring us large glasses of chilled white wine. "Anyway, I'm too old and long in the tooth not to say what I want when I want." She took a generous gulp of wine and gave a satisfied sigh. "Well, apart from work; I do try and behave there, at least on occasion."

Lila really was a force of nature. I admired her confidence,

I really did, even though it caused some inevitable embarrassment. Nobody would ever dull her sparkle. She would never change; I don't think she could if she tried. I imagined she would be the same at eighty years of age as she was now, just possibly with a touch more sass. She would be dressed impeccably with her war paint flawless, drinking pink gin and poking strangers with her walking stick to regale them with anecdotes of her fabulous life.

"So, how are things going since Daniel the Dickhead moved out?"

I sighed and took a large gulp of wine myself. I savoured the deliciousness of its crisp sharpness for a second. "It's going OK: he's still living at his mate's house, still seeing *her*, but he does come round a couple of times a week to see Jacob, so that's good. I guess I can't complain too much."

Lila was theatrically rolling her eyes. "Can't complain too much? Are you for real? You're talking as if he's a thoroughly decent chap, going to so much effort to visit his offspring now and again. I would say that's the very least he could do. He's a pig, Lottie, and he's cruel to you too: always making fun of your weight and calling you 'Lottie Big Bot'."

I grimaced at this. Daniel always liked that nickname for me, said it was a term of endearment. It felt more like a slap in the face to me.

Lila picked up a small crust of bread and dunked it into the balsamic vinegar and oil. The oily mix dripped off the sourdough and onto the table, just as Lila's words were dripping with sarcasm. "Well, I only hope he's still paying the bills and not letting things slide now he's a sugar daddy."

Sugar Daddy. Ouch. That really hurt to hear that, but I suppose that was what people would be saying. There would be hushed sniggers and raised eyebrows as they discussed him in such a manner: like he was a tired old cliché, a middle-aged man with an itch to scratch. My husband, my Daniel. But he wasn't my Daniel any more, he hadn't really been for a long time.

"He's changed his Facebook status to 'single' now. There are pictures of them together all over his feed." I dropped my head gloomily into my hands and groaned. "Everyone is going to know now. Why doesn't he realise how embarrassing this all is? I'll be a laughing stock."

Lila rubbed my arm affectionately. "No, you won't be a laughing stock. You've done absolutely nothing wrong. He's just being an insensitive bugger, that's all." She took another hearty gulp of wine, and I could see she was getting annoyed on my behalf: pink spots had appeared high on her cheekbones, a clear sign that she was riled up. "What is it with these men? They get a younger woman, and they feel the need to show her off to the world like she's a new toy. Absolutely no consideration for the woman who's stood by them all those years. You wait, Charlotte, he'll be the one with egg on his face when she dumps his sorry saggy ass; and mark my words, dump him she will."

"Do you really think so?" I asked, embarrassed by the neediness evident in my voice.

What was I doing? I needed to get a grip. The wine was making me melancholy, reminiscing about the good times with Daniel when there hadn't been that many good times; well, not for the last few years anyway. It didn't matter if they split up or not. I wasn't taking him back. Ever. Enough was enough.

Lila really thought she had the monopoly on knowing how

men's minds worked. Since her split from her husband, any relationships she entered into with the opposite sex were most definitely on her terms. She liked to have the upper hand in all aspects of her life.

"I'm telling you, Charlotte, this Roxy might think she's struck gold for now: got herself an older, successful more sophisticated man, but she'll soon wise up. She'll get bored and move on to a younger guy who doesn't need to trim his nose hair and be in bed by 10.30 pm. It won't take her long to figure him out and see what he's really like."

I wasn't exactly sure what Lila was getting at, as the wine was going straight to my head. It was a nice feeling, to be honest: the stresses and strains of the day floating away on a cloud of intoxication. However, in my rather inebriated state, my thought processes were a little laboured. I knew that Lila had never been Daniel's biggest fan, even referring to him on occasion as "Dreary Dan", but her words seemed heavy with meaning.

"What do you mean, Lila? It won't take her long to figure him out?"

Lila put her wine glass down on the table mid-swig. "He's a narcissist, Lottie. Surely you've figured that out by now? Everything is always about him and his needs; he's all that really matters; you're just an afterthought." She paused to pop an olive into her mouth before continuing. "Plus he's about as much fun as a boil on your ass crack."

I laughed. I couldn't help it, her last comment had cracked me right up. Lila really did have a way with words - admittedly a bit like a stand-up comic in a dodgy working men's club, but she was funny. It was a welcome release to laugh for a change, and as tears of mirth streaked down my cheeks, I clenched my pelvic floor to ensure there would be no tears streaking down my legs too.

When the tears of laughter finally subsided, I got to thinking. Lila's comments about Daniel being a narcissist had really hit a chord with me. Was it right what she said? Was Daniel a narcissist? Personally, I'd never used that term before. I just knew he was my husband and we'd rubbed along together well enough over the years. It hadn't been easy, but I'd thought our marriage was worth the work. Yes, he was a bit of a stiff; yes, he was self-obsessed; but he was my husband and it had just worked. Well, it had worked until it sadly no longer did.

At least it was true that he was being decent about money, making sure all the bills were covered and Jacob and I didn't have to worry about that at least. I was worried, though; I couldn't help it. How long would he continue to pay the bills and be able to finance his new lifestyle too? I only really brought in a pittance from my job, and that was soon to go. Would we have to sell the house? The thought of that felt like a sucker punch to the gut. We'd been in that house forever. Jacob had grown up there, taken his first steps there, it was all he'd ever known. It wasn't just a house, it was our home, every room alive with memories. But would memories mean anything when hard cold cash came into the equation? Would Jacob and I end up living in a poky one-bed high-rise with damp walls and no Ivy next door to feed me carrot cake and provide a shoulder to cry on? I couldn't bear to think of it.

I also couldn't shake off the conversation I'd had with my mother. Our talk in the café was weighing heavily on my mind. The serious expression on Mum's face when she was telling me just how important it was for a woman to have her own independence, something just for her so she didn't have to rely on a man.

I realised that Lila and I hadn't spoken for several minutes, both lost in our own thoughts. When I turned my attention back to her, she was studying me rather intently.

"I've got to say you're looking good, better than I've seen you in years." She reached over to feel the fabric of my cardigan. "Apart from this, though. I'm not loving the fact you're still head-to-toe in black polyester. I thought you were going to brighten yourself up a bit, be a bold new Charlotte?"

Lila of course was dressed to the nines. She had been at work since 9 am, but she still managed to look as fresh as a daisy. How she kept a cream linen shirt dress looking so immaculate was beyond me. If I'd worn it, I would have resembled a dishevelled sack of spuds within five minutes. I wondered if she had one of those little hand-held steamers in the office and kept one of her minions poised to jump into action and give her a damn good steaming once a wrinkle threatened to appear.

I, on the other hand, was wearing my stretchy black midi dress. It suited my shape well, especially now there was slightly less of a shape to fill it. It was the sort of forgiving material that would stretch if it needed to. No worries if you wanted to indulge in an all-you-can-eat Chinese buffet in this little number: it really had your back. I was also wearing my new studded leather ankle boots, which I felt gave me a slightly grungy rock-chick edge. A bit like Courtney Love, but with slightly more soap and slightly less attitude. I was happy overall with what I was wearing, but I knew exactly what Lila was getting at. Lila knew me of old, knew how I adored fashion and would lose myself in glossy magazines every month, wishing that I would someday have the confidence to dress like the models in the adverts. My friend just wanted me to have the confidence to express myself in the way that she did. I knew she believed Daniel had a lot to do with my poor self-image. It was one of the many reasons she disliked him.

"I am pushing myself," I assured Lila. "I've been treating myself to a few new colourful pieces, accessories too. I don't know, it's just easier to go with the safe option, but I am trying to push myself out of my comfort zone, baby steps, you know?"

It was true. My dress sense was improving, and having lost weight I was becoming more adventurous with my fashion, but it would take time. Rome wasn't built in a day, and sometimes it was easier to fall back, quite literally, into my old black tent-like garments. It was hard to change habits that were so ingrained and get into a new way of thinking; sometimes it was easier to revert to what was safe. My safe factory settings. But I needed to take more risks in life, I knew that. Without risk I would simply stay where I was, and that was going nowhere.

"Your hair is amazing though, Lottie. I always knew you'd suit a shorter length, but the colour is just gorgeous. It really brings your face to life, it's priceless."

I smiled at Lila, lapping up the compliments. "Priceless? Thank you, I should probably have tipped Tabby a bit more than a fiver then."

Lila was nodding her head in agreement. "First rule of life: always look after your hairdresser. Those people have the ability to ruin your looks with a few careless snips of the scissors. They hold infinite power and should only be underestimated at your peril."

She shook the last few dregs from the wine bottle into her glass, giving its bottom a spanking for good measure to ensure not a single drop went to waste. Satisfied it was well and truly spent, she glanced around the bar for any passing waiters. "Should I get us another bottle? We've a dead soldier here."

I hadn't realised we'd already downed a whole bottle. I checked my watch – 7 pm. I knew I should be heading home, quit while I was still ahead; but no, I knew I wouldn't. I was enjoying myself far too much. Lila was such a tonic; her acerbic wit and brutal honesty could always cheer me up, even in the most hopeless situations. I think it's called gallows humour. Being able to laugh and make light of disasters always seems to help, bizarre I know, but true. And it was so good to be out enjoying myself again in the world. And I was enjoying myself. There was also so much I still wanted to tell my friend. We did need another bottle of wine though, as all the talking would most certainly dry our throats out. It was the sensible thing to do.

Over the next three hours we talked and drank and laughed and cried. It was funny, it was cathartic, it was emotional, and it was just what I needed. As Lila was already up to speed with the whole Daniel situation, we steered clear of that subject for a bit - which was just what I needed. It was a relief not to think about all that stuff for an hour or so.

Lila was gutted to hear about my imminent job loss, and assured me that she would keep her ear to the ground. If she heard of anything that could suit me she would tip me the wink. I thanked her, but didn't hold out much hope. It was kind of her to offer, but it was unlikely I would fit in her office. I just didn't have the necessary experience, never mind the qualifications, and if Lila was a Rottweiler, then I was more of a Yorkshire Terrier. Hardly in the same league.

Once the subject of my approaching unemployment was exhausted, I took a deep breath and told her about Leo. Her eyes lit up, like she'd just rear-ended a 100-watt bulb.

"Now this is more like it." She refilled our wine glasses with enthusiasm. "Tell me everything, and leave nothing, I repeat nothing, out. I want every filthy detail; and if there aren't any, I give you permission to make some up."

So that's what I did. I told her everything about Leo. In truth there wasn't much to tell, but Lila was thrilled that he was taking me for lunch on Saturday. She loved to date younger men, and was a great advocate for toyboys – more stamina, less nostril hair etc.

"He obviously fancies you."

I could feel my cheeks getting hot, partly through embarrassment and partly through the copious amounts of wine we'd sunk. "No, he really doesn't," I protested, "it's not like that at all. We're just friends; he's Ivy's nephew and he wants someone to go for lunch with as he doesn't know many people and he finds me easy to talk to."

Lila was rolling her eyes theatrically. "Yeah, yeah, whatever you say, Charlotte. You keep telling yourself that, but I don't believe it for a second." She paused for a moment to retrieve her Chanel powder compact from her bag and flipped the black case open. "Look in the mirror, just look, you're a catch."

I tentatively peered in the little mirror and grimaced at my reflection. I had jolly red cheeks like Santa Claus and my make-up had all but sweated off completely. It was not my best look. "A catch? Whoever catches me needs to throw me straight back. I look a right fright."

Lila shrugged. "Have it your way, Lots, but when he starts asking you to teabag him, believe me, he doesn't want you to stick the kettle on. It's not a brew he's gagging for."

Chapter 21

I didn't remember getting home. I didn't really remember much at all after sinking the second bottle of wine. I knew it had been a great night, that much I knew for sure, but now the following morning I was feeling anything but great. You know that scene in *Cinderella* where our girl is getting ready to tend to her ugly sisters and all the delightful little animals are helping her get ready: the birds are tweeting, Cinders is singing, and all is technicolour picture perfect. Well, imagine the opposite of that and you get my drift. It felt like Iron Maiden were tuning up in my skull and I didn't have the energy to lift my head from the pillow, let alone lift myself out of bed and attempt to get ready for work. Fair to say, I had the hangover from hell.

I lay in bed like a dead fish, summoning the strength to open at least one eye; they felt as if they'd been superglued shut. Little flashes of memory kept jumping randomly into my mind. After the second bottle of wine, we had moved on to another bar, and then another, and then another... well, you get the idea. But evidently I had at least made it safely home to my bed, thank goodness.

Although large chunks of the evening had been expunged from my memory, I could still recall some excruciating moments, like little titbits of humiliation. Apparently I had been chatting complete nonsense to strangers in the ladies' toilet as we compared stretch marks and birth stories. I had also informed a bearded man at the bar that his soaring eagle tattoo resembled a startled turkey. And worst of all I had left the Ladies with half a tissue stuck to the heel of my ankle boot and my skirt hitched up into my granny pants. I had walked across the crowded room, oblivious to my fashion faux pas. I had thought I looked damn fine, you know the way you do when alcohol is involved and you have this crazy idea you might be a dead ringer for some Hollywood actress. I shuddered at this memory the most. Yep, that was enough recalling the events of the previous night. I had learned many valuable lessons in my life, and one was that over-analysing an exceedingly drunken night was never a good idea. The post-drink post-mortem with a hangover should never be done; the cringe factor was just too bad.

Eventually I managed to prise my eyes open. They felt dry and gritty, as if I'd been at the beach and the wind had blown a bucketload of sand straight into them. I dreaded the moment of looking in the mirror and assessing the damage I'd done. At least we had eaten, though. I knew that for a fact as I had a sliver of shrivelled kebab meat stuck to my forehead and my hair whiffed of garlic mayo. I had also slept in my clothes, which I'd not done in forever. I was always correctly attired for bed, with make-up removed and a thick layer of night cream applied to keep the wrinkles at bay. However, it appeared I had collapsed the previous night wearing my entire outfit, well apart from the boots: one was on the pillow next to me, and the other was randomly sitting on top of the portable TV in the corner of the bedroom. How had we let ourselves get in such a state? Especially on a Thursday? The shame of it. I was in my forties and Lila, well, Lila was considerably older than that. We were supposed to know better, be older and wiser. Hah, that was a laugh.

No matter how horrendous I felt, I still had to get myself ready for work. While I still had employment, I sure as hell wasn't going to be late and risk losing everything.

I pulled on my dressing gown and stumbled to the kitchen in search of caffeine, blinking against the fluorescent tube lighting like a tortoise coming out of hibernation.

"Wow, Mum, you look like a bag of crap," Jacob politely noted as he plastered a round of toast with butter and. He had an expression on his face that I couldn't quite fathom. Was it pity, or grudging respect?

I groaned as I lowered myself delicately onto one of the kitchen chairs. Every part of me felt sore and tender. I must have been drunkenly bouncing off the walls last night, like the little silver ball in a pinball machine.

"Lila and I went for a quick drink after work," I mumbled, squinting at my son through eyelids that felt a ten-ton weight. "Could you please get your old mum a cup of black coffee? I need something to perk me up before getting ready for work."

Jacob seemed highly entertained to see his mother rather the worse for wear. He grinned as he scooped instant coffee into my "World's best biscuit eater" mug. "Just the one drink, was it?" He gave me a cheeky wink. "It must have been a strong one."

Somehow, I managed to get myself fully dressed. It felt like a mammoth task, as I had to keep sitting down until the waves of nausea subsided. But eventually I was ready to face the world. When would I ever learn? You never go drinking on a school night. Well, at least not drinking like you're on a hen weekend in Magaluf.

I was always warning Jacob about the perils of binge drinking: how drinking was so much fun until the fun stopped; that when you drank you felt on top of the world, invincible and everything had a rosy glow to it. But it wasn't real and wouldn't last. You were only borrowing joy from the following day. And when tomorrow came, and come it would, you had to pay the joy back with interest. And that's where the misery of the hangover came into play: the nightmare of the "hangxiety" or the "beer fear", and the solemn promise to yourself that you would never ever get into such a state again, until of course you did.

I eventually made it out of the house and halfway down the street before I realised my error. In my haste I'd grabbed my most comfortable shoes, my ballet pumps, a good choice normally - nice and flat, with less chance of a hungover stumble. However, in my less than astute state I had grabbed a black one and a navy blue one from the wardrobe. I really needed to tidy my shoes and place them neatly in pairs rather than all heaped together in a massive jumble. I was in two minds: part of me wanted to think "sod it" and head for the bus; but I reminded myself that I was trying to make more of an effort to look elegant and polished, and by wearing odd shoes that would not be the impression I'd give. In fact, all and sundry would reckon I was losing my marbles.

Five minutes later and I was again ready to start my journey to work, correctly attired in matching black footwear. Ivy was at her front door in her floral dressing gown, signing for a delivery from the postman. As I passed, I raised my hand in a friendly greeting and she waved back with a smile.

"Morning, Lottie, looks like it's going to be a lovely day."

I nodded back. I had no doubt that the chance of my day being lovely was fairly slim. No matter how glorious the weather turned out to be, it would be a struggle for me to remain awake and upright.

I wondered if Leo had told his aunt about our lunch date tomorrow. I really didn't have a clue. There was no harm if he had: it was only two friends sharing a bite to eat together, after all. I hadn't had the chance to talk to Ivy in a few days, so hadn't been able to tell her myself. I really didn't think she would have a problem with it. In fact, I knew she would be pleased.

Somehow I managed to make it through the day unscathed. As was the new norm, the boutique was quiet. I would normally have found this fact depressing, but today I was delighted that I could keep my head down, count off the hours until I could go home and just see the day out without disgracing myself too much.

"You should get a couple of sausage rolls and a can of Vimto," Morgan suggested helpfully; "always sorts my hangovers out a treat."

Poor Morgan, she had a lot to learn. Hangovers in your forties could not be cured with mere pastry and carbonated beverages. Hangovers in your twenties were a mere drizzle of rain compared to the tsunami of destruction that they wreaked in later life.

"No sausage rolls for me, thank you." I picked up a pile of green sweaters that needed to be discounted. I had an inkling that my pallor was probably the same shade as the wool. The thought of sausage rolls made me a little queasy, partly from the thought of eating, but mostly the embarrassment of remembering the sausage roll incident from the day before. "I'm just going to power through on caffeine, water and paracetamol every four hours."

Morgan shrugged her shoulders. "Your choice, but I always find carbs and sugar sort me out a treat."

Somehow I managed to make it through to home time. I had never been more thankful in my life to be able to collapse on the bus and know I would soon be home. I had planned to spend the evening getting organised for lunch with Leo the following day. I had plans to pluck, wash and tan myself within an inch of my life. Not that it was a date, of course, but going out to a nice brasserie in Harrogate was an occasion for me, so I wanted to look my best. I even had one of those face mask sheets ready, the ones that make you look like something from *The Phantom of the Opera.* With that and a deep conditioning hair mask, I was going to settle down for a few hours with a nice crime documentary. You know the ones? Tales of blissfully married couples living their best lives until one forgets to replace the toilet roll and gets bludgeoned to death for the insurance money.

Once I had finished with the beautifying and Netflix, I had envisaged a nice light dinner of an omelette and then an early night by 10.30 pm for some restful rejuvenating sleep. But you know what they say about the best laid plans? In fact, once I returned home, I headed straight for the fridge, ravenous after existing all day on H_2O and caffeine. I wolfed down an entire packet of wafer-thin ham and three packets of cheese and onion crisps, then collapsed exhausted into bed at precisely 7 pm, just glad to have survived the day.

Chapter 22

The following morning, I was awoken to the reverberating sound of grunge pop music blaring out of Jacob's bedroom. I rolled over in bed to squint at the clock on the bedside table. How come Jacob was awake so early on a Saturday? Normally he wasn't one for early mornings, especially at the weekend; his sleep pattern was more dead to the world Dracula than dawn riser.

As the digital numbers on the clock slowly came into focus, I felt my stomach lurch - 10:45 am. How was that even possible? I had slept solidly for over 15 hours. Was I ill? I must be ill, surely; it wasn't normal to sleep for so long. I didn't feel ill though, in fact I felt pretty good overall. The hangover was gone, and I felt well rested and better than I had in ages. The last few weeks must have taken more of a toll on me than I had realised. But today with the sun shining high in the sky and the birds singing, I felt optimistic, as if an exciting new chapter in my life story was about to be told. I had my date, of sorts, with Leo later and I couldn't help but feel the thrill of anticipation of new adventures. Well, that is, once I had worked out what I was going to wear.

I headed downstairs to fix some coffee; I'd make a bit of breakfast too and then come back upstairs to figure out what outfit to choose. Jacob followed me downstairs, eager at my heels like a puppy. As it was the weekend, he was hoping for more than his usual weekday bowl of cereal.

"Egg and bacon good for you, love?" I began cracking eggs into my trusty old frying pan, confident what his answer would be.

"Yeah, that would bussin'. Could you do some fried bread too?"

I smiled indulgently at him and pulled some white sliced out of the breadbin on top of the fridge. "What time is your dad picking you up today?"

Jacob shrugged his shoulders and poured himself a large tumbler of orange juice. "Dunno, about 12ish, I think."

The bacon was beginning to crisp up nicely at the corners, so I added the bread. It instantly sucked up all the fat from the pan like a famished SpongeBob SquarePants. I reminded myself to stick to toast; I shuddered as I could only imagine the calories.

If Daniel was picking Jacob up at around 12 noon, that meant they should have left way before Leo's arrival at 1 pm. Phew, I didn't fancy another meeting between those two. The last thing I needed to spoil my good mood was fisticuffs over the fried slice and bacon.

I took a sip of my coffee nonchalantly. "You remember I'm going out today too?"

Jacob's face looked a little confused. "You are?"

"Yeah, just for lunch with a friend; you know, Leo, Ivy's nephew. We're going into Harrogate."

Jacob looked as if he was tickled by something, and his lip twitched at the corner. "Ah yes, your 'friend' Leo, that's great, Mum. You have a good time with your friend, he's a cool guy."

With Jacob tucking into a plate of bacon and eggs like he hadn't seen food in days, and the frying pan steeped in soapy water, I took my mug of coffee upstairs. I was going to have a nice leisurely bath and slowly get myself ready. At my age it took time to make a good impression. I could no longer rely on a quick once-over with a face flannel, a spray of deodorant and swipe of lipstick to transform me. No, now it was more of a military operation involving deft manoeuvring into shapewear and plenty of primping and applying of make-up/camouflage.

Just after midday, I was finally ready. I'd plumped for a jet black pair of high-waisted boot-cut jeans, the dark hue of the material having a flattering effect on my silhouette. They were long-legged, and I was wearing my highest ankle boots underneath to give the illusion of gazelle-like legs. Well, more Shetland pony, but still pretty good. Then I put a deep burgundy fitted T-shirt over the jeans, and a smart black blazer. Looking in the mirror I felt confident that I looked good. OK, I wasn't the slimmest of women by any stretch of the imagination, but I had a good shape now. I was going in and out where I was supposed to; my curves looked womanly and Renaissance-like. I added some subtle jewellery to the outfit, and I was good to go. My make-up had taken an age to apply, but it was worth it. I was wearing a shedload of the stuff, but it had been done in such a way that it looked virtually au naturel. How clever was that? I was learning so much from YouTube, and I could scarcely believe how much I was enjoying it. It felt good to be concentrating on me for a change.

I was nervously looking forward to lunch, my tummy doing anxious little somersaults beneath my control pants. The only fly in the ointment was that it was after 12 noon and Daniel still hadn't arrived. I wanted to avoid the meeting of the two men at all costs, as it certainly hadn't gone well the last time they had run into each other.

My heart soared with relief as the doorbell rang out. I mouthed a silent prayer of thanks and shouted down the stairs to Jacob, "Your dad's here, love."

"I'm just in the bathroom. Can you get the door, Mum?"

I padded down the stairs to answer the door and came face to face with my ex-husband. I felt a jolt of shock course through my veins. Daniel was standing solemnly in the doorway looking... well, in truth, not looking too great. His face was certainly a more natural colour than last time: a healthy pink rather than the fuchsia it had previously been. He must have finished his pot of face cream. But apart from that, I had seen him looking a lot better. His face was round and puffy, not as angular and well-defined as it had once been. Too many takeaways and cans of lager, making him a bit squidgy round the edges. I'd thought from the Facebook pictures that he had put on some weight, but seeing how much he'd evidently gained I couldn't help but wonder if he had been competitively eating hotdogs, like they do on that weird satellite channel.

He always claimed to be a man of the world. Well, he certainly looked like it now - just rather large around the equator. He was leaning against the door, and his shirt had risen a bit. I was shocked to see he had done my pregnancy button trick: you know the one where you hook an elastic band through the buttonhole to give yourself an extra couple of inches to manoeuvre with. His 32-inch-waist trousers must really be feeling the pressure of his new lifestyle. He might have to consider elasticated-waist trousers soon.

This probably sounds hypercritical, noticing Daniel's weight gain when I was a plus-size woman myself. I knew all too well how easy it was to pile on the pounds, and really it shouldn't matter. It honestly hadn't mattered to me; I would have loved Daniel irrespective of how fat or thin he was. But that was in the past, and it was his mammoth ego, not his mammoth gut that had turned me off loving him.

However, that said, it just seemed so alien to me that Daniel would allow himself to gain so much weight. He was incredibly militant about his diet and exercise, and had always been so critical of me and my size.

I realised that Daniel must have noticed I was staring, so I forced my eyes away from him for a moment and examined the chipped paintwork on the skirting boards.

"Hello, Daniel. Jacob will be down in a minute."

Daniel didn't respond. He was now studying me intensely, his gaze making me feel a little awkward and self-conscious, as if I was under a microscope. It was a good while before he deigned to say anything.

"Are you going out today?" he asked with an accusatory note to his voice.

"Actually, I am," I replied a little cagily. "I'm going out for lunch with a friend in Harrogate."

Daniel nodded and continued to study me for a few more moments. "You're looking really nice, Charlotte," he commented, half-heartedly. "Your hair, your clothes, you look... well... you look good."

I felt somewhat shocked to hear Daniel compliment me. It was a sunny day in Yorkshire, but was it a frosty day in hell? It had been so long since I had felt the warmth of a compliment from him that it unnerved me. I knew I was looking better, not comfort-eating as much and taking more care of my appearance. But for him to notice had really thrown me. I had lost a little weight, but not as much as he always made me feel I needed to. Yet I couldn't deny there was a look of grudging admiration evident on his face.

"Thank you, Daniel. I'm just taking a bit more care of myself."

"Well, it definitely seems to be working. You look quite pretty, like you did when we first met... when we were young."

It would have been nicer if he had said "pretty" and left it at that, rather than adding the "quite". Even hearing those words should have made my heart sing, but they didn't. I no longer felt I needed validation from him, or validation from anyone. I didn't need a man to make me happy. I might want one, but I certainly didn't need one. Especially not one like Daniel Potts.

I was quite surprised by the icy-edged tone when I spoke. "But I'm not young though, am I, Daniel? And speaking of young, how is the fragrant Roxy?"

Daniel's eyes dropped hesitantly to the floor, and he cleared his throat. "She... she's OK, I think. I've not seen much of her the last few days."

I wasn't expecting him to say that, and it didn't make any sense. Hadn't I just seen them all over social media together, looking like they were completely besotted? Yorkshire's answer to Romeo and Juliet without the dagger. Well, we knew where the dagger was – firmly in my back.

"I must say that surprises me, Daniel. I saw your Facebook post, the fact you're in a relationship together. How did you think that would make me feel? Didn't you even think I deserved the respect of you at least giving me the heads-up?"

He had the good grace to look shame-faced for at least five seconds. "I know I should have told you, it's just that Roxy was keen to put everything out there for the world to see. And she's hard to say no to; you know what the young are like."

Hard to say no to? The young? I couldn't help rolling my eyes at this. "And where is Roxy today? Have you just got her a Happy Meal and left her playing in the park?"

This time Daniel didn't need the spicy face cream; his face went pillar-box red on its own. "I've not seen her for a few days; we're taking a bit of a break so she can catch up with her friends."

I tried to appear uninterested in hearing this nugget of information, and turned to rinse off the frying pan to keep myself busy. However, it was clear that Daniel was in the mood to talk.

"I think it's over, Charlotte. She was never right for me really. I just don't know what I was thinking."

I laughed bitterly. "I know exactly what you were thinking, or rather what you were thinking with."

Daniel was now sitting on a kitchen chair, crossing his legs awkwardly as if worried I was going to whack his misbehaving member with the frying pan. He looked up at me with longing in his puppy dog eyes; those eyes that used to make me agree to anything, but not any more.

"I want to come home, Charlotte. I miss you, I miss our family. I should never have said you should put up with me having a fling. It wasn't fair to you. I was being selfish."

I picked up a tea towel and started to dry my hands. "The thing is, Daniel, you might say you don't know what you were thinking, but I do. I know exactly what you were thinking: that you could have your cake and eat it too. Indulge in a bit of fresh fruity tart on the side, and come home to the dry old Yorkshire pudding." Why, oh why, was I comparing myself to battered yorkies now? I was clearly losing the plot.

The thing was, I had known for a while that it was over between Daniel and me. But I don't think he had contemplated for a single second that I wouldn't take him back. I was calm, comfortable old reliable Charlotte: I knew what side my bread was buttered on; I was lucky to have Daniel, and I would take what little scraps of affection were thrown my way. But that was no longer the case.

Like it or not, Daniel was going to have to realise that things had changed, and they had changed a lot. I was evolving, reinventing myself. Yes, I was scared about the future; I often felt I wanted to run to the sofa and stay there, curled up in my safe place with my junk food for comfort and my reassuring films to escape to. But that wasn't going to be me any more. I had a life, and I was going to damn well live it.

Daniel took my hand. "We can go back to where we were when we were happy. Forget about Roxy, she's a bit of a nightmare to be honest."

I shook my head resolutely. I wasn't going to be swayed.

"You're right, she is a nightmare." Jacob's voice startled both of us. "I only met her the once, and that was enough. Talk about basic bitch: I mean I like my phone and all, but she's proper addicted to all the socials; it's proper tragic."

Jacob flopped down onto the chair next to his father. "Any-way, Mum's going out too with a... friend." He smiled to himself. He was clearly sick of his dad's behaviour too and wanted to give him a taste of his own medicine.

Daniel was a little slow on the uptake. "Yes, is it just Lila or all the girls you're meeting up with?"

I took a deep breath. Well, here goes nothing.

"I'm not going out with Lila or the girls, Daniel. I'm going out for a spot of lunch with Leo."

Daniel looked a little bemused by this. I started to count slowly in my head as I waited for the penny to finally drop. 1...2...3.

"Hang on... Leo, you mean Ivy's nephew? The one that's staying with her?"

I nodded my head and tried to explain to Daniel that Leo and I were just friends, it was a casual lunch and he should not read too much into it. But Daniel wasn't listening and had clearly lost the ability to reason. He looked apoplectic, a small vein in his temple throbbing like it was doing an Irish jig. I felt it would be wise if I River-danced away for cover.

"You're going out with him?" Daniel demanded, his voice more shocked than angry. "He's nothing but a scruffy oik. He looks like his hair has never seen a brush, and he doesn't even work."

I felt myself getting increasingly angry and needing to defend Leo. "He does work, he's just taking some time off before going back to Canada. He works in the hotel industry."

Daniel sneered unattractively. "Works in the hotel industry, doing what exactly?"

I shook my head. I had no idea. To me it was not important what Leo did for a job. I was just happy to know him.

"I bet you anything he cleans the toilets. Is that the sort of man you want, Charlotte? A loo attendant that squirts bleach around urinals and scrubs skid marks for a living?" A little smile twitched at the corner of his mouth. He was clearly getting into his stride. "I must say I'm surprised at you going out in public with a much younger guy. I never realised you were such a cradle-snatcher. Or are you simply doing your bit for charity? The poor slob's so skint you're slipping him a few quid to take you out on the town."

The cheek of him! I couldn't believe what I was hearing. Yes, Leo was younger than me by a bit, well quite a bit, roughly ten years. But what room did Daniel have to talk? Daniel had been old enough to go drinking in pubs, drive a car and start voting Tory (which he always did) before his latest squeeze had even been conceived! How was it fine and dandy for him to date Roxy, yet I was made to feel that Leo was grabbing a granny by taking me out for a bite of lunch? And to insinuate that I would have to pay him, like he was some sort of gigolo, was just so insulting.

I could feel my face getting hotter and hotter, but this time it wasn't the blasted peri-menopause; it was pure unadulterated rage coursing hotly through my veins.

"I... just fuck off, Daniel!"

Daniel and Jacob's heads shot around to face me simultaneously, their eyes wide with amazement. I never used the "f" word, and they were clearly shocked. I had shocked myself too. I was used to hearing Lila swear like a fishwife when she was in a rant, and it never particularly bothered me, that was just her way. But me? I never used expletives much, and to use this particular one meant only one thing – I was effing furious.

Daniel quickly recovered his composure. "There's no need for that sort of language, Charlotte. Your son doesn't need to hear that word coming from his own mother."

Jacob snorted with laughter. "Chill, Dad. I hear way worse than that from the ten-year-olds on the bus into town. Mum using the 'f' word once in a blue moon isn't exactly going to corrupt me." He grabbed his backpack and his earphones from the kitchen worktop. "Are we going now? I don't want to miss the start of the film and I'm starving, so I'm gonna need a bucket of popcorn."

Starving? He'd barely finished a huge cooked breakfast. That was teenage boys for you, though: hollow legs.

Daniel caught my eye and opened his mouth to say something, but upon seeing my furious expression he thought better of it and shut it tight like a Venus flytrap.

I watched them both set off and felt my anger begin to wane. Jacob called out from the hall, "See you later, Mum, and have a good time."

I smiled to myself; he was a good lad. My smile froze on my lips, though, on hearing the parting words from Daniel: "Yes, enjoy your lunch, Charlotte. I'm sure whatever fine dining establishment Leo has selected will be simply sublime. I hear you can get a decent pie 'n chips these days in a greasy spoon."

With that I heard the front door slam aggressively, shaking the whole house on its very foundations. With no one to hear I let rip: "Fuck... fuck... fuck... fuck... fuck... fuck you, Daniel."

The doorbell rang out again, startling me into silence. I bet he was back with another cutting remark to twist the knife a little further. There really was no need for him to be so vile about Leo, he didn't even know him. It was none of his business who I had lunch with. He was the one who had left, after all, not me. If I wanted to have lunch with a friend, a male friend, it was none of his damn business.

I strode to the front door. I was still mad, and I was more than ready for him. If he wanted an argument, he was jolly well going to get one. I'd had just about enough of Daniel, and this mouse was ready to roar.

I swung the door open, but it wasn't my ex standing on the doorstep; it was someone I didn't even recognise.

Chapter 23

The man standing in the doorway looked a little unsure of himself. He shuffled back and forth from one foot to the other and smiled down at me nervously. "Are you ready to go, Charlotte?"

I didn't answer straight away. My mind was still trying to make sense of what I was seeing in front of me. Clearly it was Leo, I knew that much as soon as he opened his mouth and spoke. I recognised the deep rich voice straight away, but that was all that was familiar. This Leo could have stepped straight out of an aftershave commercial or a Hollywood movie set. Gone was the bushy beard and wild shaggy hair, now replaced by a clean-shaved face and neatly combed short back and sides. He was dressed in an elegant white linen shirt unbuttoned just enough to show a hint of chest hair. I knew Lila would find this repulsive, liking her men buffed and waxed within an inch of their lives, as hairless as a shop mannequin, but not me. I liked a bit of hair, and seeing it through Leo's shirt made my tummy flutter. He looked incredible. And who could have known that under that forest of facial hair was such a fox? In short, I was very, very impressed.

I realised that I must have been gaping in shock at Leo for longer than was the social norm, as he politely cleared his throat and spoke again. “Are you ready?”

“Wow, Leo, you look so different.”

He smiled at me, his eyes twinkling. “Yeah, I can scrub up quite well when I need to, and I wanted to make a bit of an effort.” He nodded down the garden path to where a smart red two-seater sportscar was parked up on the street. “Your chariot awaits, my lady.”

I stared at the vehicle in amazement. I knew nothing about cars, but it just looked so elegant. The sun was bouncing of its glossy polished exterior. It was reminiscent of a car out of the movies: Cary Grant could have driven around the South of France in this with Grace Kelly in the passenger seat. In fact, Leo looked just as handsome as any matinee idol, and whilst I doubted my similarity to the Princess of Monaco, I had the inkling that today Leo was going to treat me like royalty.

I beamed at Leo. “It’s really beautiful. Is it yours?”

Leo brushed the question aside. “Well, it’s ours for this afternoon; I wanted us to travel in style.”

Now I desperately hoped Daniel and Jacob would return: maybe Jacob had forgotten something vital and had to come back to the house to retrieve it. It would have been priceless to watch Daniel react to Leo now. “Scruffy oik” he had called him; well, that couldn’t be further from the truth now. He had also criticised Leo for not having a car, so for Daniel to see this little two-seater beauty would have really been the icing on the cake. He would have had to eat his words, along with everything else he had been wolfing down of late.

I grabbed my clutch bag, locked the front door and walked down the garden path side by side with Leo, feeling like an awkward teenager, unsure of myself and what to say.

He held the passenger door open for me to slip in. The seats smelt of lemon and leather and I sank down with pleasure. Leo jumped in beside me, revved up the engine and we were on our way.

I stared at Leo's profile from the side: he looked so different. Yes, I had always thought he had a lovely face and kind eyes, but so much had been obscured by his grizzly beard and unkempt hair. Now that he looked so well-groomed, I noticed his long eyelashes, his chiselled cheekbones and his full, soft lips.

"Steady on, Charlotte," I told myself sternly. "Don't get carried away here. You're just friends, remember that; friends going out for lunch. Don't read any more into it than that."

"So, Charlotte, I'm really looking forward to seeing what this brasserie is like. It's had rave reviews and the Coquilles Saint Jacques are apparently to die for."

Leo pulled up at a zebra crossing to allow a pedestrian to pass. An attractive, slim twenty-something woman with long brunette hair and a cropped tank top, showing an enviably flat stomach, cast a glance of admiration at Leo as she crossed the street.

I felt my stomach lurch a little. She clearly fancied him, but what had she made of me sitting in the passenger seat? Did she wonder if I was his maiden aunt? A friend of the family that needed a lift to Tesco or somewhere before he went to meet his real, fabulous friends?

"I love Coquilles Saint Jacques," I mumbled, casting my mind back to my year 11 French school trip from many years before. If I remembered correctly, we'd had that dish one evening and it was scallops with creamy sauce, mashed potato and some sort of cheese on top. I couldn't really remember if I'd particularly enjoyed it, but to be fair, anything with potatoes and cheese was usually a pretty safe bet for me. Any cheesy dish was always better in my book. I would happily add grated cheddar to a Sunday dinner, given half a chance.

Leo smiled at me, and his eyes twinkled. Did he realise that I was nervous in his company? He seemed relaxed enough himself, and slowly I felt my own anxiety slowly melt away.

We talked for the whole car journey. I opened up about everything in my life: the situation with Daniel, work, my fears for the future. Maybe I said too much, but he was just so easy to talk to.

In turn Leo told me amusing anecdotes from his travels, funny family memories about Ivy and just general chat. He didn't go into much depth about his plans for the future or any great detail about his life in Canada. I didn't pry; it was nice just listening to him. He had such a great sense of humour, and he was charming company.

Some of his tales had me in hysterics, especially one from his childhood about catching the family dog running around the house with Ivy's false teeth. The family had been in uproar, especially when Tom had declared that Fido looked like Janet Street Porter with a better haircut.

It felt as if time had whizzed by when Leo pulled into the car park at the rear of the restaurant. It looked a smart building, with a freshly painted exterior, and must be doing a roaring trade as only a couple of parking spaces remained unoccupied.

We entered the chic interior of the restaurant through heavy mahogany doors. A friendly, efficient maître-d escorted us to our seats in front of a decorative pillar that partitioned us from the diners behind. He passed us a couple of thick, leather-bound menus. This place was classy; certainly not the greasy spoon that Daniel had envisaged.

Leo ordered some sparkling mineral water for the table.

"Would you like some wine, Charlotte?" He passed the wine menu over to me to have a look. "I won't of course, but you definitely should."

I thought a nice glass of something chilled might be just the thing to steady any remaining nerves, so I ordered myself a large Sauvignon Blanc and busied myself studying the food menu. The prices had me reeling; it certainly wasn't Wether-spoon's prices, that was for sure. Leo could clearly feel my unease and smiled at me reassuringly.

"This is on me, Charlotte. I invited you, so I'm the one picking up the tab."

I felt I should argue, but hearing the firmness in his voice, I knew his mind was clearly made up. Could he afford it? What if he didn't have enough money? And how could he afford somewhere as salubrious as this when he wasn't working? I didn't want him to spend what little he did have on me. Maybe I should just let him pay and then I could slip some money to Ivy tomorrow and she could give it back to him. It was so sweet of him to treat me, but this restaurant was incredibly extravagant, and I would feel bad, as if I was exploiting him.

I turned my attention back to the menu. It was in French, but thankfully the English descriptions were printed just underneath in small lettering. My rusty GCSE French wouldn't stand up too well in this sort of establishment; the few words of French I remembered would only deliver a ham sandwich and a strawberry ice cream, and that wouldn't pass muster here.

The young waiter returned to our table and smiled politely at us. "Monsieur, Madame, are you ready to order? Or do you perhaps need a little more time?" He stood poised with pad and pen in hand.

Leo proceeded to place his order in fluent French, the waiter a little taken aback by this turn of events, but not as completely gobsmacked as I was. I was seriously impressed. I couldn't help but think back to Daniel's efforts at conversation with Disneyland Paris staff many years before. His phrasebook had been open, trying with much gesticulation to establish how far it was to the Dumbo the flying elephant ride, as Jacob had little legs so couldn't walk much. The exasperated Frenchman had muttered something about there already being one dumbo in the vicinity, whilst looking pointedly at my husband. Leo, however, spoke French fluently with such a perfect accent that he could pass as a native Parisian.

The waiter now turned his attention to me, his eyebrows raised slightly in anticipation. I felt my order was rather an anti-climax after Leo's, mine being delivered in English with a flat Leeds accent. I plumped for the scallop dish too and then the duck confit with dauphinois potatoes. Part of me, a very small part, felt guilty: I should probably opt for something lighter and less indulgent, like the salad niçoise. I should make Leo think I was one of those women who was happy to munch on a lettuce leaf and chase a lone olive around their plate for their lunch. But let's face it, that wasn't going to fool anyone. Plus, how often did I get to come out to a lovely restaurant like this? The answer was never, and therefore I was going to order exactly what I fancied. In fact I fancied every dish on the menu, each one sounding more mouth-watering than the one before.

The waiter scrawled hastily on his pad, deftly nodded his head and then left. Once again it was back to just Leo and me. I shouldn't have worried, though; the conversation flowed along nicely. He really was incredibly easy to be with. There were no awkward silences at all. I was feeling relaxed, helped in no small part by the deliciously chilled white wine I was enjoying. I simply was having the most fabulous time.

A loud honking laugh erupted from the table behind us, nearly causing a passing waitress to drop her frogs' legs. The noise cut through the serene ambiance of the dining room like a chainsaw.

Leo smirked. "If something is that funny, they really should share the joke with the rest of us."

I smiled back at him, but something was troubling me. That braying laugh seemed too familiar, but I couldn't quite place it. My curiosity got the better of me, so I excused myself by taking a trip to the Ladies.

"Leo, would you excuse me a minute? I'm just going to powder my nose."

"Of course." He stood up for a few seconds whilst I left the table and then returned to his chair. He really did have lovely manners.

I walked towards the restrooms. I had just passed the dividing pillar behind our table when I realised why that laugh had seemed all too familiar. There seated at an intimate table for two was Imogen Dyer, hand in hand with her lunch companion across the table. And the lunch companion was clearly not her husband.

Chapter 24

I felt a jolt of shock at seeing my friend. You know what it's like, you're used to seeing certain people in certain environments, so it throws you to see them out of context. Especially when they're seated at the table behind you in a restaurant you have never visited before, far from where you both live. And even more so when they seem to be on an intimate date with someone who is not their spouse.

How could I get past the table without them noticing? They were both clearly into each other and staring intently into each other's eyes, so there was a good chance I could slip by unnoticed.

The devil on my shoulder wondered what would happen if I just plonked myself down at their table, grabbed a piece of bread from the basket and settled down to enjoy the show. I could really make her squirm. But of course I'm just too nice for that; that would be much more Imogen's style.

I crept surreptitiously past their table, and had almost made it out of their sightline when I bumped my hip against another table. Thankfully there were no diners seated there, but the noise of the wine glasses shaking alerted Imogen and her companion to my presence.

Her face paled in shock as the realisation dawned on her.

"Ch... Charlotte... I... I..."

Never had I seen her so flustered. The seconds ticked by as the three of us stared at each other without a single word being uttered. Finally, Imogen appeared to regain her composure. "How lovely to see you." But her face announced it was anything but lovely. She dropped the hand of her companion as if it had suddenly scalded her.

"Hello, Imogen, lovely to see you too. I've never been to this restaurant before, but I must say I love it. I'm having the most fabulous time here with my friend..." I tailed off, realising that I was gabbling for England, as I always do when confronted with an awkward situation.

Imogen nodded her head valiantly, her smile forced. "Yes, I'm enjoying lunch with my friend too." She gestured to her companion who nodded her head at me and smiled weakly.

"You really should try the chocolate mousse, it's absolutely divine."

I stared at the half-eaten dessert in the middle of table with the two spoons sticking out of it that they had clearly been enjoying. How romantic.

Imogen dropped her head into her hands and let out a slow groan of resignation. "Oh, what's the point any more? You're not an idiot, Charlotte, so why am I treating you like one? Please let me introduce you to Natasha... my girlfriend."

I smiled at the pretty dark-haired woman sitting opposite Imogen, and she held her hand out for me to shake, which I duly did.

Well, this certainly was a turn up for the books. Perfect Imogen Dyer with her perfect husband, perfect child and perfect life was having an affair. And with a woman to boot. I would never have seen this plot twist coming in a million years.

I should have felt triumphant, but I didn't. All the years of Imogen's subtle and not so subtle digs at me suddenly seemed to make perfect sense. Her passive aggressiveness towards me that sometimes bordered on the plain aggressive. Her constant need to belittle me, was that because of this? Had she pulled me down to lift herself up? What do they say - hurt people always hurt people? Like me, had she been trapped and unhappy but not willing to admit it, least of all to herself?

Seeing her here today, she looked like the Imogen I had always known, but a much improved version. She wasn't wearing her usual heavy shield of make-up and high-end fancy clothes; instead she had a little lipstick and a sweep of eyeliner and was clad in a plain unstructured T-shirt and smart fitted jeans. Her blonde hair was pulled back into a simple ponytail. She appeared finally relaxed and at ease with herself. But it was more than that, it was her whole aura. The haughty air she always possessed was gone. She no longer had that pained look on her face, as if she had inadvertently sashayed through a pile of dog turd in her designer heels. She looked as if a cloud had been lifted from her. She looked lighter, younger. Well, she just looked happy.

"I suppose you're really shocked?" Imogen couldn't quite meet my eyes as she spoke.

In truth I was shocked. But then again what business was it of mine what she did in her private life? I was beginning to realise that so much in life was never as it seemed.

"It's really none of my business, Imogen. You don't have to explain anything to me."

"But I do, Charlotte, I really do." Her eyes filled with tears. "Please don't think badly of me, this isn't just some tawdry affair. I love Natasha... we're in love." She looked across the table shyly at her companion, who reached over and reassuringly squeezed her hand. A loving gesture of solidarity.

"I've just been living a charade for years," she continued. "How could I admit to everyone that I loved a woman? That I was a lesbian? I live in Alwoodley, for goodness' sake."

I nodded at her as if I understood, but I didn't. What did the area you live in have to do with your sexual proclivity? The fact that she was a school governor and ran various charitable committees wasn't dependent on her being a signed-up card-carrying heterosexual, surely? It wasn't the 1950's any more. But I knew what the problem here really was: Imogen was scared, scared of being true to herself, of how that truth would impact on her life. I understood that fear. I had been scared too for most of my life.

"Things with Alistair aren't good, haven't been for a long time, we have an... arrangement." Imogen picked up her wine glass and drained the contents. "He does his thing and I do mine, but he won't even talk of divorce. He says he would make my life a living nightmare if I went down that path. So, I keep everything normal and that in turns keeps everyone happy... well, everyone apart from me."

Normal? It sounded anything but normal to me.

Imogen raised her eyes from the table and met mine. "You do understand, Charlotte, don't you?"

I did understand, but I wanted Imogen to realise that this was no way for her to live.

"You say you're keeping everyone happy, but what about you? You're not happy. And your family only think they're happy because they're living in ignorant bliss. Don't you think it would be better to come clean, better for you all in the long run?"

Natasha was nodding earnestly at this. From the expression on her face, it was clear she was besotted with Imogen. This clearly wasn't a new thing, this relationship had history.

Imogen's eyes sank back to the tablecloth, and she spoke in an imploring tone. "Please, Charlotte, promise me you won't say anything."

Of course I would never have said anything. I wasn't in the habit of homewrecking, but I really hoped Imogen would do the right thing in time.

"I know it's difficult for you to understand, with you and Daniel being so happy."

It took all my restraint not to erupt into laughter at this; but I just self-consciously shifted my weight from one foot to the other, very aware that I was loitering by their table like an unpaid member of staff. "Maybe we were never as happy as you thought. I was living a bit of a lie myself; in fact, to tell you the truth, Daniel and I have separated."

A look of shock returned to Imogen's face. "I'm so sorry, Charlotte. I didn't realise; I would never have seen that coming."

Part of me wanted to invite her to take a little walk behind the pillar so that I could introduce her in person to my rather gorgeous lunch companion; show Leo off as if he was a prized possession, like one of her designer handbags. But I decided against it. It would be a bit naff, and anyway I wanted to keep Leo to myself for as long as I could. Plus there had already been enough soap-opera-style revelations for one lunch time. Any more would completely wreck our digestion.

"Could we meet sometime for lunch or a coffee?" Imogen asked hopefully. "I know we always say we will, and it never happens. I realise that's because I've been a bit of a cow to you over the years, but it was only because I was jealous of you, and it was my way of making myself feel better. Given half a chance we could be really good friends, I'm sure of it."

Well, this was certainly a turn-up for the books. Imogen Dyer had been jealous of me. It beggared belief. I had never thought for a second that someone like her could have possibly coveted anything about my life. The gorgeous, glamorous Imogen Dyer had been envious of frumpy old Lottie Potts? Who would have thought that? I reckoned the odds on that would be less than all six numbers dropping on the Lottery. Life really was surprising at times.

Maybe she was right, and we could have been good friends all these years, and all that time had been wasted. Both of us had disliked the other when we really had more in common than we could have imagined. I thought she had the perfect husband and perfect life; she believed the same of me. How wrong we both were. Mind you, she still had the perfect arse and designer wardrobe, so on balance things were still very much in her favour. That said, I wouldn't swap my life for hers in a million years - no thank you. Any resentment I had felt towards her had well and truly gone. I smiled at her warmly and assured her that we would meet up very soon. And this time I wasn't lying.

In the Ladies' room I washed my hands with the fancy complimentary toiletries, and my mind was whirling. It just went to show that you could never take anything at face value. I would have thought it a safe bet that Imogen's life was just as perfect as it had always appeared, but how wrong had I been. Keeping up the pretence of a loving happy marriage to a man you had been with for decades whilst you desperately wanted to be with the person you really loved must have been soul-destroying. Had Imogen always known she was a lesbian, or had it taken meeting Natasha to admit the truth to herself? One thing was for sure: I had never seen a person look so calm and at peace as Imogen today sitting with her lover. Surely the trappings of her married life couldn't be worth living a lie? Wouldn't it be better to be free to live the life you really wanted? I knew that was what I wanted to do for myself.

I made my way back to our table where Leo was sitting patiently waiting for me. "Oh, there you are, Charlotte. I was worried you'd done a runner for a moment."

I laughed and sat down, placing my napkin back on my lap. "And miss out on all this amazing grub? You must be joking."

The waiter was just setting down our starters and they looked phenomenal. I heard my belly give a little rumble of anticipation. "I just bumped into a friend at another table, so I stopped to say hello."

Leo seemed happy enough with the explanation, and without another word we tucked into our platefuls. They were even more delectable than they looked, and so was the rest of the meal. Each course was a delight to the tastebuds. I was being well and truly spoilt.

Once we had finished our main courses and the plates had been cleared away, the efficient waiter was back. "Could I interest either of you in one of our fine home-made desserts, or a coffee?"

I knew I shouldn't. I had already eaten so much that any more would simply be greed, but then again who could turn down home-made *tarte tatin*? Anyway, I was always saying I needed to eat more fruit, and what could be healthier and more virtuous than apple tart? Well, unless you were in the Garden of Eden of course.

The drive home was perfect. Zipping along the roads in the smart convertible with the roof down and a handsome man by my side felt thrilling. Life was good. And it wasn't just the wine and food that made me so content and mellow; it was Leo's company. He had such a knack of putting me at ease. Everything I said seemed to matter; he really heard me and valued my opinions. Whatever the subject, he was interested to hear my point of view. It made me feel valued. I'd often felt with Daniel that he merely tolerated me, felt my intelligence not quite on a par with his own. Sometimes when I spoke he would have this strained half smile on his face, as if to say, "Here she goes again." That look of Daniel's would always stop me dead mid-flow; it was not as violent as a physical slap, but in some ways just as hurtful. I would slink away without finishing the point I had really wanted to make. No one ever wants to feel unappreciated and unheard.

In no time at all Leo was pulling up at the kerb outside our houses. I felt a wave of disappointment wash over me; it had been such a lovely day that I genuinely didn't want it to come to an end.

"Well, thank you for such a lovely lunch. The food was amazing and the company even better." I looked up shyly at Leo, suddenly feeling a little unsure of myself.

"The pleasure was all mine." He smiled back at me. "I had a lovely time too."

With that, Leo was out of the car and bounding around to open my door. I scrambled out of the low seat as elegantly as I could, and we walked silently up to my front door where we both stood rather awkwardly for several seconds. I felt like a tongue-tied teenager and desperately fumbled in my clutch bag to retrieve my house keys.

What had the time we had just enjoyed together meant? Quite clearly we relished being in each other's company and had both had a great time. The chat had flowed, but had it been flirtatious at all? I wasn't sure. I was too out of practice in the laws of attraction. The thought of a male finding me fanciable was such an alien concept to me after all the years with Daniel. At times I had felt there might be a little spark of something, but then again I could have been completely off the mark. All I knew was that we were friends. Which was great: you could never have too many friends. But if all I wanted was to be friends, then why did I have this little gnawing feeling of disappointment in the pit of my stomach?

Suddenly everything became clear as I felt Leo wrap his strong muscular arms around me and draw me close. I felt my heartbeat accelerate in my chest as his face came ever closer to mine. He smelt intoxicatingly of mint and woody aftershave. It was as if time stood still for a few moments with his eyes looking deep into my own. Then his lips were on mine, powerful yet gentle. He was kissing me deeply. And what a kiss it was. Strong and tender all at the same time, and I experienced feelings that for so long had been repressed. It was as if I were Snow White being woken from a dream with love's first kiss. And I was kissing him back fervently, feeling desire burning through me like wildfire. His hands were now in my hair, and mine were running up and down his back.

How could I have forgotten that it could be like this? Suddenly I was the heroine in my own MGM love story, being kissed passionately by my leading man against a backdrop of a technicolour sunset as sweet music played off in the distance. But the music wasn't actually that sweet; in fact I may have been mistaken but it sounded very much like The Red Hot Chilli

Peppers.

"What the bloody hell do you think you're doing?" An angry male voice boomed out, rudely pulling us out of out of our glorious shimmering moment.

Leo and I jumped apart like a pair of scalded cats just in time to see a furious Daniel striding up the path at speed towards us. The red face was back again in all its glory.

Jacob was standing by Daniel's car, which was now parked just behind Leo's, looking rather less elegant and much more conventional than his. My son was watching the scene with a look of curious amusement on his face. That explained the music that had been playing. Jacob was a big fan of The Red Hot Chilli Peppers.

My shock was quickly replaced by anger. What right did Daniel have to shout at us like that? We weren't doing anything wrong. OK, we might be smooching outside our semi-detached for all the neighbours to see at tea-time on a Saturday, but there was nothing illegal in that. Daniel and I were separated. If I wanted to kiss half the eligible men in West Yorkshire, I bloody well could. Hell, I could set up a revolving door on the porch and invite the rugby club up to my bedroom for a quick tackle if I so wished. He had moved out and moved on with at least one woman that I knew about. He had no right to start taking the moral high ground. It was a bloody cheek.

Daniel was only a few feet away from us. He looked incandescent, little drops of spittle flying out of his mouth as he turned towards Leo, poking a demanding finger in his face. "And just who the fuck are you?"

"It's Leo, Dad, you've already met him." Jacob strolled nonchalantly up to the three of us. "Can I have the key, Mum? I've left mine in my bedroom."

I nodded silently and passed him the door key that was still pressed in my right hand, now somewhat sweaty.

He took it with a brief nod. "Cheers, Mum." He appraised Leo for a few moments. "All right? Looking stylish, mate, but I liked the grunge look too; less stuffy and middle-aged."

"Thanks, Jacob... I think." Leo looked a little unsure of himself. His eyes were troubled as he glanced back and forth between me and Daniel. Clearly, he didn't want any trouble.

Jacob quickly unlocked the front door and dumped his rucksack in the hall. "Going to play some tunes in my room. The film was OK, by the way." With that he was off.

Daniel was still eyeballing Leo. He had an expression on his face as if he was trying to figure out an exceedingly difficult maths equation in his head and something just didn't add up right.

"You're Leo?" he finally demanded, his tone incredulous. "Leo? As in next-door-neighbour Ivy's nephew, Leo?"

"For goodness' sake, Daniel, yes, he's Leo, the same Leo I was having lunch with. Who did you think he was? Just some random guy I'd picked up on the street?"

"I... I didn't know... It's just..." Daniel's voice trailed off to nothing. I saw his eyes travel to the vehicle parked in front of his own. "And is that *your* car?"

Leo nodded his head.

Daniel's confused look was slowly turning into something far more unpleasant; he looked as if he had been sucking on a crate full of lemons.

Evidently I was not the only one to find Leo's transformation staggering. Daniel was looking him up and down so much that I was worried he was going to get a crick in his neck. He seemed barely able to comprehend what his eyes were seeing.

I felt obliged to repeat both Leo's and Daniel's words from earlier in the day.

"Yes, Daniel, I think you'll find that Leo scrubs up quite well... In fact far too well to scrub skid marks off toilets."

Chapter 25

"Should we all get Pina Coladas, or be like the *Sex in the City* girls and stick to cosmos?" Lila was impatiently tapping her long scarlet fingernails on the glass tabletop. "Come on, ladies, chop chop, we only have 40 minutes of quaffing time left."

"*Sex in the City*? Haven't seen that in years," Jayne admitted with a little boozy hiccup. "I bet they're all nearing pension age now. Honestly, Lila, if we keep on drinking so fast, we'll be more Wrecks in the City than sophisticated ladies who lunch."

Jasmine nodded in agreement. "Yeah, more like ladies who lose their lunch."

I was out on the town at Olive Affair. Again with my girlfriends, but this time for a Saturday mid-afternoon bottomless brunch: little dishes of delicious tapas to share, and as many cocktails as we could happily sink in 90 minutes max. Lila was true to form, taking the whole brunch thing very seriously, as if it were a personal challenge to her; she was therefore treating the ticking clock as enemy number one. We might as well have been top athletes taking part in a competitive sport, the way Lila was haranguing us like our highly motivated coach. She was not impressed with our leisurely sipping and savouring of our drinks. Not on her watch: we were clearly letting the side down and needed to get our drinking heads on.

Jayne tucked a wayward strand of auburn hair behind her ear, considering all the options. "Or we could plump for a margarita. I'm not too good with Pina Coladas: the cream upsets me and gives me a runny tummy."

Lila snorted, a rather unattractive sound for someone dressed head to stilettoed toe in top-end couture. She began humming the tune to *Escape* by Robert Holmes, only changing the lyrics to better suit the current mood: "*If you like Pina Coladas and getting caught with the shits*," she sang in a lilting voice, "*better find the ladies' toilet before the diarrhoea hits.*"

Jayne laughed good-naturedly and shook her head at her friend. "You really are the limit, Lila; you know that?"

Lila smiled at us all, completely unfazed, and tapped her watch again. "Time is a-ticking, girls. Come on, I could die of thirst waiting for you lot to pick your next tipple."

We collectively decided to stick with the Cosmopolitans, and gave the harassed waitress our order. Lila was finally content. It was daft, really: out of all of us, she was the one who could best afford to pay full price for her drinks; but like everything in her life, Lila liked to feel she was on top, and if that meant imbibing cocktails like her very existence depended on it, so be it.

It had been an entire week since I had seen Leo. We had shared a few sporadic text messages, both saying how much we had enjoyed ourselves the previous Saturday. The kiss had not been mentioned at all. It was just hanging out there in the ether. Yep, hanging like one of those child's piñatas you have at parties. But I really didn't want to whack this particular donkey with a big stick in case shit fell out of it rather than candy. Bad metaphor, I know, but in other words I wasn't going to be the one to bring the kiss up in case I heard something I really didn't want to. I didn't think my fragile ego could take it.

Leo had said, "We should do it again soon." I just wished I knew what "it" was and when "soon" would be. Was he referring to our delicious three-course meal, or our even more delicious kiss? Was it soufflé or seduction he had on his mind? I just wished he would set a date. I didn't want to be pushy, but the man was on my mind. On my mind a lot.

As for Daniel, I hadn't heard a peep out of him since he had so rudely halted the smooch. At least he wasn't making trouble, so that was a plus. I'd been guilty of doing a little low-level stalking on his Facebook, and it seemed to be all on again with Roxy. However, the many photos that he shared with the young woman seemed to have a rather different vibe to the previous ones I had seen. They still appeared to be living the high life: out and about in chic pubs and night clubs, but the happy smile on his face just didn't quite seem to reach his eyes any more. In fact, he had more of the expression of a kidnap victim who was trying to signal for help via the camera lens.

I looked around the restaurant. It was as busy as could be expected on a Saturday, and we were by no means the only group of ladies enjoying the challenge of a bottomless brunch. It did, however, feel a little surreal to be back at the venue that had kicked off that infamous girls' night out. We had all enjoyed such a lovely meal here before moving on to Eduardo's for what was now commonly known as the "shitstorm end of the evening". That night seemed like a million months ago, but in fact was barely two.

Lila gave me a playful nudge. "What we all really want to know is how Charlotte's date with the mysterious Leo went?"

Jasmine and Jayne's eyes both lit up simultaneously.

"Ooh yes, spill the tea, Lottie, we want to know every sordid detail." Jasmine leaned closer towards me over the table. The arm of her dusty pink jumpsuit soaked up some of her cocktail as it sloshed out of the martini glass in her eagerness to hear the latest gossip. She looked fabulous in head-to-toe pink, the soft colour working so well against her dark skin. I couldn't help thinking that if I wore her jumpsuit, I would look disturbingly like a big lump of Spam straight out of the tin. Jasmine squeezed some of the excess liquid out of her sleeve. "We want to live vicariously through you."

So I took a deep breath and began my tale, from our first meeting in Ivy's house until our much-anticipated kiss. It was the truth, the whole truth and nothing but the truth, m'lud, and it was anything but sordid. Even so, by the time I'd finished I could feel myself blushing as if I'd been caught with my granny pants around my ankles. It was just so strange for me to be talking about a man, and moreover to be talking about one romantically. Although my cheeks were flaming, it was still nice to be able to tell them about Leo and get their opinions.

"Blimey, it's very Mills & Boon, Lottie," Jasmine commented, her eyes shining; "the romantic rendezvous, the passionate embrace, the will they/won't they suspense of it all." Jasmine, very much like me, was an old romantic at heart.

I sighed deeply. "It's the will they/won't they that's worrying me. I mean, yes, we kissed, but does he want anything more than that? And even if he does, do I? He's younger than me after all, and he's planning to go back to Canada. So is it even worth pursuing anyway?"

Lila rolled her eyes. She seemed to be forever rolling her eyes or tutting at us. "What's the worst that can happen? You have a fling with a younger man and then he leaves the country. I wish most of the men I shagged would bugger off to the other side of the world afterwards." She caught my eye and gave me a cheeky wink. "Just don't overthink it, it takes all the fun out of it. So, what if you end up shagging him? At least you'll get the cobwebs blown out of your knickers. I'd say that's definitely a win in anyone's books."

A new waitress arrived at our tables carrying a tray of yet another round of colourful cocktails. She must have been at least eighteen years old, but looked about twelve. She couldn't quite mask the grimace of horror that crossed her face upon stumbling across Lila discussing sex. Clearly in her mind nothing was worse than hearing a group of older women talking about such matters. She probably thought that knitting and crossword puzzles with a mug of cocoa were about as risqué as old crones like us should get. In turn Lila winked at her as she deposited a glass in front of each of us before scuttling off. We duly fell upon the cocktails like a pack of dehydrated wolves.

Jayne polished off half of hers in one go with a satisfied sigh. "Well, putting aside Lila's rather crass way with words, she does have a point. Maybe it would be good for you to just have a fling; see what you've been missing all this time."

I nodded slowly. I knew she had a point. The kiss had awoken something in me that had been dormant for way too long. Maybe this old lady wasn't ready to be put out to pasture just yet.

"Let's see a picture of the man in question," Jayne insisted, rubbing her hands gleefully together. "We need to assess who may be the one tasked with unflowering our Charlotte."

"It's hardly unflowering," I protested indignantly. "I'm not exactly a wilting virgin, you know."

"You might as well be, it's that long since you had a good old rattling," Lila mumbled through her straw. "You've got a bloody lot of lost time to make up."

I pulled my handbag onto my lap and rummaged through it for a few seconds until I located my handset. I scrolled through the few texts I had exchanged with Leo. We had sent each other a couple of pictures, so I had a few images of him. I selected the one I felt best represented him: the one where he looked the dishiest.

Lila perked up. "He's sent you pics? Now this is sounding promising."

"No, Lila, not the sort of pics you're thinking of." I held my phone out of her grasp as she made a swift grab for it. "He sent me one of himself before he went to meet some friends, asking if I thought his shirt was smart enough, that's all. He's fully clothed."

Her face fell about a hundred feet, her disappointment evident.

I found the image that I was searching for and placed my phone screen side up on the table for them all to see. I couldn't help but feel proud to show them Leo. He was a catch, after all.

"Not bad... not bad." Lila nodded appreciatively; he'd clearly got her seal of approval. "I wouldn't kick him out of bed for dropping toast crumbs on the Egyptian cotton." As if Lila would ever eat toast in bed; more likely oysters and champagne.

Jasmine picked up the phone and scrutinised the image of Leo thoughtfully. "Charlotte, what did you say Leo's surname was?"

I was confused. Why would she be asking about Leo's name? "I didn't... it's Knight... Leo Knight."

Jasmine continued to study the image of Leo for a few more

moments, her beautiful brown eyes clearly troubled. Then she clicked her fingers. "I bloody knew it." She suddenly looked jubilant. "I knew I had seen him somewhere before."

I was totally confused now, and couldn't help but feel the icy shivers of dread creeping down my spine. "Oh no, please, please, don't let it be bad news," I silently prayed. I couldn't bear it if Leo was all over the dating sites like a professional lothario. Or what if it was worse than that? What could possibly be worse? Maybe he was a serial seducer of the elderly? OK, I wasn't elderly, but I was certainly a fair bit older than he was.

Jasmine had replaced my phone on the table and was now scrolling through her own device, clearly trying to locate something. A few moments passed excruciatingly slowly while we all stared at her, waiting for the inevitable bombshell. Our table was completely silent, punctuated only by the occasional slurping of liquor or crunching of ice cubes. After what seemed like an eternity but was probably less than a minute, she triumphantly placed her phone on the table next to my own. "Look at this, girls."

It was a news piece all about Leo, and it made for interesting reading.

It appeared that there was much more to Leo than I had ever imagined. He wasn't just the laid-back Leo that worked casually in a hotel in Canada and bummed his way around the world travelling like a penniless hippy – Daniel's words not mine. No, in fact Ivy's nephew Leo was none other than the millionaire Leo Knight: self-made man, philanthropist and owner of the exclusive chain of Knights Lodge hotels that were dotted all around North America.

None of this made the slightest sense to me. How could it be true? Leo was living with his elderly auntie in the smart but most definitely modest semi-detached house next door to ours. How could he possibly be the hotel magnate that this article was describing? This highly esteemed man of wealth and means. It all seemed so surreal. Suddenly I felt very sober indeed.

Jasmine picked up her phone and found other images of Leo for us to see: ones of him with various celebrities that looked vaguely familiar to me; a few of charity events where he was awarding prizes. I had to admit he looked bloody dreamy in his tux. I started to look around the restaurant to see where the infant waitress had gone. I really needed another drink asap.

Jasmine was nodding to herself. "I just knew I'd seen him before. I met him at a dinner party with Ash a couple of years ago. Leo was interested in using Ash in his new hotel venture. He was looking to open a Knights Lodge in the UK."

Jasmine's husband Ash was a chartered surveyor and very well regarded in his field, so it was no wonder that someone as successful as Leo would want to employ him.

My mind was blown. How could I not have known any of this? Leo was just so unlike this impressive businessman that was being described to me. Yes, Leo was incredibly impressive in his own right. But mainly for being a gentleman, kind to his elderly auntie and making fine mugs of strong Yorkshire tea. This entrepreneur Leo was not someone I knew.

Lila was first to echo my thoughts. "How could you not have known, Charlotte? Haven't you Googled him? That's the first thing I do before I even agree to go on a date. You need to take precautions, you know. And I don't just mean rubber johnnies. You need to check that they're not an axe murderer or something even worse."

Jayne shook her head at Lila. "Seriously, Lila, what could be worse than an axe murderer?"

Lila smirked to herself. "Plenty... I went on a date with a lovely chap, or so I thought. What I didn't know at the time, because I hadn't taken the time to have a little stalk, was that he collected china dolls and spent his spare time sewing little outfits for them. Believe me, I would cheerfully take a quick slice and dice with a rusty blade any day over having to spend another dreary afternoon with Derek embroidering lederhosen for his dolly 'Fraulein Helga'."

Jayne held her hands up. She had to surrender to Lila on this one.

I shook my head. Lila was right, though, and I was angry at myself. Scrap that, I was furious. I had been too busy checking up on my ex and his Lolita girlfriend to even think about having a quick snoop on Leo. Why had I not checked him out? I suppose part of me thought he was probably not even on social media. He seemed the type who would have just thought all that a little "uncool" and would rather live in the moment than endlessly document it.

Lila rolled her eyes yet again, showing the whole world she clearly thought I was as naive as a new-born. "First rule of dating is to Google the guy; everyone knows that. It's the best way to get the heads up on any red flags there may be. You don't want the first time you get an inkling that a guy's a bit dodgy to be when your decapitated head turns up in his fridge next to a jar of out-of-date mayonnaise, do you?"

There really wasn't any way to answer that. I looked at each of my girlfriends in turn; they were all regarding me with an expression that clearly told me they were of the same opinion as Lila.

"I just didn't think. I mean it's not even as if I'm dating him, is it?"

"Well, that's true," Lila admitted grudgingly, "but Lottie, you really do need to wise up a bit. The dating game is brutal, and there are a lot of nutters out there." She paused for effect. "And they're not the ones you necessarily think. There was another guy I went out with: a lovely respectable lawyer who liked nothing better on a weekend then to don a saddle and have me ride him around his town house shouting 'yah' at him while I whipped his bare arse with a wooden spoon."

Well, that had taken the spotlight off me for a moment, and Jasmine and Jayne were now staring slack-mouthed and wide-eyed at Lila. She never failed to entertain.

I could see that she had a point though. Even though I loved my classic old films, I had to realise that I wasn't living in those bygone days. There was no David Lean directing my life; I really needed to get with the times and possibly buy a new wooden spoon. Mine was ancient, and the handle would surely break if I tried tapping it against an eager derriere.

I couldn't help but think about Leo for a moment. He really did have a lovely bum.

A little seed of doubt was now taking root in my mind. "Jasmine... about Leo... he's not married, is he?" The very thought of me having kissed a married man sickened me to my already gurgling stomach. I couldn't be the other woman. Not after Daniel. I just couldn't.

Jasmine was shaking her head at me, her words reassuring. "No... no he's not married, never has been, I believe, and he doesn't have any kids either. He's most definitely a bachelor, and a pretty eligible one at that."

Chapter 26

"Charlotte, how lovely to see you!" Ivy's face broke into a wide smile, finding me on her doorstep early the following morning. "Come in, come in and I'll stick the kettle on." I followed the slightly stooped figure as she made her way back into the house, and once we were both comfortably settled on opposite armchairs, cradling mugs of piping hot tea, I could hold my tongue no longer.

"Ivy, how on earth could you not tell me about Leo?"

The old lady looked somewhat taken aback. "What do you mean? Tell you what about Leo?"

I eyed Ivy with what I hoped was my most withering glare. "Oh, I don't know, perhaps the fact that he's not at all who I thought he was."

Ivy looked thoughtful as she selected a piece of shortbread, the largest one, from the open packet on the table. "But my dear, he is exactly who you thought he was, he's Leo... just Leo."

I shook my head vehemently. Perhaps my dear friend was getting a bit doolally in her old age. "But the money, his business, all of that, it's just..."

Ivy lifted her hand to silence me. "Leo is and will always be just Leo to me: the sweetest, most lovely nephew I could ever have wished for." She smiled to herself, her eyes misting a little. "I was thrilled when you and Leo hit it off so well after all these years; you're both such special people to me." She reached up the arm of her chunky woollen cardigan for her hanky and dabbed at the corners of her eyes before reaching over to retrieve the open packet of biscuits from the table. "Do have a piece of shortbread though, my dear, and I'll tell you everything you want to know."

And true to her word, that's exactly what she did: told me everything I needed to know, chapter and verse. After listening to Ivy speak for nearly an hour, I felt that my mind had been put well and truly at ease.

Ivy had never felt the need to tell me about Leo because his success barely registered with her. Yes, she knew he was a prosperous businessman, but to her mind he was still her beloved nephew who couldn't get enough of her home-made shepherd's pie, wore tatty old jeans when he mowed the lawn, and always had time, no matter how busy he was, for his Auntie Ivy. Leo was just her Leo, the Leo she had always known and loved, no more and no less.

When Leo and his mother had moved to Canada, he had worked hard, often in multiple jobs. After some time, he and a friend had taken the risky punt of opening a small bed and breakfast-style guest house. It had proved to be a very canny move on their part. On the back of their hard work and some sound investments, the business had flourished. They had gone on to open another and another, and well, the rest is history.

Leo had always managed to remain grounded. Wealth and all the trappings had not changed him in the slightest. In fact, the greatest upside for not having to watch the pennies any more was the fact that he was now able to help out many charities. It seemed he was quite the philanthropist whilst never losing his humility and respect for his humble beginnings.

It just seemed the most natural thing to him that when he was in the UK he should stay with his aunt, and Ivy was of course delighted to have him. She was his family and he loved her, so there was no other place he would rather be.

I had liked Leo very much, but hearing everything that Ivy had to say was endearing me even more to him.

"Talk of the devil." Ivy's face broke into a wide smile. "How long have you been standing there?"

I twisted around quickly, nearly giving myself whiplash to see Leo's tall frame standing in the doorway. He was dressed more casually than when I'd last seen him, and he had an amused expression on his face.

"Not long... any tea left in the pot?"

My face was hot. Why did I always have to blush? Too much hot tea, no doubt; I was damn near awash with the stuff. I felt tongue-tied. This was the first time I had seen Leo since our kiss, and so much had transpired since then. I was at a loss what to do: too worried that if I spoke, I couldn't trust the words that would spill out of my mouth.

"Better make a fresh brew, love," Ivy advised, breaking the silence, "and bring another packet of the shortbread too. I really shouldn't buy them, they're so blooming moreish that I make a pig of myself." She struggled out of her chair and Leo reached over to steady her. Smiling, she gave his arm an affectionate pat. "Just make tea for you and Charlotte. I'm going to go upstairs to finish my Agatha Christie and have a little lie down."

I smiled affectionately at my friend. It was obvious that she was making herself scarce so that Leo and I could talk in peace.

Five minutes later, Leo and I were sitting awkwardly across from each other. I tentatively blew on my cup. The last thing I needed was yet another cup of tea, but at least it gave me something to focus on.

"Are you OK, Charlotte?" Leo's eyes were rather troubled. "You're very quiet. I hope Daniel didn't give you too hard a time about us going out?"

I quickly shook my head. "No, it's not that. Actually, Daniel is being very quiet at the moment; I think seeing us together was a bit of a shock to him, hurt his male pride or something." I took a deep breath before continuing.

"That's not what's bothering me, it's you."

Leo looked confused. "Me?"

"Yes, you. When were you going to tell me about your life? The hotels and your business, for a start? I feel a bit of an idiot knowing so little about you."

Leo smiled indulgently and settled further back into his chair, looking completely relaxed. He knitted his hands together behind his head. "None of that stuff's important, you know. I'm just me, my job is what I do, it's not who I am."

He was pretty much echoing what Ivy had told me. He was the same guy; he hadn't changed in his eyes, and none of it was a big deal. To me, though, it all seemed a very big deal indeed.

Leo reached across and took my hand in his. "Yes, I've got money, which is very nice; and yes, I can jet around the world if I want to on a whim; but I'm still the same guy I always was, the kid you were so kind to. It hasn't changed the person I am."

"But what does this mean for us?" I heard the tremble in my voice and hated myself for it.

"It means whatever you want it to mean, Charlotte. I like you,

I really do, and I would like us to go out again and see where it could go... if you want to?" He sighed, concern furrowing his brow. "I suppose I didn't really want to tell you the whole truth about me, as I wanted you to like me for who I was, Ivy's nephew, not for you to get caught up in everything else."

"I understand that, but what I don't understand is that you can have your pick. Why would you waste your time with me?" I could feel a tear betray me, trickling down my cheek and plopping into my cup. "I'm nothing special."

Leo dropped my hand abruptly, and when he spoke, his tone was firm but not unkind. "I really don't want you talking like that about someone I care for, and I do care for you." He reached over and pulled me closer, taking me into his arms, all the time looking meaningfully into my eyes. "You're a beautiful woman, Charlotte, inside and out, and the fact that you're the only one who doesn't realise that makes you even more special."

It was on the tip of my tongue to chime in and say I knew at least one person who would take issue with that: Daniel, for a start, who clearly thought I was about as appealing as day-old toast, but I held my tongue. I didn't want to spoil the moment.

A second later he was kissing me, and it was just as thrilling as I remembered. My heart soared in my chest. If this was falling in love, then in that moment I was happy to hurtle off that particular cliff at a thousand miles an hour.

I pulled away from him for a second. "Does this mean that we're going on an actual date?"

He laughed, looking a little confused. "I thought we'd already been on a date. What was the lunch at the restaurant, if not a date?"

"I wasn't sure. I thought we were just friends."

He kissed me again. “I think it’s fair to say we’re now more than just friends. If I kissed any of my friends like that, they would file a restraining order against me.”

Chapter 27

So it appeared that Leo and I were dating. We were a bona fide couple, like Romeo and Juliet, Bogie and Bacall, George and Mildred. Charlotte Potts, middle-aged mum with a muffin top, had a younger boyfriend and I could scarcely believe it. If I could just lose the nagging worry that people might mistake us for mother and son, all would be fine. I had to stop thinking like that. I didn't want to sabotage this before it had even started. Leo clearly didn't have a problem with me being rather older, so why should I care? I knew I really shouldn't.

But it wasn't just that Leo was younger, but he had shedloads of money and a business empire to boot. I felt I needed to pinch myself. Surely I must be dreaming? But no, I was wide awake and appeared to be experiencing, for the first time in years, what could be considered a life worth living. But was it the life I really wanted? I couldn't help but question myself. Yes, I found Leo intensely attractive, and he was great company, but wasn't everything happening a little too quickly? I felt I had barely drawn breath since I'd discovered Daniel's deceit, and here I was already rushing headfirst into dating again.

It was intoxicating to feel that a wonderful man like Leo could want me, but what was it I truly wanted? Everything seemed to be happening too fast. And nothing had ever really happened to me in years. Until recently finding a buy-one-get-one-free deal on teabags in Sainsbury's was about all the excitement my poor old heart could take.

And what about Daniel? He was surely going to explode when he heard the news that Leo and I were a couple. Or maybe he would implode, or perhaps spontaneously combust, you know, like in those documentaries where they just disappear into a smoking hole in the Axminster carpet with only their slippers remaining and a half-finished sudoku. Well, whatever happened, he would not be happy, and it would most certainly not be pretty.

I spoke to Lila about my concerns, and true to form I got a typical Lila response. She told me to stop overthinking everything, pull my head out of my arse and go for it.

"Lottie, just enjoy yourself," she said. "Why must you always go to the far ends of a fart worrying about the worst thing that could possibly happen? Just go with the flow, it's only sex and it's supposed to be fun. After all, you're not doing a cryptic crossword, you're just having a shag."

And with that, Lila alerted me to yet another problem. I had so far only been concerned about the ramifications of dating: what people would think of seeing Leo and me "out on the town". And going out was all we had done so far: nice restaurants, the cinema, romantic walks. The idea of "staying in" was an even more terrifying thought. I hadn't even considered the prospect that at some point Leo might actually want to see me naked.

Lila had, naturally for her, assumed we had already taken it to the next level; indulged in some "adult-themed behaviour", as my mother would whisper. But the very notion of getting undressed in front of a new man, after being with the same, albeit very critical man for decades, had me in a complete tailspin.

So far Leo and I had just been in our little romantic bubble. I was happy to take things slowly, preferably at glacial speed. It was also in the back of my mind that at some point he would be returning to Canada, so what future did we really have?

We had enjoyed plenty of lovely kisses, but I knew the next inevitable step would be sex. The thought of flashing an abundance of flesh was the stuff of my worst nightmares. I would happily watch a zombie marathon with Jacob every day of the week rather than drop my drawers in front of a new man. I had only ever been with Daniel. And he had never really shook my world, barely shook the headboard in truth. It had always been more lacklustre than lust filled.

Was sex even the same any more? Would I still remember how to do it? Maybe there were a plethora of athletic new moves I wasn't even aware of. I sincerely hoped not. I wasn't exactly limber, and my right leg tended to get sciatic spasms if I jerked it the wrong way.

So now I wasn't just worried about what I would look like, but also how I would perform. Maybe Leo wouldn't notice that my boobs were more pendulous than perky, and that with my stretchmarks my tummy resembled a relief map of the Himalayas, so long as I appeared to know what I was doing in the boudoir.

Should I get a manual? Maybe *The Joy of Sex*? But it had been many decades since I had giggled over that particular handbook with schoolfriends in a dark corner of the public library. No, maybe I should be thinking more twenty-first century. There was nothing for it, I needed some inspiration. I was going to have to change the habits of a lifetime and watch some porn.

Ten minutes later and I resolutely snapped the top of my laptop firmly shut. I now felt a gazillion times worse. Did those women have to angle-grind their lady gardens to get them so smooth? And the boobs: they certainly didn't need to wait 30 minutes after eating before they swam, given those inbuilt flotation devices. And they were just so accommodating. I felt exhausted after watching them and in need of a serious lie-down, but for sleep, not for anything saucy.

I had to talk to someone. And in this instance there was only one of my friends who would do.

It took Lila a good few minutes to curb her laughter before she could get any words out. "What were you thinking, Charlotte? Of course watching porn isn't going to make you feel any better about yourself."

She was trying to calm me down as I had been rambling on to her, pretty much incoherently for the past twenty minutes.

"You can't go comparing yourself to porn stars. Hell, porn stars don't even look like themselves when the cameras stop rolling and they put their sweatpants on."

I could hear the faint sound of plinky plonk jazz in the background and imagined my friend was relaxing after a hard day at work with some music to unwind and a large glass of something highly alcoholic in her hand. I really shouldn't be bothering her with all my nonsense.

"But did you learn any new tricks?" There was a hopeful note to Lila's voice. "Anything you can pass on to the lucky gentleman?"

I sighed. "Not really. To be honest, everything seems pretty much the same. The odd flourish here and there, but nothing that was too off-putting. Mind you, I did try and stick to the categories that sounded relatively tame. Some of them were a bit mind-boggling and seriously outside my comfort zone."

"So the main problem was that you felt intimidated by the beautiful actresses and their inflated assets?"

I nodded my head vigorously, although there was no one to see. "Yes, that's definitely it. They made me feel about as alluring as a soggy suet dumpling bubbling in a pot of gravy."

"Problem solved then. Next time you have a little browse, make sure you Google BBW. That will be right up your street and much less intimidating for your viewing pleasure, you can trust me on that."

After I had ended the call, I thought about what Lila had said. BBW? No idea what it was, but I certainly wasn't going to Google it. I had most definitely had more than enough excitement for one day, thank you very much.

Chapter 28

I was due to have a date with Leo again on Saturday night, a mere three days away, and the thought of the topic of s-e-x arising, or anything else rising for that matter, was scaring me witless. That wasn't the only thing that had me rather fearful. I had this awful nagging feeling of impending doom that was gradually building momentum in the pit of my stomach. Daniel had missed this month's mortgage payment, and when I'd tried to speak to him on the matter, he had promptly brushed me off with a terse "it's getting sorted". Needless to say, that hadn't put my mind at ease at all.

I had always just assumed that Daniel would continue to honour his financial commitments. After all, he had said he would, and I never thought for a minute that he would put his own son's home at risk. But then again there was a lot Daniel had done of late that I really hadn't seen coming. I knew he had been throwing money around like confetti, living the middle-aged man's dream. But he was the one that worked in banking, for goodness' sake. He had always preached fiscal responsibility to Jacob and me. He'd even tried to get me to recycle teabags; but as Daniel was someone who did not appreciate a good cup of tea, he hadn't realised that such nonsense was close to sacrilege to me.

I looked down at my bitten fingernails, a sure sign I was stressed. So much for trying to look more well turned out and polished; my hands looked as if they'd been attacked by a horde of ravenous hamsters. I'd picked the skin away from the sides of my nails until they bled: my equivalent of worry beads.

My salary from the shop was not going to cover the mortgage, that was for sure, and anyway that particular revenue stream was drying up very soon. My finances were looking very arid indeed.

I tried to push the worries aside. As it was Wednesday, I was meeting Mum for lunch in one of the vast department stores in Leeds, the same one she had always taken me to as a child. Mum did like familiarity, and I understood that. So much was changing in life, and at such a speed, that to hold onto something that felt reassuring could only be a good thing. Thankfully lunch today was her treat. I was beginning to worry that in my current financial state, I might need to turn tricks in the red-light district to afford even a tuna baguette with a small salad on the side.

I was rather surprised at how much I was looking forward to seeing my mother. Although we were like chalk and cheese and could squabble for England, I had to admit that when it boiled down to it, we were as close as could be. We often annoyed the heck out of each other, but wasn't that always the way with mothers and daughters? Anyway, I really needed to bring her up to speed on everything. I had a feeling that Mum might think my life was getting a little too close to one of her beloved soap operas for her liking.

I received a rather cryptic text message from her that morning, and I hoped everything was OK. She had, as was her usual style, typed it all in capitals: "CHARLOTTE DEAR I

HAVE SOMETHING EXTREMELY IMPORTANT TO GIVE TO YOU AT LUNCHEON". Mum really hadn't mastered the art of the succinct text and could give *War and Peace* a run for its money. I felt sure that she wouldn't have the faintest clue what an emoji was, probably thinking it was that weird green bean I'd served up in my chicken stir-fry on one of the rare occasions I'd cooked for her.

As I showered and washed my hair, my mind once again returned to Leo. I had been playing over all the different scenarios in my head vis-à-vis me and Leo actually "getting it on", copulatively speaking. It was always my way of dealing with any situation to expect the worst, and then anything not totally horrendous was just an added bonus. But when I conjured up the worst scenario in my head, it included Leo taking a quick gander at me in my finest silky two-piece from Marks and Spencer and running for the hills with shrieks of "my eyes, my eyes".

I shuddered at the thought. Of course, the best scenario would be him struck dumb in rapt appreciation of me in all my satiny viscose glory and us enjoying the most wonderful of nights. But somehow, I just couldn't convince myself of that.

I still had the nagging doubt in my mind that this wasn't really what I wanted. I knew I should, of course I should. Leo was gorgeous, and I was very attracted to him, and he was very much into me too, but still something felt a bit off and I couldn't quite put my finger on it. But then again, as Lila had said, I needed the cobwebs blowing away and who better than someone as lovely as Leo to do the blowing?

Anyway, being the endlessly organised creature I am, I had prepared everything in case of any eventuality. If an intimate situation should occur, then Charlotte Potts had it covered.

There was the aforementioned Marks & Sparks undies, and I had purchased enough vanilla candles that should there be a West Yorkshire power cut, I would possess flattering lighting for several months. I had decided that the candles were an essential buy. My feminine form in all its naked glory might be somewhat more appealing if it were viewed in semi-darkness. Ideally, I would have preferred a full black-out, but candlelight was the next best thing.

We were planning to stay in on Saturday night and watch a film. I was cooking. No slow-cooker concoction this time, no, I was pulling out all the stops and trying my hand at a Gordon Ramsay dish. But no doubt with my culinary skills I would be swearing just as much as the chef whilst preparing it.

Jacob was spending the night at a friend's; he was seeing Daniel first for a meal, but reluctantly. My son was not at all delighted to be invited to go for a Chinese meal with his father and Roxy. The plan was to eat together so that he and Roxy could get to know each other better, after which they would drop him off at his friend Joe's. I knew that Jacob felt bad for me that he was going to share prawn crackers and crispy duck with his father's dim sum of a girlfriend, but I reassured him that I was fine with it. I even made a joke about Roxy maybe dumping his father over the fortune cookies if fortune favoured him, but Jacob was not impressed. He just couldn't understand why his father was still with her. He felt she wasn't really interested in his dad and was wasting his time, and moreover his money. But I understood. After everything Daniel had given up for his girlfriend, he had to try to make it work, at least to save face. If he didn't, what had it all been for? Whether it be squash, Trivial Pursuit or matters of the heart, Daniel simply hated to lose.

So lost in thought was I that I hardly noticed I had arrived at my destination. The store was a tall, imposing Victorian building with a slightly weathered façade. Rather like me. I pushed firmly on the revolving glass and mahogany door, on the way to meet my mum.

I wandered casually through the first department – lingerie. I was startled to see a group of elderly ladies admiring the garments on display. They were clearly impressed with the merchandise and some of the stuff was pretty racy: push-up bras fit for Madonna and thongs that made my eyes water and my buttocks clench just looking at them. Wow, these ladies were really putting me to shame. I pulled my navy trench coat firmly around myself, imagining that these old dears possessed X-ray vision and could see my mismatched greying bra and granny pants through my clothes. The only frills my underwear possessed was the fraying around the edges where the elastic was poking through. Maybe I should have worn the new set that I had bought for if things got steamy with Leo? After all, what was the point of keeping them for best? Doing that meant there was a very real possibility that nobody would ever get to see them. At least if I wore them every day, I wouldn't be so embarrassed if I got hit by a bus and taken to hospital. But then again, what would be less embarrassing to be cut out of by medics: greying saggy cotton or overtly sexy satin?

I glanced quickly around the closest lingerie display. Some of the knickers were miniscule and would barely cover one of my cheeks. A woman in her late seventies was standing to the right of me, sorting through a rack of balcony bras with a look of steely determination on her ageing face. She turned to address me: "These are amazing, my dear. They make my bosoms look like they did when I was eighteen, and believe it or not that was nearly sixty years ago." I believed her.

I reached over to the rack of bras and selected a lavender-coloured one in my size. Should I get it? From what this lady was claiming, there was enough scaffolding in these things to force the leaning tower of Pisa up straight. I felt the material: buttery soft, and the colour was lovely with pretty little rose buds embroidered around the cups. Could I pour my ample cleavage into this garment without making Leo want to pour himself an arsenic or something similar upon seeing me in it? Of course, that was if we ever actually got to that stage.

The old lady was still chatting, and I forced myself to focus on what she was saying. "They give my husband a real twinkle in his eye. He's given me his bank card and told me to get one in every colour." She let out a little sigh of regret. "Mind you, once I take it off the spell is sadly broken."

I smiled at her agreeably. It was interesting to get an insight into the love life of someone apart from Lila, and this lady clearly proved that old age didn't have to mean a diet of hot cocoa and cold celibacy. No, this old dear was clearly still getting her muffin buttered on a regular basis.

Then out of the corner of my eye I spotted my mother sitting some distance away at a small table in the open-plan restaurant. She was seated straight-backed in her chair, dressed smartly in a checked trouser suit, tentatively sipping on a tall latte. I was surprised at this. Mum was not one for wasting precious calories on milky beverages. She was one of only a few diners seated in the tired-looking eatery. Clearly most shoppers had the good sense to go to one of the more chic dining establishments in the city. This area was designed to make you believe you were eating al fresco, with a few dusty-looking fake plants dotted about and an abundance of small brick walls partitioning the diners off from the rest of the shoppers.

I quickly replaced the bra on the hanging rail, deciding I would return after lunch to buy it.

"I must go," I told my new acquaintance. "Have fun with your husband."

She winked conspiratorially at me again. "Oh, don't you worry, my dear, I fully intend to."

I hurried over to meet Mum. She was waving her teaspoon impatiently as I approached. "Oh, there you are, Charlotte, I've been waiting simply ages for you."

I glanced down at my watch: it was 1:05 pm and we were due to meet at 1 pm.

"Hello, Mum, sorry I'm late." I pulled off my coat and flopped into the chair opposite her. "Are you going to have something to eat?"

She shook her head firmly. "No dear, I'm just having a coffee for my lunch."

This was not in fact sarcasm. That was exactly what she intended to do – have a cup of coffee for lunch. Not wasted calories at all when your latte made up the entirety of one meal.

I was starving after having skipped breakfast, so made my way over to the canteen-style food court. It boasted an impressive selection of sandwiches: fillings ranging from the ubiquitous cheese and pickle right up to the rather forward-thinking and most definitely stomach-turning beetroot, boiled egg and hummus. There was a special of fish and chips, and that sounded right up my street. I ordered a large portion, bread and butter and a pot of tea for one. As I returned to our table my mother looked critically at my tray of food and opened her mouth to speak, but then clearly thought better of it and took a sip of her coffee instead.

I happily tucked into my food. You simply couldn't beat a good plate of fish and chips. Which this wasn't, but I was ravenous so it would have to do.

"I see you've got mushy peas," Mum commented, obviously unimpressed with the choice of vegetables. "You should really have got garden peas, they're much better for you, you know."

I inhaled a forkful of the sloppy mush. "Ah yes, Mum, but didn't you know that mushy peas are in fact the caviar of the North?"

She rolled her eyes at me to suggest she was less than impressed with my idea of humour and drained the remainder of her coffee. "I haven't told you about Belinda's daughter yet, have I, dear?"

I hadn't the foggiest idea who Belinda was, never mind her daughter. My blank expression clearly told Mum the same.

"Belinda Trotter, she's a very good friend of mine, I met her a while back doing my salsa dancing class for the over 60s at the church hall. I'm sure I must have mentioned her before."

I honestly didn't have a clue who she was, but then again I'd probably been told and simply expunged it from my memory. Mum had an awful lot of "very good friends" that she met through bridge and various other classes.

"I don't remember you mentioning her." I took a hearty swig of tea, waiting for the no doubt earth-shattering bit of gossip I was about to hear.

"Well, Belinda's daughter is vegan now, would you believe?" She tutted to herself as if she couldn't quite believe some people and their silly notions. "She was a vegetarian, but apparently cheese has feelings now, or some such rubbish, so she touches no animal products at all."

I tucked into my fish and nodded my head. "Yeah, a few of Jacob's friends are vegan or plant-based too. I admire them and their principles, but I couldn't do it myself. My weakness for fried egg sandwiches and toad in the hole would always prove my downfall."

"Well, apparently she can't even eat nuts now. The poor girl has developed some sort of allergy to them. One whiff of a walnut and her face blows up like a balloon. It's frightful for the poor thing." Mum shook her head sadly as if she couldn't believe the sad state of the world she was now forced to live in. "Can you believe it though, a vegan with a nut allergy? Belinda is beside herself. She hasn't a clue what to give her for Christmas dinner now, as obviously the Waitrose nut roast she was planning is completely out of the question."

Christmas? It was barely May.

Mum fished around in her handbag to locate her pearlised pink lipstick for a post latte touch-up. "The stress of it all is really getting to Belinda, the poor dear, and she really should avoid stress. It makes her condition so much worse."

I knew I really shouldn't ask, but I was a glutton for punishment.

"What condition?"

Mum leaned conspiratorially across the table towards me, her voice dropping to a delicate whisper. "Poor Belinda had her appendix out a few weeks ago, but the general anaesthetic constipated her something rotten in the days following. She really had to strain on the toilet for hours to even pass a bowel movement the size of a raisin."

I felt myself pale and was pleased I hadn't plumped for the spotted dick for pudding after all.

"But she has met the most fascinating people online in her Anal Fissure support group, so that's a great bonus. It really is wonderful how the internet can bring such diverse people together these days."

The internet? Diverse people? Anal Fissure Support Group? Suddenly my mind was back to the scenes I had viewed on my laptop the previous evening and I winced. A few of those actors might actually be friends with the salsa-dancing, Waitrose-shopping Belinda Trotter.

I pushed the remainder of my fish and chips away. My appetite had gone.

"Full, dear? Well, you really shouldn't have gone for such a big portion, should you? You always did have eyes bigger than your stomach." She made a pig-like snorting sound to demonstrate my greed.

I didn't think I had eyes bigger than my belly. I would resemble an alien from a very weird and terrifying 1970s sci-fi movie if that were truly the case.

"So how are things with you, Mum?"

"Can't grumble really. Well I could, but who would listen?" She looked at me pointedly, and I made a mental note to concentrate more closely in future when she talked about her friends. "I'm delighted that the terrible scoundrel from my soap has been bumped off. I wouldn't wish ill on anyone, but I must admit that I cheered when he choked on his pickled egg in the Woolpack."

I nodded, but again had no clue what she was talking about. I had been a bit remiss in keeping up with the soaps the last few weeks. In truth, I often felt like I was living in a soap opera myself.

"And you, my dear? How are you bearing up with everything?

It can't be easy now that Daniel's gone." Her eyes narrowed as she mentioned his name. There was no love lost there.

I felt unwelcome tears welling up in my eyes; and through sniffs I filled her in about Daniel failing to make the mortgage payment and how worried I was with everything.

It felt good to be unloading everything to my mother. Cathartic, I guess. I had wanted to tell her all about Leo too, but it just didn't feel like the right time. I still had to figure things out in my own head first. What did that tell me? I really didn't know.

"There, there." Mum dabbed at my eyes with another pressed linen handkerchief she had extracted from her leather handbag. That bag really was huge, like a Mary Poppins number, and I wondered what else could be lurking in its cavernous depths. I didn't have to wonder for long. She rummaged around inside it for a few more moments, pulling out a Ruth Rendell thriller, a sewing kit and a Travel Scrabble before she located what she was looking for: a thin white envelope with my name printed neatly on the front in my mum's distinctive swirly handwriting.

"This is for you, Charlotte dear. I was thinking about everything we talked about last time we met: what I said about a woman needing to have her own independence and not relying on a man too much, and I really want to help."

She slid the envelope across the table to me. I eyed it with suspicion. It wasn't my birthday and Mum normally wasn't in the habit of handing out white envelopes willy-nilly.

I started to tear open the corner of it, keen to discover the contents, but she quickly placed her hand over mine and squeezed it gently. "I'd prefer you didn't open it now. Keep it until you're on your own. But I want you to know that it's something important."

I nodded and popped it into my own bag, making sure it was safely tucked away. Mum was being very cryptic. I hoped it wasn't a letter informing me she had a nasty disease; I really couldn't cope with that on top of everything else.

The remainder of our time together passed quickly. Mum regaled me with tales of more people I didn't know and would probably never meet. I learned that the bridge club in the neighbouring village to hers was a hotbed of rampant wife-swapping. Apparently, they passed the wives around like they were hot appetisers. Honestly, it seemed like everyone apart from me was getting some.

When it was time to go, I hugged Mum and we arranged to meet the following Wednesday. I even convinced her to break with tradition and meet me in a wine bar. She took some persuading, but eventually relented with protestations that she would only be having one small glass of something fizzy, as daytime drinking was simply not ladylike. I gave her a hug, holding on for a few more seconds than was strictly necessary, and then we said our goodbyes. Despite our differences, we both knew how much we loved each other.

Sitting on the half-empty bus on the way home I retrieved the envelope from the recesses of my bag. My hands were a little sweaty and shaky as I ripped it open. There was a neat handwritten letter inside, and a cheque for a considerable amount of money; a life-changing amount of money, well, in my little life anyway.

I slowly read the letter.

"My dearest Charlotte,

I want you to know how incredibly proud you make me every day. I know I don't always show it, but that's just the Weaver way. We women just get on with things and struggle through, but I don't want that for you, I want better. You deserve to be happy, and you deserve to live your very best life.

I hope this money will give you options. And life is all about options. You're my only child and you will get everything I have once I'm gone (don't worry though, I'm as fit as a flea; I always told you that starting the day with a bowl of prunes would see me to 90), but I want to see you happy now, not when I'm gone.

Stop settling for second best. When you were a child, it was always as if a light burned in you and you shone so brightly. But I haven't seen you shine for such a long time. Now I feel the light is flickering again.

Take time to smell the flowers and realise how beautiful it all is. You have so much to offer. Never let a man, any man, define who you are or make you less than you are meant to be.

Your father would be so very proud of you. Now make yourself proud.

All my love,

Mum xx

P.S. But please stop wearing that shade of lipstick you had on last time we met. The red is so draining on your skin tone; a pale pink would be far more elegant (and less tarty), in my opinion."

I finished reading the letter, a half laugh, half snort escaping me at the last line. That was so like my mother. Suddenly I felt a great rush of emotions overwhelm me. Love and sadness and regret and hope washed over me like waves crashing against my soul.

I didn't care that the other passengers on the bus were viewing me with morbid curiosity and embarrassment in equal measure. I let my tears flow freely.

Chapter 29

I re-read my mother's letter many more times over the following few days, the words swirling chaotically around my mind. Did I make myself proud? I knew I was certainly prouder than I had been, but was there still room for improvement? I felt the answer was a firm yes.

The words Mum had written about never letting a man define you had truly struck a chord with me. I knew that was what I had done with Daniel. I'd only ever existed in his shadow, feeling I was insignificant and of less importance than him. As my wise matriarch mother said, I needed to let my light shine.

The cheque was still tucked safely away in my handbag. I was incredibly grateful to Mum for her generosity. It had been such a shock to receive it, but for once a shock that had been very welcome, unlike the many other ones I had received recently.

There was one thing I knew Mum was right about: money gave you options. It couldn't necessarily guarantee your happiness, but then again it was nicer to cry in a Mercedes than on the top deck of the number 12 bus. At least now I could stop worrying myself sick about the overdue mortgage payment and my imminent unemployment. I had the funds to sort that immediate problem. But what about the future? Now, thanks to this money, for the first time in years I had options. But what was it I really wanted?

It was mid-afternoon on Saturday, a lovely warm spring day where you could almost smell the tantalising hint of summer coming. Ideally, I should have been outside in the garden enjoying the fresh air, but instead I was drinking a glass of wine at the kitchen table with a daily newspaper and the letter spread out in front of me. I read it again. I knew the words by heart now, even though some of them were smudged and ineligible, thanks to my heartfelt tears causing the ink to run like little rivers down the page.

I glanced quickly around the kitchen; I had all the ingredients and utensils set out in preparation for the meal I was going to cook for Leo. We were having lemon herb chicken thighs with a crispy bacon gravy. I certainly needed to start the prep soon as Leo was due at 7 pm, and with my culinary skills and ability to burn water we would be lucky if the house was still standing by that time.

I picked the letter up from the table, folded it neatly and secreted it back into my handbag in the inner zipped compartment, along with the cheque. I clapped my hands together, a definite call to action. It was time to make culinary magic. I opened my cookbook to the desired page, grabbed the chicken thighs and began to rinse them thoroughly under the kitchen tap.

At a whisker after 7 pm the doorbell rang out, causing me to jump and nearly drop the bottle of wine I was uncorking. I hadn't realised just how anxious I was, but my jangling nerves confirmed it. Even though I was expecting Leo, I still felt the adrenaline jolt through my system. I steadied myself with a couple of deep breaths, hastily smoothed my hair down as no doubt it was frizzing with the heat from the cooker, and checked my teeth for any wayward lipstick in the hall mirror. I looked better than I felt, so with a deep steadying breath I answered the door.

"You look great." Leo greeted me enthusiastically and thrust an expensive-looking bottle of red wine into my hands. He looked me up and down and certainly seemed impressed.

I self-consciously ran my hands down the front of my fitted black midi dress, smoothing out the creases in the process. Ironing was not my forte. I glanced quickly at the label on the front of the wine bottle. It claimed to have won many prestigious-sounding awards. Very nice; certainly not one of my usual two for a tenner supermarket deals.

"Thank you so much," I graciously accepted the compliment and the wine, and directed him to the living room. "You're looking very handsome yourself."

He certainly did scrub up well, dressed in a form-fitting ice-blue jumper and black jeans, his hair neatly swept back off his handsome face.

Once Leo was settled comfortably, I scurried to the kitchen to fetch the wine and a bowl of cashew nuts. Minutes later, both nursing a large glass of wine and Leo nibbling on a salt and pepper cashew, my nerves returned with a vengeance. Why exactly was I so apprehensive? I was a fully grown woman for pity's sake, but sitting here sipping my wine, I felt as skittish as a newly born kitten.

"How has your week been?" Leo asked, taking a large sip of his wine and sighing contentedly, obviously relishing the taste. It must be good; he'd brought it, after all. I'd left my less fancy supermarket plonk chilling in the fridge, next to Jacob's fizzy orange pop.

"It's been quiet, not much happening." I didn't feel the need to tell him about the letter from my mother or the cheque. I hadn't told anyone yet. "How about you, how has your week been?"

Leo commenced a long-winded tale about a business deal he was involved in that wasn't panning out as he had hoped. He also spoke about the fact that he would still like to open a hotel in the UK with his business partner, but securing the perfect location was proving to be more troublesome than expected.

I was really trying my best to concentrate and keep up with what he was saying but was finding it difficult. The stupid new knickers I just had to buy were proving a little more of a snug fit than I had anticipated, and I was beginning a low-key panic that the elastic was cutting off my circulation. Could someone lose a leg to lingerie? Was that actually a thing? Also, the bra, whilst making my knockers look a knock-out, was nipping under my arms terribly. Who first said that there was no beauty without pain? Whoever it was, I wholeheartedly agreed.

I excused myself to check on the food and to have a furtive rummage under my dress and try to get the torturous under-garments to play nicely. All looked good on the cuisine front: the chicken smelling delicious, and nothing burnt to a crisp as yet. Maybe I wasn't as bad a cook as Daniel had always led me to believe.

Thirty minutes later and I had confirmation that this was indeed the case as a satisfied Leo scraped his plate clean, nearly taking the china pattern off in the process. The problem with cooking was all those hours slaving away in the kitchen for it to be gone in a couple of minutes. Although I was chuffed the food had been a hit, it just seemed a monumental effort to end up with nothing. At least when you created a painting, that work of art could be enjoyed for ever. My beautiful culinary creation was now nothing more than a tangle of greasy chicken bones and a few random peas.

"That was delicious, a fabulous meal, cooked for me by a beautiful woman." Leo's eyes twinkled mischievously. "I really am a lucky man."

I felt my cheeks flush a little and busied myself clearing up the dirty plates, escaping to the kitchen for another sneaky extraction of underwear from my nether regions.

"There's chocolate cheesecake for dessert too," I called out from the kitchen. I could not take the credit for this as I had bought it earlier that day from the local delicatessen. I carried the decadent concoction through to the dining table, it looking very impressive atop my grandma's crystal cake stand.

Leo's eyes lit up. "Chocolate too... Mrs Potts, you're trying to seduce me."

My stomach lurched so much that I nearly fell off my hugely uncomfortable high-heeled shoes, perilously close to dropping the dessert too all over the carpet. I was horrified. Was Leo making a joke about our age gap? Making it all seem a bit seedy and quoting a line from *The Graduate*? Just replacing Mrs Robinson with Mrs Potts? Oh, the absolute horror of it.

Leo clocked the look of startled dismay on my face and immediately flew to my side, taking the cake stand from me and hastily setting it on the table well out of harm's way.

"I was only joking, Charlotte." He gave me a reassuring smile. "I'm not expecting anything like that tonight; it was just something I said without thinking. I think I'm a comedian sometimes, but I really should know when to shut up." He took my hand and led me back into the lounge where we resumed our seats on the blue floral sofa. "I know you're probably not ready for our relationship to go to the next level, and that's OK by me, everything can be at your pace."

How did he know I wasn't ready? He was right of course; I wasn't, but how did he know? Did I give off frosty "don't touch the goods" signals? It wasn't until he had made that flippant joke about me trying to seduce him that everything had suddenly become clear in my mind. I knew I wasn't ready to sleep with another man. For me it was just too soon.

I liked Leo very much. More than liked him. He was wonderful. To use the hackneyed old phrase, "it wasn't him, it was me." I just wasn't ready to fall headlong into bed with any man; frilly knickers and scented candles aside, I just wasn't ready. There was only one person I needed to have a relationship with at present, and that person I saw every time I looked in the mirror.

"Leo, I think we need to talk."

Leo's face dropped about a mile. "Oh dear, I know I'm not going to like what's coming."

And talk we did. Talked until the early hours of the morning. The dirty dishes were left abandoned in the kitchen and the beautiful cheesecake uneaten. I tried to explain how I was feeling, even though I didn't really understand it all myself.

Lila would think I had taken leave of my senses. Here I was with a hot younger man who was crazy about me, wanting to take our relationship further, and I was giving him the heave-ho. She would consider me certifiable and needing to be marched to the nearest funny farm pronto.

Thankfully, unlike Lila, Leo was much more understanding.

"I get it, Charlotte, I really do. You've only just split up from your husband, whom you'd been with for most of your life. I should have realised you didn't want to jump into anything else too quickly."

I felt a little pang of regret, but I knew that what I was doing was right for me and therefore right for Leo too. He deserved someone who was completely invested in him, not a messy work in progress like I knew I was.

"But if I did want to jump, Leo, I hope you know I would want to make that leap with you."

He smiled, his eyes tinged a little with sadness, and I felt my heart break just that little bit more. "I know it isn't our time, but you're a wonderful woman, Charlotte, truly you are, don't ever doubt that. And if we can't be anything more, I would still be honoured to be your friend."

He stood up, all determined and gracious and walked towards the front door, his tall frame only needing a few steps to get there. We stood in the narrow hallway for a few seconds, awkwardly avoiding each other's eyes. I knew his thoughts must be mirroring mine. Should he hug me? Kiss me? Would it just be more appropriate to shake hands formally, seeing as we were now just friends?

I made the decision for both of us and hugged him tightly. I held on for longer than was necessary, but when I began to pull away, Leo's lips were on mine, warm and strong and passionate. It was a lovely kiss, but I knew it was to be our last.

I felt regret when our bodies eventually moved apart, but I knew in my heart that it was the right thing to do. I needed to rebuild myself first; discover who I really was and where I belonged in the world before I became part of a couple again.

"Friends?" Leo gave me a cheeky grin to lighten the sombre mood.

"Always." I hugged him again. And I was confident we would always be friends.

Leo was halfway out of the door when he stopped abruptly and turned back to face me.

"I'm not giving up though, Charlotte. I know the time isn't right for us now, but life is a long time, so never say never."

With that, the door shut firmly behind him, the sound echoing around the emptiness of my home. I was alone again. But I didn't feel empty. I didn't feel lonely. No, I felt alive and hopeful and somehow very brave. I had turned down a wonderful man, but I had done it for the right reasons. I felt empowered. I now knew that there was nothing I couldn't do if I set my mind to it.

There was, however, something I really didn't want to do though I knew I must. I turned on my heel and returned to the kitchen. Yes, there was a hell of a lot of washing up that simply had to be done.

Chapter 30

"You did what?" I moved my phone away from my ear for fear I might be deafened. Lila's shrieks were so loud and piercing that there was a real possibility she could perforate my eardrum.

It was the following afternoon and I'd just received a phone call from Lila, keen to get all the juicy details of my dinner date with Leo.

"I've told you, Leo and I are just going to be friends," I explained really slowly, as if talking to a toddler. "It's just not the right time for us. I'm not ready to get into another relationship, and he'll be returning to Canada soon. It's the sensible thing to do and he understands that."

"Sensible?" Honestly, her voice was so shrill now that I could hear the cocker spaniel two doors down howling mournfully in the distance. "Who gives a rat's arse about being sensible? Charlotte, he's a millionaire for fuck's sake, and he's bloody gorgeous. What were you thinking?" I could hear her moving around her home from room to room, her voice cutting out when she lost the Wi-Fi signal. The price you have to pay for those thick old Victorian walls. "Well, clearly you weren't thinking, or you would realise how unbelievably stupid you're being. You must have had a bang to the head or something;

you're obviously not in your right mind." She paused in her rant for a few seconds. I wasn't sure if it was to let her words sink in, or whether she had her head buried in her fridge selecting a chilled bottle of wine, but I could definitely hear the clinking of a bottle. "You need to sort this out now. Tell him you've changed your mind, tell him before he finds another woman and you've lost him forever."

Lila just didn't get it. I was happy with my decision, and I knew that Leo understood. Maybe if we had met further down the line, when my life felt more on track, then things would be very different. But things were as they were, and this was the right decision for now for us.

My words were in vain and fell on very deaf ears.

"What did you buy all that fancy underwear for if you had no intention of testing the bedsprings with him?" She demanded to know.

"I bought them because at the time I did I think there was a real possibility we would end up in bed. But now I'm just going to wear them for myself, to feel good about me."

That wasn't strictly true. I had no intention of ever putting those grisly garments on again. I had been married to Daniel for over twenty years. Had I not suffered enough? The bra and knickers were now in a messy heap in the corner of the bedroom, most likely destined for the bin. But that wasn't to say I wouldn't treat myself to some more new underwear in the future; just nothing that felt like it was bearing a grudge and wanted to physically hurt me one butt cheek at a time. It would be nice to wear pretty things, but wear them just for me and just for the hell of it, and they would most definitely have to be comfortable. Now I was all about comfort. Chic but comfortable were my words du jour. I pulled my trusty old dressing gown tighter around my naked body. Bliss.

Lila was back in full swing again. Clearly a good swig of chardonnay had enlivened her. "Men like Leo don't just come along every day, you know, Lottie. At our age most men that we like just aren't interested in us, and the ones that are tend to be at least two inches shorter than they state they are, with all their hair having migrated to their ears and up their nostrils." I could hear her physically shudder. "And don't get me started on their scrotums, believe me, they look like Alice Cooper on a bad day. These men have all the sex appeal of over-cooked pasta and are just as limp."

More information than I needed, and certainly more than I wanted.

"But don't you see, Lila, I'm just not interested in a man – any man. And don't worry, it's not that I'm hung up on Daniel and want him back." I nearly laughed at the very notion. "Believe me, that ship has well and truly sailed. Sailed, been shot down and is now at the bottom of the ocean in tiny unrecoverable pieces. It's just that I need to find me again, not a love affair, and if it is a love affair that I need, then I want it to be with me."

Lila tutted, but I could sense her mellowing. "I still think you've lost your marbles, but whatever you want, I guess it's your life after all." Finally, she was getting it.

"Thank you. I'm just going to concentrate on me and Jacob for the moment, make sure we're both OK, and then whatever happens in the long term happens, no expectations."

"When you say concentrate on you and Jacob, you'll still have time for your friends, won't you?" There was a little edge of concern now to her voice. I smiled to myself. As if she even had to ask. If there was one thing I knew I needed, it was my friends. My close group of girlfriends were my tribe. With them I had strength.

"Oh, don't you worry, Lila, there will always be time in my life for you and a large glass of Pinot." I heard her audible sigh of relief. I knew she needed me just as much as I needed her.

My phone pinged in my ear, alerting me to an incoming text from Jacob. "Hang on, Lila, just getting a message from Jacob. He's out with his dad and the Barbie bint tonight, so I just want to check he's OK and all hell hasn't broken loose."

I moved the phone away from my ear and squinted at the screen, clicking on the message icon from my son so that his words appeared on the screen.

"Mum... you're blowing up!!!!"

I slowly read the text out loud so Lila could hear, not understanding a single word of it.

Blowing up? What the hell? I jumped up from the bed and marched to the dressing table to check myself in the mirror. No, I looked fine, no extra chins, in fact my face was much more defined than it had been in years. Not slim by any means, but it was a nice face, even if I admit it myself and it certainly wasn't ballooning up or blowing up or whatever.

Maybe Jacob hadn't sent the text at all. Perhaps it was Rancid Roxy. She could have taken his phone when he wasn't looking, too busy inhaling his hot and sour soup, and decided to send a vile text to me. Maybe taking my husband from me wasn't enough for her and now she wanted to twist the knife a little. More fool her, twist away, dear, twist away. She could have the two-timing twit with my full blessing, I really wasn't interested any more.

I was still staring at myself in the mirror when Lila's voice snapped me back into the here and now. Unbelievably her voice was even more screechy than it had been. It sounded like a soprano singer inhaling a helium balloon. I considered hitting the floral bedroom carpet ninja style, just in case the dressing table mirror shattered into a billion pieces.

"Jacob's right, you... you've gone viral... hang onto your hat, I'm coming over."

I was back up and staring into the mirror, checking myself out again. Viral? What the hell was she going on about now? I looked fine. Perhaps I had used a little more blusher on my cheeks than usual, but I certainly looked healthy enough.

Chapter 31

Fifteen minutes later, Lila was bursting through my front door like a hurricane, brandishing an expensive bottle of champagne and trailing a cloud of even more expensive perfume in her wake. She must have driven like Lewis Hamilton to get from her home to mine so quickly.

"Get the glasses out, Lottie. Believe me, you're going to need a drink."

I accepted the proffered bottle from her, briefly examining the label. It was good stuff. I'd only ever drunk anything as fancy as this at the wedding of one of Daniel's snooty colleagues, and it seemed a bit decadent for a Sunday afternoon. "What are we celebrating?"

Lila looked concerned and her forehead wrinkled slightly, as if she needed a top-up of her Botox. "Celebrating? Commiserating? I haven't a bloody clue. To be honest you're the one who's going to determine that. But this was the only booze I had left in the house, so this is what we're drinking."

She was being very cryptic. I pulled two of my fanciest champagne flutes out from the back of the faux antique mahogany display cabinet in the dining room. They were more than a little dusty, so I gave them a quick once over with my dressing gown sleeve. They can't have seen the light of day for many a year, as there was never much need for celebration in the past.

Lila took the bottle back from my grasp and was carefully tugging the foil off the top and prising the cork out of it with a look of concentration on her face. "Let's get this bad lad open, shall we?"

The cork shot out of the bottle like a high-speed runaway train, colliding with the Ikea chandelier light fitting and leaving a smudgy mark on the ceiling rose as it hit it with immense force. My hands flew to cover my eyes. The cork was nowhere near me, but I was taking no chances. The last thing I needed on top of everything else was a black eye. If I was sporting a shiner at work, I didn't think anyone would believe it was from brut champagne, not the hands of some brute.

Lila efficiently filled our glasses, determined not to waste a single drop of the expensive foam. She passed me a flute and we clinked our glasses together momentarily. I couldn't help thinking this was all a little bizarre.

"What's going on, Lila?"

She paused for a second, clearly deciding what was the best course of action to take. Then with a "What the hell" she pulled her mobile phone out of her Chanel quilted handbag and passed it over to me. "You'd better take a look at this."

I saw that her phone was opened to TikTok. Not an app I knew a great deal about, always believing it was more for Jacob's age group and full of dance routines, glamorous twenty-something makeovers and singing chihuahuas.

I studied the image on the phone. It was a short video, and the people starring in it seemed a little too familiar to me. Who was the rather heavyset woman in the padded anorak who was waving a paper bag at a seated couple in a smart restaurant? "Oh yes," I thought with a sudden sinking feeling of dread and horror. That woman would be me.

It was indeed a video of me throwing down Daniel's psoriasis medication on the table at Moonlight Lounge. The recording was a little grainy and the sound not the best quality, with my words sounding rather jerky but clearly audible. I listened to my own voice playing in my ears in abject horror. Did I really sound like that? The shame of it. But never mind what I sounded like, it was what I was saying that was even worse. I must have wiped this particular little speech completely from my memory, out of self-preservation, no doubt. But here it was for everyone in the entire world to hear, loud and nearly clear. But a monologue from Shakespeare it certainly was not.

"It's his special ointment for his psoriasis. He gets it particularly badly on his bottom, the poor love. Just make sure he rubs it in often, or you can do it for him if that's more your bag. The main thing is just to apply it regularly, because if the psoriasis isn't treated, his arse cheeks will flare up and resemble a flaky old Hobnob biscuit."

I stared at Lila in horror. "I don't believe it," I wailed, my voice several octaves higher than usual. "It's from the afternoon when I followed Daniel; he said he was playing squash, but he met Roxy for a drink, but how... why?"

My mind slowly ticked back as I recalled that particular Saturday afternoon: following Daniel to Moonlight Lounge, going into the chemist next door and then surprising him with his lover. Now that I thought about it, I did remember other people listening to our heated exchange, and there was a group of girls at the next table, some with their mobile phones out filming. One of them must have uploaded the video to social media at some point.

I drained my champagne flute in one fell swoop and held it out for Lila to refill it. Expensive or not, I had barely tasted the first glass. "The shame of it, Lila. I'll be a laughing stock." I took another deep swig of my glass, shaking my head in despair. "I sound like an old fishwife embarrassing myself like that. What will people think?"

Lila was shaking her head too, but for a different reason. "No... no not at all, people are loving you. It's not you that should be embarrassed. You really need to see the comments."

I looked up at her dubiously, my voice a hopeful whisper. "Really?"

Lila was nodding, a large smile spreading across her pretty face. "Yes, it's incredible, they're calling you the 'Biscuit Queen'. It's absolutely hilarious. It seems you're a role model for the cheated-on and down-trodden woman. You're not a laughing stock, you're a bloody icon."

Disbelieving what I was hearing, I clicked on the little speech bubble next to the video. She was right. The video had been viewed thousands of times, with many hundreds of comments. Most of them were incredibly positive, calling me a voice for the oppressed, a woman who refused to skulk away into the shadows, but instead stood proud and had the last word, likening me to strong women from history – women I really admired. Others applauded me for the guts to embarrass my cheating husband in public while he sat there with his bit on the side and just took it.

There were a few meaner comments, making rude jibes about my appearance and how they could understand why my husband had cheated with a young filly when I was such an old boiler. These people must be what they called trolls. It hurt a bit. How could it not? But in all honesty, I'd heard much the same from my dear husband over the years, so I really wasn't going to let a few random strangers upset me too much. I had now learnt to be the bigger person, both literally and figuratively speaking, and I could certainly rise above it all. The truth of it was that happy people didn't need to pull others down in order to lift themselves up.

"It's not just TikTok; you're on Instagram too." Lila seemed to be physically buzzing with this development. "It's unbelievable, and you want to see the amount of stick they're giving dastardly Daniel."

Lila reached over to retrieve her phone from my shaking hands, and found another video to show me. It was the same footage as before, but this time Daniel's face had been replaced by a bright green cartoon lizard. It was quite realistic in a Disney sort of way, with its pointy tongue darting in and out of its reptilian mouth.

They were calling Daniel a "Lounge Lizard", obviously a play on the fact that they were in the Moonlight Lounge. Somebody who went by the username "RadicalRose84" had commented that he was a lizard lothario, and he gave her the creeps.

There were also lots of jokey dessert-inspired comments. Clearly there was a lot of mileage to be had with puns around my flaky Hobnob comment: stuff about Daniel just being a dirty old geezer wanting his oats; him having his cake and eating it too, that sort of thing. There was the odd rude one about Roxy wanting to suck the cream out of his éclair, it being hard on the outside and nice and gooey in the centre. You get the drift.

I felt secretly pleased to see there were quite a few people unimpressed with the twenty-odd-year age gap: saying how he was far too old for her, and his nuts would be dried up and shrivelled, not nice and moist like they should be. Somebody called "BabyboyBryn" had simply posed the question "Lady fingers?" To which a plethora of people had replied, one in particular commenting, "Bet she does, right up his doughnut hole." I couldn't help but laugh at that one.

Truthfully, it was all incredibly adolescent and childish, but Lila seemed to be enjoying it immensely, finding more and more content that made her whoop in delight. Many of the comments tickled her funny bone so much that they had her in stitches. She could barely breathe for laughing, tears streaming down her face, her make-up blotchy under her eyes. So much for her top-end waterproof mascara.

My mind was reeling. Yes, it was funny, but it also wasn't good, not good at all. Daniel was going to be beyond furious when he cottoned on to what was happening. And it would only be a matter of time before someone showed him all of this. Honestly, he probably already knew. Like Jacob had said, Roxy was permanently glued to her phone and proudly referred to herself as an "influencer"; so she was bound to have stumbled across it by now. The young woman struck me as someone who was incredibly image-obsessed, I didn't imagine she would relish her older, sophisticated lover being mocked and ridiculed. Not on her watch.

I felt embarrassed, too, seeing myself plastered over the internet. I wasn't exactly looking my best, and I was ranting on about flaky bottoms, for heaven's sake. But at least I seemed to be getting a positive response overall from the general public. The same could not be said for Roxy, and especially not for Daniel.

It appeared that I was on the receiving end of a lot of admiration from a whole host of people who loved the fact that I had confronted my cheating spouse and managed to embarrass him and have the last word. Others felt I should have given him a well overdue punch in the face too, as a farewell gesture, but that was never going to happen.

It was fair to say that Daniel was not coming out of this at all well. He was being seen as someone rather odious who rightly deserved to be ridiculed.

I looked over at Lila and saw that she had valiantly managed to curtail her laughter. She was now carefully studying me to see what my reaction to everything was.

"It's not good, is it?" I questioned her, my voice wavering.

"Not good?" Her face broke into a smile again. "I would say it was bloody marvellous and just what the snivelling little git deserves."

She jumped up from her seat and started pacing round the dining room, rubbing her hands together in glee. "Give him a bit of reality for a change. He's always walking around judging everyone else, like he's better than them and his shit don't stink." She held her phone out again for me to see, and jabbed her finger at one comment from a very angry subscriber who had been cheated on herself recently and had no time for philanderers. "Well, his shit stinks now and everyone knows it."

Suddenly there was an almighty banging at the front door, so loud it sounded as if it would knock the door off its hinges. Lila and I leapt out of our skins in shock. The furious hammering was at deafening level. I was on edge anyway, but the ferocity of the din nearly sent me hurtling over. I knew without a shadow of a doubt who was at the door: it was Daniel.

His face was angry. And when I say angry, I mean ready to explode, spitting venom in fury. He pushed me aside to enter the house and strode into the living room as if he still lived here. Still the same Daniel, it would seem.

True to form, his mobile phone was in his right hand and he was waving it angrily at me. "Have you bloody seen this?" He demanded, sitting down at "his" place on the sofa. "I can't believe it... what have you gone and done now, Charlotte?"

Me? Why was it all my fault? Yes, I might be the one centre stage in the video, putting him and Miss Fancy Knickers in their place, but I didn't ask for any of this. I didn't ask for it to be filmed, and I certainly didn't ask for it to end up on social media for the world and his wife to see.

Daniel was now concentrating hard on the small mobile phone screen in his hand, scrolling through it, his face darkening by the second. "They're making me look like a right pillock. It's unbelievable... and you should see some of the comments."

"No less than some may say you deserve," Lila commented pleasantly as she strolled into the living room from the kitchen, a refilled glass of champagne in each hand.

Daniel's eyebrows shot up like two stupefied slugs. "Lila... I didn't know you were here." His brows dropped again, and his eyes narrowed dangerously. "I might have known you'd be in the middle of the drama though. You couldn't stay away, eh? Just had to come and gloat!"

"Who, me?" Lila's voice was saccharine sweet as she smiled innocently and took her place on the chair in the bay window. She studied Daniel for a few seconds, as if he was a bug under a microscope. He was clearly her adversary, and she was ready to fight.

"You're wrong though, Daniel, this is nothing to do with me. I just wanted to have a little drink and a catch-up with my friend." She took a delicate sip of her champagne. "The fact that I get to witness you squirming over this embarrassing development is just the icing on the cake."

Trust Lila. She had to get on board with the cake quips too, it seemed. The comment wasn't lost on Daniel, and his face was like thunder. Yes, the weather forecast was very grim, better batten down the hatches and hunker down as a storm was coming.

Lila reached over and passed one of the glasses to me, sending Daniel's brows up again. They were up and down now more than his girlfriend's knickers. "Champagne? Tell me you aren't celebrating this. What's wrong with you women?"

I sat down on the empty place on the sofa next to my irate ex. "No, Daniel." I spoke in a soft, measured tone trying to calm the situation down. "We're not celebrating anything. I'm as shocked as you are. Lila just saw the video and came around to see me, that's all... nothing else."

Daniel shook his head, clearly not believing a word I said, and quietly continued to scroll through his phone. The only sound coming from his direction was the occasional tut, lengthy groan or "What the actual fuck, you must be kidding me". His head suddenly jolted towards me. "What about your fancy man? Does he know all about this?"

Clearly the thought of Leo rattled him. His ego was wounded by the fact that the younger man was clearly richer than him and drove a much fancier car. Fine to judge him when he believed he was penniless, but now he saw him as a threat.

I was not going to let Daniel know that Leo and I were over before we had even really started. Like most things in my life, it was really none of Daniel's business.

"I've no idea if he knows." My tone clearly indicated that the subject was not up for discussion.

Daniel tutted and returned to his scrolling.

Lila caught my eye and gave me a little wink. She then pulled a ridiculous face, her eyes crossed and her tongue sticking out of the corner of her mouth. For someone so beautiful, she could really make herself look comically absurd. Daniel, still busy reading another comment on his phone, was oblivious to her antics. Despite everything, I desperately wanted to laugh; I had to summon all my strength not to dissolve into a fit of schoolgirl giggles. When all was said and done, the whole thing was ludicrous.

I successfully managed to maintain my composure, and glanced over at my husband sitting on our ancient floral sofa, in the exact place he had sat for so many years of our marriage. He had an ample posterior, certainly not keeping up with the gym sessions, which was imprinting even more of a dent into the velour fabric; this served as a constant reminder of his presence, and was impossible to remove no matter how hard I plumped the seat cushions. The last few years of our marriage, he had sat in that very spot barely communicating with me, and now I tried to remember what I had ever seen in him. Yes, there was no denying it, he had been a handsome man. But what I now realised was that looks weren't everything; they weren't the be all and end all. It didn't matter if you looked like a Greek god if you were still a bad-tempered devil and ugly inside. Maybe I wasn't being fair to him; he wasn't completely bad, just bad for me.

He was dressed in skinny navy jeans and a Ralph Lauren shirt. This seemed to be his signature style now he was no longer with me. His shirt was creased, though, which he would never have tolerated while we were together. He was not so well groomed now that he had to do his own laundry, it seemed. I felt a little twinge of sadness for him: sitting there in his too tight jeans, he cut a slightly pitiful figure. His skinny legs and his burgeoning gut hanging over the waistband of the denim looked so uncomfortable. He was clearly trying to give off an air of youth and vitality, but try as he might, he was still nudging 50 and starting to look his age. His hair was visibly darker than normal, an effort to recapture the shade from his youth. I had always liked his wavy brown hair with its flecks of grey, which had been distinguished and given him character; but now it was darker and more matt looking. Quite clearly, he was attempting to keep up with the younger crowd he was now mixing with but wasn't succeeding. He was fighting a losing battle. He simply looked exhausted.

I no longer felt such seething anger towards him, but I knew I was no longer in love with him either. Looking at him just made me feel a little hollow and very, very sad. Sad for the "us" we used to be; so in love and ready to take on the world together, content in the knowledge that our love would see us through any hurdle life threw at us, and determined to live happily ever after. But real life wasn't like the fairy stories, and if mine was, it was the unexpurgated Brothers Grimm blood and guts account, and not the happy smiley Disney version.

I had loved Daniel before, and I was glad I had married him. Without Daniel, I would never have had Jacob. And having Jacob meant we had both done something very right with our lives.

There was no way that Daniel and I would ever be together again. I knew that. Too much had happened. He had changed. I had changed. Too much had changed, and it wasn't changing back.

Another groan emanated from Daniel's vicinity. His fragile

ego was clearly taking a severe hammering. I knew he was worrying about what his workmates would say, and what stick he would get the following morning at the coffee machine. I felt some sympathy for him, but in truth I just wanted him to leave. He didn't live here any more, and I needed to speak to Lila on our own.

I suddenly realised something. He hadn't brought our son with him.

"Where's Jacob? I thought you were bringing him back."

So far Daniel had made no mention at all of our son.

"Eh?" He glanced up from his phone, his eyes a little dazed and unfocused. He looked at me as if I was speaking in tongues. "What did you say?"

I repeated myself more slowly this time. "Where's Jacob?"

He flapped his hand at me dismissively, as if I were an irritating fly that needed swatting. "He's still with his mates. Sam's father's dropping him off here later."

I nodded. Probably for the best: the last thing Jacob needed to see was his parents going at it hammer and tongs. I really hoped that wouldn't be the case though, and Daniel would just get up and leave.

From Daniel's expression it was clear that he thought his world had come to an end. I was beginning to feel rather irritated now. Yes, it was all embarrassing, for me too, not just him, but there were much worse things that could happen and were happening in the world. It wasn't as if someone had died.

"Well, my reputation is dead and buried now," he commented, his voice sounding flat as if he was resigned to the fact that his name was mud.

I offered him an encouraging smile. "Come on, Daniel, I

know it's embarrassing, but it's really not that big a deal. Yes, people are having a laugh about it now, but it will all blow over in a couple of days. Everyone that's important to us already knows that we've split up, and they must know about Roxy too by now, so what does it matter in the big scheme of things?"

If looks could kill, the one Daniel was currently shooting my way would have seen me zipped into a body bag heading for the morgue with a tag on my big toe. He clearly thought I had lost my tiny mind.

"Blow over? Blow over?" He was out of his seat now. Standing tall and imposing, he looked directly at me and pointed an accusatory finger. "It's all right for you, everyone thinks you're marvellous, a bloody comedy legend, it seems. But me? They're treating me like I'm a serial killer." He was marching around the room now, in full flow. "And it isn't just going to blow over like you say. It's not the 1980s any more. Today's newspapers aren't tomorrow's fish and chip wrappers – no, stuff like this lives forever."

"Yes, one Google of your name and up pops your lizardy face."

Up to that moment Lila had managed to keep her trap shut, but quite clearly the effort of biting her tongue to keep herself quiet was proving too painful. "It's such a shame, Daniel." Her face was the picture of sincerity, but I knew she was being as disingenuous as was humanly possible. "All those silly pudding jokes at your expense about spotted dick and cream horns. It really isn't fair, you poor thing."

Daniel's eyes were bulging furiously now. "Well, I'm glad you think it's so funny, Lila, but it's not your reputation that's in ruins, is it?"

"You should have thought of that before you cheated on my

best friend, Daniel. I'm going to say this to you because your lovely wife, the woman you've treated like absolute shit for years, is too pathologically polite to say it herself."

She paused as if for dramatic effect, and I felt the atmosphere in the room shift. It felt charged with kinetic energy. I tensed up, waiting for whatever she was going to say next. I had absolutely everything clenched, from my jaw right down to my wobbly bits.

"You're an absolute prat, Daniel Potts, and what people are saying about you is nothing less than you deserve. I suggest you buckle up, boy, because it's going to be one hell of a bumpy ride."

And she wasn't wrong. Lila talked and for once Daniel listened. In no uncertain terms he heard a few home truths that he really had had coming for a while. She told him how wrong he had been to treat me the way he had: to take me for granted, to undermine me at every turn, and then after years of loyalty to thank me by cheating with a little strumpet from his office. She said how pleased she was to watch me rediscovering who I was always meant to be: no longer worn out and burdened down by life and lack of love; happy to see me finding happiness, not just in the biscuit tin and my classic movies, but in the world outside the safety of these four walls. She was glad that I could now own my own story, be the heroine of my life and maybe in time go on to find love.

As I listened to my life being dissected by Lila, I felt anger; righteous anger; anger at Daniel and anger at myself. I had really let myself down. But I was a different person now. The Lottie of old was no more; there was only the new and improved version now.

I hoped Lila's speech had hit home, but I wasn't sure. Daniel seemed to be slowly digesting her words for several minutes, but it appeared they were giving him a nasty case of indigestion. Slowly a sly sneer spread across his face.

"You really are the Rottweiler they say you are, Lila."

Lila hooted with delight, her eyes narrowing. "You say that like it's a bad thing."

You had to admire Lila's style. I imagined this must be how she was when in full flow at work, her demeanour so calm and in control.

She looked Daniel dead in the eyes whilst she delivered her final killer blow: "You've lost Lottie and she's the best thing that ever happened to you. I've always said it, but I'll say it once again for the cheap seats at the back... Daniel, you really are one dozy dickhead."

Chapter 32

Unsurprisingly, Daniel left shortly after that. He literally flounced out. Or rather he would have done if it hadn't been for the unfortunate accident of him stumbling and falling. He had always nagged me to make sure that the woollen rug in front of the fireplace was smoothed out correctly, as it was a tripping hazard. Know-it-all Daniel was right again. Thanks to my slovenly rug flattening, he caught his converse trainer on it mid-flounce and sprawled unceremoniously to the floor. It was a bit surreal to see him lying there in a messy husband-shaped heap on the shagpile. He tried his best to style it out and swiftly leap to his feet, but this was hampered by his skinny jeans. His legs were vacuum-packed into them, so his range of movement was restricted by the stiffness of the denim. It took three attempts to get to a standing position, with him glaring at Lila and me for the whole episode, daring us to laugh.

We did laugh, but somehow managed to wait until he had safely left before the hooting commenced.

"I can hardly breathe!" Lila was gasping for air. "I wish I could have recorded that; we could have enjoyed it for many years to come!"

I wiped the tears from my eyes. "Poor Daniel, he was trying

to leave with such dignity too."

Lila pointed to a spot on the carpet beside the rug. "And it looks as if he's left you a little something to remember him by."

There was a small dark streak there. Neither of us had to say anything, we both knew it had to have come from his hair dye.

Lila carried the empty bottle of champagne over to the recycling. "Did I go too far with Daniel and speak my mind too much?" Her voice sounded unsure. "I just couldn't stop myself once I got started. He's so unbelievably smug, it really boils my piss!"

I grimaced inwardly as I rinsed the champagne flutes under the kitchen tap. I really hated that expression, it was so crass, but in fairness it truly described her feelings towards Daniel.

I dried the glasses thoroughly with a tea towel. "It's fine, you're allowed to say how you feel, and let's be honest, it's nice to have someone stick up for me every now and then. I always know you have my back."

I flicked her arm good-naturedly with the damp tea towel to show her there were no hard feelings.

Daniel and Lila had never been each other's greatest fans; more like sworn enemies. He didn't like driven career women like Lila, feeling that they were taking a job that could be better suited to a man. And she in turn hated chauvinists. Daniel would scornfully inform me that Lila was "one of those feminist types of women" and a "man hater". That couldn't have been further from the truth. Yes, Lila was an advocate for women's rights and proudly so, but a man hater? When it came to men, Lila was most definitely a lover and not a hater.

Lila glanced at the champagne bottle languishing at the bottom of the recycling box. "Should I nip out and get us another one? I could go to the offy on the High Street."

I yawned and glanced at the time on the kitchen clock: 9.15pm. I felt exhausted, really exhausted. The last couple of days had been eventful, to say the least.

"I'm pretty whacked, Lila. Jacob should be home any time now and I could really do with heading to bed once he's gets in."

She nodded her head. "You're right, it's been a strange kind of day. I'll leave you be. We can catch up in the next day or so."

She reached over and planted a kiss on my cheek. I inhaled her perfume, as she always smelled so good. I doubted very much that I was quite so fragrant. Less Dior and more dustbin, I imagined. I could really do with a long soak in a nice hot bubble bath.

I walked Lila to the front door and was just about to reach for the handle when it swung open wide. In strolled Jacob, a sight for sore eyes: tall and lean, fair hair dishevelled, and his tatty rucksack slung over his arm. I felt an overwhelming impulse to hug him.

His face lit up when he saw Lila. Out of all my friends, she was by far his favourite.

"Yo, Lila. Whassup?"

"Jakie boy!" She too was delighted to see him. "Would you look at how tall you're getting."

Jacob beamed at her. "I know, right? I'm almost the tallest one in sixth form. Mum says it's because I eat so much; she says I've got hollow legs."

Lila gave one of his knees a little serious tap with her manicured hand. "Nope, sounds just fine to me."

Jacob laughed at her silliness, clearly delighted. "Hey, did you know that Mum's famous now?"

"Ahhhh yes, indeed she is," Lila replied sagely. "The feisty Biscuit Queen, no less. You'd better make sure you look after her, though; she's had quite the day."

Jacob looked suddenly concerned. "Dad?"

She nodded at him, her face deadly serious, which spoke volumes. I could see that Jacob understood the situation without a single word being uttered.

"Right, I'd better be offski." Lila was unzipping her bag to locate her car keys, and a couple of seconds later the keys along with their Bentley keyring were dangling from her index finger. She quickly thought better of it, remembering the half a bottle of champagne she had just quaffed, and pulled her phone out of her pocket to call an Uber. She blew us both an exuberant kiss and with a "Syanara superstars" she was out of the door and gone into the night, with as much finesse as when she had first arrived.

I was glad it was now just me and my son.

"You hungry?" I enquired, knowing only too well what the answer would be. I had never known Jacob be anything but ravenous.

"Could murder some cheese on toast." Jacob was nearly as much of a cheddar fiend as I was.

I pulled a half loaf of bread out of the breadbin. I should really have shares in a bakery, the amount of white sliced we got through in a week, and popped a couple of thick slices into the toaster. I grabbed a large block of mature cheddar from the fridge and began to cut it in thick, uneven slices. Like me, Jacob preferred his cheese sliced straight from the pack onto his buttered toast. He liked "raw cheese" as he called it on toast. "Cooked cheese" was only for pizza, lasagne and such like. He could be quite specific in his tastes.

"Did you have a good time last night with your dad... and Roxy?" I spat out her name as if it were stuck in my throat. Sometimes I still found it difficult to bring myself to speak of her. I just couldn't stand the woman. In my mind there was a special place in hell reserved for the type of women who dated married men.

Jacob picked up the slice of cheddar I had just finished cutting and popped it into his mouth, chewing slowly. "Yeah, it was OK, bit of an atmosphere to start off, to be honest. I think they'd had a row before they picked me up, but then they cheered up a bit."

Oh dear, sounded like there was maybe more trouble in paradise; what a shame.

"So you didn't see the video until after the meal?"

Jacob shook his head. "Nah, Roxy saw it on TikTok in the car on the way to Sam's house." He chuckled to himself. "Man, was she livid? She couldn't believe her eyes when she saw you; and then, when she realised the stick she and Dad were getting, and the way people were loving on you, she got ten times worse."

Oh well, at least they had managed to enjoy their Chinese meal before everything went pear-shaped. The calm before the storm; the condemned man had eaten a hearty meal of Char Sui pork before the atmosphere had turned from sweet to sour.

The food was ready, so I passed the plate with two rounds of cheese on toast to Jacob who took it eagerly. I had added a bit of chutney spread thinly on top, just the way he liked it.

"Thanks, Mum." He took a hungry bite and chewed for a few seconds before swallowing. I waited patiently for him to finish so he would tell me more.

"I didn't get to see the vid properly till I got to Sam's house. Then I couldn't believe it when I clocked you dissing them both like a badass. But full respect, Mum, you stood up for yourself and it was wicked."

I guessed he meant wicked good.

"Roxy really thinks she's something. She gets a few endorsements from brands for advertising make-up and stuff, and now she reckons you're ruining her brand." He rolled his eyes. "She's proper delusional, fancies herself as a bit of a celeb." He laughed again at the very notion and picked up the second piece of toast. "She's dating a celeb now, I guess, but not in the way she'd like. I think she always fancied bagging herself a footballer or suchlike, not a wanker banker like Dad."

"That's not very nice, Jacob." My tone was stern. "He's still your dad."

"I know, Mum, but he has been acting like a right idiot, you know he has."

I couldn't really argue with that. "Tell me about Sam's then, did you have fun?"

Jacob's eyes lit up. "It was awesome. His dad made the most amazing burgers, with three patties in each one, and Sam and me discovered our own condiment."

"You did what?"

"Yep, we couldn't decide if we wanted mayonnaise, mustard or ketchup with our chips, so we thought we'd have them all. We mixed a dollop of each one together in a bowl and it was lush."

I felt ill at the thought, and certainly not convinced by this new gastronomical discovery, no matter how convincing my son was.

"Yeah, it's quality, we're thinking of patenting it, calling it "Mayochupstard". It could go global; we could make some proper bank, be like gazillionaires."

His enthusiasm seemed to wane slightly. "But the only thing is if you have too much, you feel like you want to hurl. Honestly, I really thought I was going to spew all over Sam's kitchen at one point, like chunks of chunder everywhere, but I didn't," he announced proudly. "Sam's mum says I've got a cast-iron stomach."

I smiled affectionately at Jacob. My big, tall son looked so grown up, but in many ways he was still a little boy. I was so glad he had managed to contain himself. I'd had the pleasure of having coffee with Sam's mum only once in the aforementioned kitchen. I had been incredibly impressed and rather in awe of it as I had sipped my espresso from its tiny cup. The room was like something straight out of a showroom catalogue: shiny white units and high-tech appliances that gave the impression of a sanitised operating theatre rather than somewhere to whip up an omelette. The only nod to it being a kitchen was the odd decorative bottle of olive oil artfully positioned around the perimeter of the marble worktops. It was hard to imagine triple burgers and chips with hybrid mayo, ketchup and mustard dressing on the side being prepared in that spotlessly zen room.

I glanced around my own rather more homely kitchen, with its tired oak farmhouse units and chipped worktops. You could tell that many happy meals had been prepared here over the years, some of which were still stuck rock-hard to the roof of the ancient combination oven.

I left my son gobbling his cheese and chutney and went into the lounge to fetch my handbag. I needed to show him the cheque and letter from Mum, to see what his take on it was.

I sat back down at the kitchen table opposite him and spread the letter and cheque on the tablecloth next to his nearly empty plate.

"What's this?" Jacob wiped a few crumbs from his fingers and picked up the letter first.

"Just read it."

His brow furrowed as he studied the words on the page. When he was finished, he placed the letter down on the table and picked up the cheque. His eyes widened in disbelief when he saw the amount.

"Mum, that's... a lot of zeros there. I never knew Gran was seriously minted." He let out a long whistle. "Do you reckon she would get me those trainers I want? The ones the rappers wear."

"Jacob," my voice was stern, "your Gran's trying to give me... well, us... an opportunity. I just wanted to see what you thought about it."

Jacob was quiet for several seconds, mulling it over.

"I think it's really nice of her. She wants you to have the best life you can, but it's up to you to decide what that is. I'm going to be off to uni this year, if I get my projected grades, so you need to have a long think about what it is you want, and not just everyone else." His eyes lit up for a second. "But can we please talk about the trainers?"

I laughed at him. "We'll see."

Jacob had finished his food and I could tell he was itching to get up to his bedroom and fire up his computer. No doubt there was a plague of bloodthirsty zombies he needed to dispatch.

I made myself a mug of strong tea and cheese on toast for me too and wandered back into the living room. Settling down on the sofa, I turned on the TV, trying to find something that would hold my attention for more than just a minute or so, but nothing did.

I kept re-reading the letter. Jacob was right, I really did have some serious thinking to do.

I must have nodded off at some point as I woke up hours later, my head lolling to one side and drooling unattractively on the floral cushion. I felt uncomfortably chilly and had a crick in my neck. I blinked a few times to refocus my eyes and checked the hands on the mantelpiece clock: 6:15 am. It was too early to make a phone call; but I had decided before I fell asleep what it was I wanted to do. The fitful dreams I had experienced confirmed it too.

It felt good to have a plan for once and to know what I wanted to do with my life. In that moment, I felt excited and hopeful. There was one person I needed to speak to, but it really was too early. Maybe I could send a text message. I weighed up the pros and cons and decided I would. I was going to start things as I meant to go on and throw caution to the wind.

I grabbed my phone and started scrolling through the address book until I located the contact details I wanted.

I sent a message and said a silent prayer to myself.

"Ring me as soon as you can. I have a proposition for you. xx"

Chapter 33

Six months later

I looked around the tastefully decorated living room with appreciation. It really was a chic room: all the furniture new, yet with a timeless elegance about it. Not uber modern by any means, but nor was it old-fashioned and dated. There was a sleek minimalism to the space, but it still managed to feel homely; all clean lines with a definite lack of clutter, save for the occasional knick-knack or framed photograph. The only real giveaway to the taste of the owner was a sturdy walnut bookcase, acquired from a little antique shop and now in pride of place in the corner of the spacious room. It was heaving bountifully with books in all manner of genres. The owner of this apartment most certainly had taste, and the owner of this apartment just happened to be me.

I had finally taken possession of the keys three weeks ago, and it had been a whirlwind of activity since then. Jacob was now away at university in Newcastle studying Law. I still couldn't quite believe he was gone, and his decision to read Law could mostly be attributed to Lila. He really admired her and wanted to follow in her footsteps. I just secretly prayed he wouldn't emulate her too much: if he could be more reliable Golden Retriever and less power-hungry Rottweiler, that would be a good start. He was already back from uni with a mountain of dirty washing and appeared to have grown another half inch. His first term had gone well, or so I assumed; he hadn't said much either way, but when he didn't realise I was looking, he would have a soppy smile on his face and he was permanently attached to his phone. I knew there must be a girl involved somewhere.

I really should have got a Christmas tree by now and some decorations, since it was less than a week to Christmas Day. I would go shopping tomorrow and get a few things to make the place look more festive. All the decorations we had previously owned had gone to the charity shop when we moved, including most of everything else from the past. I had of course kept the few decorations that Jacob had made as a child. They were completely priceless, especially the robin with one eye and no beak that always had to sit on the third branch, even though it terrified young children. It was tradition, after all. I had also kept a few keepsakes: Jacob's wrist bands from the hospital where he was born, Dad's old wristwatch that he had to wind by hand every night after work, and some love letters from Daniel from when we first met. I had to keep the letters; they were part of my story. The past might be a foreign country, as they say, but it was good to take a short break there every now and then. Everything else had gone on a journey to the Help the Aged charity shop. I had bought so much from them in the past that it was only fair to replenish their stock.

It hadn't been too much of a wrench to leave our old home; not nearly as hard as I thought it might be. But so much had changed in life, and I knew that moving on was the right thing to do; and it was the right time to do it.

Ivy had been mortified and refused to speak to me for a week when the For Sale sign was first erected outside the house. Although I had already told her it was happening, I don't think she truly believed it until she saw with her own eyes the wooden sign being hammered into the rockery. After a week had passed, she grudgingly accepted the box of chocolates I bought her as a peace offering. I thought a soft centre might soften the blow: Ivy had such a sweet tooth that she could never resist the lure of a caramel.

Although my dear neighbour had slowly come round to the fact that we were selling the house, she absolutely refused to discuss any of the details; and I did catch her semi-hidden behind her net curtains, shooting daggers at would-be buyers.

The house sold quickly. Apparently, our little semi was in a highly sought after area. Who would have thought it? It was in the catchment area for one very good primary and two exceptional secondary schools, well according to Ofsted anyway. So there was no shortage of eager buyers traipsing muck through our home, criticising the pale pink bathroom suite and pouring scorn on the carpeted rather than stripped wooden flooring. However, none of those things proved too much of a stumbling block: we had several offers, and were able to accept one near the asking price from David and Jo. They were perfect first-time buyers with no chain, and eager to move in as soon as possible.

Once we had accepted their offer, I suggested bringing them round to meet Ivy after one of their viewings for a chat and cup of tea. But Ivy was adamant that she had no interest in meeting either of them, and could I please leave her be to watch *Dickinson's Real Deal* in peace. Honestly, I think if her beloved David Dickinson had been moving in next door with his tanning bed under one arm and a pile of pin-striped suits under the other, she would still have feigned lack of interest.

David and Jo were a lovely couple in their early thirties. Both worked in marketing and had the cutest border collie called Mr Scruffy. It was Mr Scruffy who succeeded where I had previously failed. Ivy was a sucker for a pair of sad puppy eyes, and when she encountered the dog out for a stroll on the High Street with his two human owners, a couple of weeks after they had first moved in, she was instantly smitten; in time she grew nearly as fond of David and Jo too.

I might have been concerned about how Ivy would react to Jo being non-binary. Being in her late eighties, she was stolidly convinced that too many women wore jeans these days, and what was wrong with a nice floral dress from Marks and Spencer and a pair of 40 denier American tan tights? I needn't have worried though, as a firm friendship between the three was quickly formed through a mutual appreciation of *Coronation Street* and a love of all foods pastry-based.

Ivy wasn't fazed in the slightest by Jo's gender fluidity. In her own words, "I couldn't give two hoots about all that stuff. Just as long as they aren't twats and don't vote Tory." Those two things were non-negotiable in her book.

Ivy told me how they stamped their own personal style through the house. I was glad. I really hoped they would be happy there. We had been for many years. I still had my memories. It was a good home, it had good bones.

It was such a relief that Ivy finally forged a friendship with her new neighbours. I had felt a little guilty moving on after so many years living in the leafy-lined cul-de-sac. I had actually only moved a couple of miles away, but for decades there had been just a brick wall separating our two houses. I would always know when Ivy was putting on the kettle and wanted me to drop in for a chat and a cuppa. She used to knock on the dividing wall, and that was my cue that the biscuits were hitting the plate and the mugs were full: get my arse around there quick!

Nearly four months ago, Leo had returned to Canada after his extended stay. I knew that Ivy was missing him, and I was missing him too. I could feel a little emptiness in me, a hole that couldn't be filled, not even with reality TV and tiramisu. I hadn't expected to feel so bereft when he left. We had continued to have our little chats over the garden fence and wave at each other in the street, but it was all strictly platonic. We were just friends. I had wanted that, and Leo being Leo had respected my feelings. I did feel wistful at times at how things could have been, and I wondered if he did too. It just hadn't been the right time for us. In another lifetime, who could tell?

Daniel initially hadn't wanted to sell, and as expected had thrown a little hissy fit when I first brought up the subject. However, in time he came round to my way of thinking; he knew it was the sensible thing to do. He really didn't have much of a choice. He couldn't continue to kip in Jon's spare boxroom indefinitely, especially now that their relationship was somewhat strained, thanks to a particular unfortunate incident.

Daniel went out to collect a takeaway curry from the Moulin Raj for himself, Jon and Roxy one evening after work. It was his favourite of all the takeout joints he frequented, and he frequented many. Since our break-up he was a seasoned connoisseur of all foods served in polystyrene containers. Moulin Raj was an Indian restaurant that also boasted some French dishes on their menu: a sort of fusion of French and Indian cuisine. Daniel couldn't get enough of the place; "Frenchian cuisine" he pompously liked to call it. However, that would be the last meal he ever ate from his favourite restaurant. He had returned home, peshwari naan in hand, to discover his erstwhile friend and girlfriend locked in a passionate embrace in the living room. They were going at it hot and heavy. Not quite as hot as the lamb curry which Daniel then furiously hurled at them, amid a torrent of expletives. The spicy Indian dish exploded onto the shocked couple at high speed. It was like a Vindaloo volcano erupting, followed shortly after by a pot of lime pickle which was just as sour as the expression on Roxy's face as it dripped down her expensive blonde extensions.

It later transpired that Roxy had decided Jon was a better option for her, long term, than poor Daniel. Jon was in line for promotion at work and had promised Roxy a week away in sunny Benidorm. How could Daniel possibly compete with that? Poor Daniel, it really wasn't much fun to be cheated on. It's a cliché to say that what goes around comes around.

After that little discovery, Daniel again harboured hopes of returning home to me with his tail between his legs. No chance! I knew exactly where that tail had been. He had no other option but to face facts. There was no way in hell that our marriage could be saved. So with staying at Jon's no longer an option, he needed to find himself a modest bachelor pad of his own, and find it fast. The family home had to be sold.

Back to my new pad: my living room was gradually filling up with guests. The party would soon be in full swing. Lila had been stationed by the front door to greet the guests. That is once they had scaled the three flights of stairs up to the apartment, out of breath and desperate for a glass of something strong and festive. I had strict instructions from Lila that I was to stay put in the lounge, so that I could be the "hostess with the mostest and mingle".

Mum was standing straight-backed in the corner of the room, in her smart, Chanel-inspired black and white wool suit, nursing a small gin and tonic. She was making polite small talk with Lila's date for the evening: a pleasant-looking man in his early fifties with a receding hairline, called Seb. He was clearly besotted with Lila, but her feelings towards him were rather more tepid. She felt he was a nice guy, but far too stick in the mud and dull to stand a chance of winning the much-coveted prize of becoming her one and only. They were strictly just friends, and she went to great lengths to ensure that everyone knew that. He worked at her firm and was a safe pair of hands as a "plus one" to accompany her to social events. But that safe pair of hands would definitely not be getting frisky under her pencil skirt on the Uber ride home.

My old friend Imogen was sitting on the pale pink sofa, holding hands with her partner Natasha. They were openly dating now. Imogen smiled happily at her dark-haired companion, clearly enamoured. Contrary to what I thought would happen, Imogen had for once in her life taken my advice and come clean about her sham of a marriage. It hadn't been an easy time for her family, but it had been the right thing to do. She seemed so happy now and completely at ease, sharing secret little glances and smiles with Natasha, as people in love often do. It was very sweet to see. Imogen was looking amazing too. Long gone was the smart couture and full face of camouflage-type make-up. She appeared younger, and although she had always been a stunning woman, she now looked even prettier, as if she was finally the authentic version of herself, who she was always meant to be. I knew how that felt.

My hairdressers Tabby and Martina were standing in the

bay window chatting animatedly. Tabby threw her head back and laughed raucously at something Martina said. They had closed the salon an hour early to attend my party, as they insisted there was no way they were going to miss it. I was very touched by that. I tucked a strand of hair behind my ear. Thanks to Tabby, I was now sporting a shorter, even choppier do. I'd plumped for more blonde highlights, and I felt bright and happy. Like they say, blondes really do have more fun.

Then my work colleagues: Diane was lounging next to the hairdressers, slurping down a large glass of red wine. I hoped she was enjoying it. It was one of the more expensive bottles from Daniel's exclusive wine club. Somehow in his hectic new life, he had forgotten to cancel his membership. The pricier bottles he had always liked to keep squirrelled away from me; they were to be strictly reserved for schmoozing important work contacts. He would be appalled if he could see his cherished bottle now being glugged down by Diane, who openly admitted she wouldn't know a good Côte du Rhone from a cooking sherry. Diane paused from her drinking to chat to Morgan. True to form, her niece was looking drop dead amazing: dressed in a black faux leather bustier top over a tartan blouse and sprayed-on denim with the highest platform boots I had ever seen; a couple of inches higher and they could have been classed as stilts. Her hair was now platinum blonde with a few lilac highlights scattered through it that gave the sleek bob shine and movement. I was pleased to see how happy Morgan seemed - how happy they both seemed.

Lila was slowly making her way into the lounge, escorting a somewhat dazed-looking Ivy by her elbow. My dear neighbour was clutching a crumpled brown paper bag, which I knew contained a bottle of her home-made rhubarb wine. That stuff was lethal. I had lost entire nights to that particular delight in the past, memories that I would never get back. I would need to hide that bottle discreetly away from my other guests, for their own good of course; as well as being more alcoholic than absinthe, the innocent-looking pink fizz went straight through your digestive system like a freight train. My little apartment only boasted one toilet, so I couldn't take the chance.

David and Jo were slowly following the cautious figure of Ivy into the room, and I was delighted to see that they had come too. I had asked Ivy to extend an invitation to them both, as I was keen to stay in touch. It was always lovely to make new friends.

Lila now positioned herself next to the buffet table and was delicately nibbling at one of Mum's devilled eggs. I had catered the party myself, mostly from the local deli, but as usual my mother had felt the cuisine on offer was a little too "modern" for her tastes. She had never seen the point of taramasalata or hummus: to her mind, chickpeas would never be a suitable offering for hungry partygoers. No comparison with the heft of a good sausage roll or corned beef and pickle bap. So on arrival, Mum had opened her colossal handbag to extract with pride that ancient Tupperware box. I recoiled in horror when I saw it. Who could forget the disheartening farting noise it made when you managed to prise off the lid and access the sweaty interior? Oh, those not so fond memories of rainy picnics from my childhood: soggy egg sandwiches and weak tea from a tartan flask at some historic ruin or other. Like a magician, Mum had always extracted food items from the Tupperware with a flourish. With a look of scorn on her face, she had pushed aside platters of charcuterie, olives and flatbreads to substitute her home-made meat and potato pie and sherry trifle.

"Lovely grub, Mrs W," Lila commented, enthusiastically helping herself to yet another curried hen's egg.

Mum's face lit up with delight. "I'll let you into a little secret, my dear: you can never go far wrong with mayonnaise." She tapped the side of her nose wisely and glanced at the guacamole with disdain. I wondered if she believed it was made from liquidised frogs, or something equally unappetising.

Lila turned her attention back to Jayne and Jasmine and resumed her narrative. She was evidently regaling them with a tale of one of her latest conquests. I couldn't hear what she was saying over the Ed Sheeran CD, but from her energetic gesticulations and jerky hand movements, I could hazard a guess. Jayne had paled slightly, looking rather queasy, and two stuffed olives slid from Jasmine's plate onto the floor. Quite clearly it was some story.

I picked up my champagne flute and drained the bubbles in one fell swoop. I needed some Dutch courage. It was only prosecco, but it was Asda's finest, and it tasted bloody lovely. I tapped my manicured fingernail against the empty glass in an attempt to capture everyone's attention.

Jacob took the cue. "Speech! Mum has something she'd like to say."

I cast a sweeping glance around the room at all the assembled people: family, work colleagues, friends old and new. My heart felt full to the brim with love. All my favourite people were together in this room. I took a deep breath and began.

"First of all, I wanted to thank you all for coming tonight to this little celebration. It's a joint celebration, the first reason being our housewarming."

There was a small ripple of applause at this, and I caught my mother muttering, "But it hasn't got a back garden. Where are they going to sit out when it's a sunny day? And how are they going to dry their smalls?"

I smiled at her, so typically Mum. I loved our apartment and could easily live without a garden. Roundhay Park was only a short walk away, and anyway how many sunny days did we ever get in Yorkshire?

I continued my speech once the applause had faded away. "But the other cause for celebration is to celebrate the fact that Zaftig and Raven has now been trading for three whole months... Morgan, would you come over here, please?"

The room erupted into applause again. Morgan normally had a very pale, ethereal countenance, but was now blushing furiously, her face as red as the cherry tomatoes on the buffet spread. She looked mortified at being the centre of attention, but I had an inkling that she was enjoying it too.

The early morning text I had sent some six months before had been to Morgan. After the restless night on the sofa, I had awoken with the germ of an idea that would set in motion a plan to change our lives forever. I wanted Morgan and me to go into business together; to make the little pipe dream we'd always talked about become a reality.

Our vision was to provide accessible fashion to every woman; to ensure that all women, irrespective of size or style, could feel thoroughly amazing in their own skin. We would offer plus-size fashion for women who wanted to flaunt their curves and feel a million dollars while doing so; to be proud and fabulous in a world that somehow expects you to be more invisible the larger you become. We wanted to change that; I wanted to change that. No longer would I apologise for being the size I was. I was size 18 now, and happy with it. I might even go so far as to say I was a bit of a bombshell. It had taken me a journey of many years to feel this way, and I hoped I could help other women gain confidence the way I had. "Lottie Big Bot" was no more; now there was only "Lottie the Hottie".

The world might want to shrink plus-size women, make us fit into a niche designed for women of size. But Zaftig and Raven was going to blow that apart; give badass big girls a choice of frocks that rocked. We believed in shoulders back and flaunt the rack. All whilst being comfortable; naturally, I was still all about the comfort.

We weren't naïve, though; we knew there was a lot of competition out there. Online you could find a glut of plus-size boutiques and alternative fashions, but we were confident that Zaftig and Raven could offer something just that little bit different. We lived this life. We embraced this fashion and we wanted to help other women do the same. It had taken me a long time to feel fabulous, but here I was feeling it every day: a plus-size woman on top of the world. And now we had our little boutique where we could sell a limited range of what we offered; somewhere shoppers could see and feel the quality of the clothes we stocked, rather than everything just being available online.

All our range was of course available online too. We had even modelled many of the outfits ourselves in a photoshoot to give a true representation of how they would look. Too often plus-size fashions were modelled by "plus-size fashionistas". Yes, technically they might be a size 18 or 22, but if they had well-defined arms and abs of steel, then they weren't the typical woman we were catering for. We wanted the woman with the wobbly tum to feel empowered; the cellulite legs to look chic in well-fitting pants; the muffin top to amaze in silk. We wanted to sell the dream, but we wanted the dream to be a reality.

And then the business also catered for the girl who desired fashion a little bit left of centre: style for those who hankered after wearable yet edgy clothes that would make a statement without completely overshadowing the girl within the fabric. In essence, girls as fabulous as Morgan.

We were lucky that through Diane we had been able to obtain some amazing contacts in the fashion world who were proving invaluable. We also had Gemini, one of Morgan's best friends who just happened to be a fledgling fashion designer. She was inexperienced and wet behind the ears, but with a flair for design and a real understanding of our vision. She was hands down one of the most talented women I had ever met, and I was ecstatic we now had her on our little team.

I had used much of the money Mum had given me to invest in the venture, keeping a little back for a rainy day and to give Jacob something for his future. Diane also had been only too happy to invest in Morgan's dream. She was a shrewd businesswoman, and she knew without a doubt that her niece was on to a winner.

When Leodis Chic's lease was up for renewal, Diane had called it a day for her fashion boutique. It was sad and felt like the end of an era, but Diane had been stoic, saying she realised that times were changing and you needed to change with them too or risk becoming a dinosaur. The shop had been sectioned up by the owner into smaller units to maximise rental income. Morgan and I had managed to obtain one of these units and were using the small space as a shop window for our business and a way to showcase a select range of our fashions.

The majority of our business was online, as everything seemed to be these days. I was now taking a business course at the local college to hone my skills, such as they were. I was seriously considering enrolling as a mature student at university part-time the following academic year, to study fashion. I couldn't believe that in my forties I might finally be able to realise my girlhood goals. It just went to show that you should never ever give up on your dreams.

I hugged Morgan tightly. If I had ever been lucky enough to have a daughter, I would have loved her to be just like Morgan: bright and funny with such a strong sense of who she was. No one was ever going to dim Morgan's sparkle.

"Thank you so much, Lottie." Morgan was wiping a stray tear away as she spoke. "It's so exciting that we're actually making our dream happen; and so far, it couldn't be going any better." She blew a kiss at Diane. "And to my Auntie Diane, thank you so much for believing in me and helping me so much; you're one in a million and I love you."

There were shouts of "For she's a jolly good fellow". Diane blushed furiously: like auntie, like niece.

I walked across the room and took my mother's hand. She backed away slightly, clearly startled, hating ever to be the centre of attention.

"And to my mum, thank you for making me see what you always did: that there was a strength in me I didn't know existed. You were so sure that I could change my life if I could just find the confidence to do so."

Mum nodded her head proudly, and a small smile played on her lips. I knew she was wistfully thinking of my dad, wishing he could have been here today to see how far his little girl had come.

Mum had really embraced my venture into fashion. As our apartment only had two bedrooms, most of the surplus garments were stored in the second bedroom. Now Jacob was back from uni, he was having to shift boxes around just to reach his bed at night. Mum had generously offered her spare room up as a workspace and to store stock. She had really been terrific; only a little worried at times about all the changes happening so fast, since it was in her nature to worry. But she supported me one hundred percent. After all, it was her words that had prompted me into doing this in the first place. Well, her words and her generosity of course. Without her help, my reinvention would never have been possible.

And business was booming. I would be lying if I didn't acknowledge that social media had played a large part in the beginning. Who would have thought that an uploaded clip of me ranting at my husband about his crusty bum would have been so invaluable as a marketing tool? The world really was bizarre at times.

After the video had gone viral, I had become a bit of an overnight celebrity. It had calmed down again now; as I had anticipated, yesterday's chip wrappers and all that. However, for a short time my life had been turned upside down. I would have strangers smile and wave at me in the street, local journalists wanting a few words. I even had some women calling me their hero. Me, a hero? All I had done was stand up to a bully, but then again isn't that the definition of a hero to some? It had been surreal. I had felt like royalty for a while, well a minor royal – the Biscuit Queen.

Now the commotion had died down and things were getting back to normal again. There were no more waves on the street, no calls from the local papers. It had been three weeks since an old man had stopped me while out shopping and asked me to sign his packet of Hobnobs at M&S in Alwoodley. All was quiet again. But it had been enough exposure to help our business get off to a flying start. Now the future would be solely up to Morgan and me.

I walked over to the CD player sitting on a shelf of the bookcase and selected a disc to play. It was nearly Christmas, after all; it was time for a bit of Slade. As Noddy Holder's voice screeched out through the room, I turned to all my guests with a happy smile.

"Merry Christmas, everybody!"

When the last guest had finally departed, I contemplated hitting the hay myself; but seeing the left-over food on the buffet congealing by the second, I thought better of it. I should at least take the left-overs into the kitchen; some could be salvaged, warmed up for lunch tomorrow when the hangover might prevent me from doing more than punch a button on the microwave.

"I'll help you clear up, Mum." Jacob was already picking up the half-eaten prawn ring, wrinkling his nose with disgust. It had been another offering from his grandma. Jacob really despised seafood called prawns, the cockroaches of the sea.

"Thanks, love, we'll just tidy this lot up and leave everything else till tomorrow... I'm done in."

Suddenly there was a sharp rap on the front door. One of the guests must be back, having left an umbrella or scarf.

Jacob put the prawn ring back down. "I'll get it."

Less than a minute later, Jacob returned with a visitor in tow. When I saw who it was, my heart sank into my slingbacks. This was all I needed after such a lovely evening.

"Hello, Daniel."

Daniel was standing awkwardly in the lounge, looking furtively around at his surroundings. He hadn't been in the apartment before, and clearly felt ill at ease there. He was warmly dressed in his navy cashmere winter coat and jaunty purple scarf, too warmly by the evident layer of sweat glistening on his brow. I couldn't help but notice that there was a button missing from his coat and the ones that were fastened were straining around his stomach area.

He smelt of cheap booze and expensive cologne. His face was waxy and pallid, resembling a sweaty baked potato: not a nice crispy one straight from the oven, but one you've banged in the microwave for ten minutes and it's got that doughy wet look about it. Not appetising at all.

"Jacob said you were having a party."

I picked up the remnants of the trifle and the one remaining devilled egg, to show him I was in no mood to make small talk; I had things to do. "Yes, we just had a few people round to see our new home and celebrate the success of the business."

He nodded slowly, his eyes darkening a little. For some reason Daniel was not at all pleased that I was becoming a successful businesswoman in my own right. After all those years when he had scathingly told me I was nothing but a housewife, you would have thought he should be happy for me to be finally making something of myself. But no; in fact I had even been told by friends that he was saying to all and sundry that I was on a hiding to nothing and would fall flat on my arse. Wishful thinking on his part. After all, if I made a success of things, what would that say about him? I was going to prove him wrong, though my arse was staying well and truly upright.

"You've got this place really nice... really tasteful."

I smiled graciously. "Thank you... and how are you settling into your flat?"

"OK, I guess. It's good for the short term, I suppose... but still living out of boxes at the moment."

Short term? I didn't like the sound of that. I was worried where this might be heading.

Jacob carried a few more plates into the kitchen. They were wobbling precariously in his hands and I was glad when he deposited them onto the worktop. "Is it OK if I go to my room now? I want to play some music."

I nodded at him. "Yes, sure you can, just don't stay up too late, please. I thought you might fancy coming into town with me tomorrow to get a few Christmas bits to decorate the apartment...

"Sounds good." He paused for a few seconds. "I'll be wearing my headphones in my room."

I knew that was his way of letting us know that he wouldn't be able to hear us if we started arguing. However, it was clear from his expression that he was really hoping we could be civil to each other. I hoped that too. It was Christmas, after all.

Daniel reached over and gave his son a brief hug. "Night, son, and I'll see you on Sunday. I thought we could go to the driving range to hit a few balls if you like?"

Jacob gave the thumbs up and loped off towards his room. Once I heard the door shut firmly behind him, I turned to face Daniel, my expression stern.

"What do you want?"

"You really do have this place very nice, Charlotte." Daniel walked slowly over to the bookcase and extracted a couple of titles, studiously reading the blurbs. He was stalling for time. Clearly there was something he needed to say.

"Daniel, I'm really tired. It's been a long day and I want to get to bed, so if you don't mind, what actually is it you want?"

When he eventually turned around from the bookcase, I was surprised to see tears in his eyes. "You look beautiful, you know; really beautiful... you are beautiful."

I stood stock still and fixed him with a steely glare. At one time those words would have been priceless to my ears; but now they didn't even amount to pennies. I didn't believe a word of his.

"I want to come home, Charlotte. I want us to try again. I'm miserable on my own. I just don't work without you."

No, what he meant was that now he was without me, he actually had to do some work.

He had such a hopeful expression on his face, like a puppy waiting patiently for an imminent treat. After all, I had always backed down in the past. As Daniel often said, he knew me better than I knew myself.

I shook my head resolutely. "No, Daniel, it's never going to happen. There is no us any more, and you can't come home. Anyway, this isn't your home. We sold it, remember?"

His expression was no longer expectant and full of hope. Now he was raging. "Why do you have to be like this?" He shoved the books back into the bookcase, clearly not giving a second thought to how valuable they might be. "I've said I'm sorry more than once now. What is it you want... blood?" He held his wrists out towards me in mock contrition. "You're in your forties, you know, Charlotte? Hardly a spring chicken." He gave a sarcastic little half laugh. "Plus you might be scrubbing up a bit better of late, but let's not forget, the fact is you're still fat."

The last word was spat out with such disgust that his face no longer looked in the slightest bit handsome. Now he looked quite hideous.

I let a small smile play on my lips for a few seconds as I let his words sink it. Quite clearly, I was supposed to feel hurt and humiliated, wounded by his words. But in truth I was not. I laughed in his face: a loud, confident sound indicating that his words had washed over me, having no effect whatsoever. As if I could forget I was fat. I could clearly see who and what I was every time I looked in the mirror. But how stupid was he to think those words would hurt my feelings? Once they would have, but that time was long gone.

Daniel had clearly not finished. Warming to his theme, he paced around the room, his hands deep in the pockets of his coat, making the buttons strain even further.

"Why do you have to be such a bitch? You were always lucky to have me, you know. I was and am way out of your league. Just because that Leo showed you a few seconds of attention, you think you're something you're not. But just remember you're on the scrap heap again now."

Of course, Daniel would assume Leo had dumped me, not the other way round. He would never think for a single second that I could have taken the initiative: his frumpy old wife the dumper not the dumpee. Perish the very thought.

I looked him over slowly, as if studying some lesser form of life in all its miserable glory. Standing there so dishevelled and clearly in need of a squirt of deodorant, he was a pitiful sight. And that was all I felt: distaste and pity. The man was delusional. And still, after everything was said and done, his ego was bigger than... well bigger than his bald spot was becoming.

I walked over to the door. "Please leave, Daniel... now!"

He sauntered to the door and walked slowly out, his leisurely pace intended to express to me that he was still very much in charge. He was muttering to himself under his breath. I was about to shut the door behind him when he turned to face me, his expression growing softer. Clearly browbeating and insulting were not having the desired effect, so it was time for a change of tack. He shot me a needy smile.

"We're still married, Charlotte. Could we not at least get some help? Have some counselling? How about Relate?"

One hand was on my hip and the other I shoved into his face, the middle finger fully extended. Yes, I gave him the finger.

"Relate to that!"

His face was a picture of shock. So I took my parting shot.

"Just remember, Daniel, the attitude comes for free, but the divorce certainly won't."

I slammed the door firmly in his face. And then I smiled.

Chapter 34

Christmas came and went quite uneventfully: those lazy days when everything passes in a bit of a blur or television repeats and left-overs. It was nice, though; quiet with just Mum, Jacob and me on the actual day. We enjoyed a medium turkey crown with all the trimmings from Waitrose, and of course Mum's obligatory sherry trifle while seated round the old mahogany dining table, stiff linen napkins on our laps and small glasses of pale sherry in our hands. I had offered to host the meal at our home, a break from tradition, but Mum had been adamant she wanted to cook herself. She liked things done "a certain way." Who was I to argue?

Jacob went to his dad's flat for Boxing Day. They were having their own festive afternoon of beer and football repeats. This gave me a whole day to myself to do as I pleased: which meant curling up on the sofa in my pyjamas watching my favourite old films and picking out all the nut chocolates from a family tub of Quality Street. It was absolutely perfect.

Things were still a tad frosty between Daniel and me. And when I say frosty, I mean like those abandoned peas at the bottom of your freezer drawer that you have to chisel off with the side of a butter knife. Tensions were running high. I had decided to be the bigger person and had generously sent Jacob off to his father's with a cheery wave and a neatly wrapped present for my ex. How kind was that? I could only imagine the look on Daniel's face when he unwrapped the old slow cooker that I had re-gifted to him. He had bought it for me for Christmas five years earlier, and it seemed high time to return it to him. After all, he had always nagged me to recycle more when we were together, so he should appreciate the effort. I never used it any more, and now he was a single man in a poky bachelor flat with a miniscule kitchenette, I reckoned he might appreciate the gadget. Not likely, but you never know.

I was now on my way to Olive Affair to meet the girls for lunch. It seemed fitting we should arrange our rendezvous there, since it was the same venue that had kicked off that fateful night out, many months before. This time, however, I wasn't dreading attending in the slightest. The fear I had felt before was now very much a thing of the past. I hadn't had a single second's worry about what I was going to wear, or fear that I wouldn't fit it. No, I simply couldn't wait, and I was dressed to kill, or at the very least to thrill. I was wearing one of our new designs from the boutique: a pin-striped navy trouser suit, cut to accentuate the curves, with a thick lattice gold belt. I felt a million dollars in it. The confidence a good outfit could instil in you was simply priceless.

As I confidently strolled into the bar area, my head held high, I immediately spotted my friends. They greeted me with enthusiastic waves.

Jayne was on her feet, beckoning me over: "Charlotte... come on, we've got the cocktails in, and tequila shots too just for the hell of it."

I joined Jayne, Jasmine and Lila at their table. This was going to be a good, albeit sozzled day.

"Sit down, Lottie," Jasmine instructed in a businesslike tone, pushing a small plate of lamb koftas to one side with a queasy shudder. "Lila is in the middle of one of her dating disaster tales and she's putting me right off my food."

I slipped off my jacket in one graceful movement and slid into the chair opposite Lila. I was all ears. "Oh, really? Well fill me in, I need to know all the details immediately."

Ten minutes later, I really wished I hadn't asked.

Apparently, Lila had ended up back at the abode of one of her younger suitors after a thrilling night of dingy bars and too many tequila shots. Things had heated up somewhat on his lumpy futon, and in the throes of passion they had decided to indulge in a little "back door" action.

I squirmed a little uncomfortably in my seat at the mention of this activity, having never really been an advocate of it myself. Strictly "exit only" from that area, if you know what I mean? Lila announced that this wasn't usual bedroom etiquette for her either. She wasn't against it, full stop; it just wasn't on her usual menu, more of an occasional side order; a bit of "à la carte anal" every now and then, mainly as a treat for birthdays and bank holidays or an expensive piece of jewellery. And especially if, like this current young beau, her partner was hung like a button mushroom.

At this point Jasmine had pushed aside her garlic mushrooms with a look of distaste. If this carried on much longer, she was unlikely to eat any of her tapas dishes at all.

Lila took lengths to explain that her lover had then left her mid flagrante to locate a bottle of lubricant from the bathroom, but after failing to find any had returned to the bedroom with some olive oil that he had grabbed from the kitchen counter.

Bedroom activities had recommenced in the darkened room

with wild abandon and a generous dollop of the olive oil. After a minute or so had passed, Lila had smelt a not unpleasant aroma wafting from their entwined nether regions.

"I could smell roast lamb," she announced matter of factly, clearly enjoying regaling us with her juicy tale. "I kid you not, I just kept thinking, why can I smell Sunday dinner?"

We collectively shook our heads. Her story was making no sense.

"I'll tell you why." She in turn shook her head as if not quite believing it herself. "Because the gormless sod had picked up rosemary and chilli oil and had rubbed it all over his todger."

We all exploded with laughter at this point, the balsamic and olive oil bottles shaking on the table as if there had been a mini earthquake.

Jayne was wiping her eyes with her napkin. "I can't believe what I'm hearing. So that's why you thought you smelt lamb, because of the rosemary in the olive oil?"

Lila nodded enthusiastically. "Exactly! And that was fine until about five seconds later, when the chilli kicked in."

All four of us erupted into laughter again.

"Talk about burning loins," Jasmine hooted.

Lila shuddered at the memory. "Let's just say it wasn't particularly pleasant, and brought to an unsatisfactory end what could have been the start of a beautiful friendship."

Trust Lila to bring in the drama. There was never a dull moment with her around. She really was one of a kind.

I was wiping my own eyes now and trying to curtail my laughter. "Well, it brings a whole new meaning to the phrase 'slam in the lamb'!"

We were all laughing hysterically again, the condiment bottles shaking in time with our guffaws, as if they were performing a jubilant jig.

I felt my mobile phone vibrate in the pocket of my trousers. I was going to leave it, check on it later as I was having such a great time with my friends; but something told me to have a quick look.

There was a message from a number I hadn't seen for quite a while.

"I'm back in the UK next week and wondered if you fancied meeting up? Maybe for a coffee and a biscuit? xx"

It was from Leo. My heart simply soared.

The End

Printed in Great Britain
by Amazon